The Bystander

The Bystander

The Lemaster Files

John David

TULE
PUBLISHING

The Bystander
Copyright© 2025 John David
Tule Publishing First Printing, September 2025

The Tule Publishing, Inc.

ALL RIGHTS RESERVED

First Publication by Tule Publishing 2025

Cover design by Croco Designs

No part of this book may be used or reproduced in any manner whatsoever without written permission except in the case of brief quotations embodied in critical articles and reviews.

This is a work of fiction. Names, characters, places, and incidents are products of the author's imagination or are used fictitiously. Any resemblance to actual events, locales, organizations, or persons, living or dead, is entirely coincidental.

AI was not used to create any part of this book and no part of this book may be used for generative training.

ISBN: 978-1-966593-89-8

Dedication

To Ann Nickodemus David, 1939-2002
She would have gotten a kick out of this.

Chapter One

4 p.m., Friday, Jacksonville Waterfront

ANYONE WORKING FOR a news outlet within fifty miles of Jacksonville knew what was coming to the Waterfront on Florida-Georgia weekend. And every news station sent somebody like me to dive into the thick of it. My news director at WJAX-TV dispatched me there to tape a video package and do a live shot for the evening newscast. He told me to interview the college football fans and maybe stir up the rivalry a bit.

In today's journalism racket, I'm known as a "one-man band." There was a time when a local TV story was covered by a whole crew that included a reporter, a camera operator, and maybe even a sound person who dangled a boom microphone. Today, due to new technology and budget cuts, one person does it all, and in this case, that's me. Back in journalism school, I learned how to operate cameras, position mics, test sound, edit tape, and so on. And now, all those skills have made me a valuable asset as a general assignment reporter for WJAX.

Typically, after getting the footage, I edit on my laptop or even on my phone, add a voice-over, and create a package that's aired old school or shown on cable or a streaming platform like Hulu, YouTube TV, or Sling TV. You get the idea. The package is also uploaded to the station's website so it can be viewed online and searched for years to come, which is good for search engine optimization. "Who clicks what" drives our coverage as much as newsworthiness or traditional ratings. I do my best to give my bosses a visually interesting and entertaining take on the day's news. While I certainly didn't get into journalism to chase clicks, review analytics, or drive ratings, I recognize that's the business I'm in today. What I do is pretty far from hard news, but frankly, that's a whole other conversation, better suited for a barstool.

I arrived at the Waterfront retail complex in midafternoon, glad to find that not everybody was drunk yet. The football game between the University of Florida and the University of Georgia draws thousands of fans to Jacksonville every October for a weekend of partying; it's viewed as one of college football's great spectacles. The pregame tailgate action used to be known as "The World's Largest Outdoor Cocktail Party," but that name has been canceled by politically correct sorts. Even so, many fans still reminisce about great moments at "the cocktail party." Call it a term of endearment—they don't want to drop it just yet.

I had a good time getting some fun sound bites from the fans—lots of "this is our year" comments, recollections of legendary plays, tales of woe, and of course, infinite complaints from armchair quarterbacks about what actual quarterbacks should do. Three Georgia fans tied a noose around a toy stuffed alligator the size of a German shepherd and dragged it around the Waterfront to alternating choruses of jeers and cheers. The fans were into it, so I shot some footage.

Although I'd be cheering on my Gators tomorrow, I kept it to myself when I shoved a microphone toward their painted faces. When they asked me where I went to school, I didn't lie. I omitted where I went for undergrad and told them I went to Columbia for journalism. Around the world, that grad school's pedigree opens a few doors, and New York is where I really learned to be a television reporter.

After I'd gotten enough interviews, I returned to my station-issued SUV and started editing my footage in preparation for the Five O'clock News and a live shot from the Waterfront. The stuffed gator bit turned out to be pretty funny, and I was satisfied the package would give my editors the lighthearted intro to the weekend that they were looking for. I seemed to have carved out a space for myself as the station's go-to reporter for events like this. I'd covered my share of hard-hitting news events but have always felt more comfortable talking to people and doing more feature and lifestyle stories. I do know I would need a well-rounded reel if I want to get promoted out of this market, but today's story was my kind of assignment because I understood this crazed football culture: The party is silly, but the game is serious.

For the live shot, I found a spot near a large concrete planter so my tripod would be less likely to be bumped by a tipsy fan. I positioned my camera to face out toward the St. Johns River but with plenty of room to catch the fans walking back and forth.

I checked my sound levels with my earpiece and lapel mic.

I listened as one of the anchors introduced the segment: "We are going live at the Waterfront with WJAX's Pete Lemaster, who's talking with fans before tomorrow's big game."

I flashed a big smile and consciously dipped into the deep end of my voice's register; then in three, two, one. . . I was on the air.

I had a quick and breezy on-air chat with the anchors back in the studio, and then I played the video package. As it ran, the crowd of beer-guzzling fans grew bigger and louder, and then the anchors were back in my earpiece with a few witty remarks. They asked me who I would be rooting for, and I made my Columbia joke and then said, "But you guys know I bleed orange and blue," which drew some yelps and howls from a mixed group of fans who had stopped to watch. And then I was out.

I was slated for another live shot but not until six p.m., leaving me time to catch up on messages and grab a snack. The wings, burgers, and fries, not to mention the beer, looked and smelled great, but the camera adds ten pounds, and one wing might turn into a dozen and a test of willpower, which I wasn't quite ready to endure. Looking fit on camera is as important as having a strong chin and a full head of hair. And a brain.

As I put away my handheld mic and pondered whether to down a bun-less cheeseburger, I saw confused faces running away from the Waterfront. Then people started running and screaming like they were in a disaster movie.

The fast runners were slicing through slow ones, shoving people aside and knocking people down.

Women were crying.

Children were screaming for their parents.

Some of the bigger men picked up the women they were just holding hands with and carried them as they ran like firefighters sprinting out of a burning building.

I froze. *What the hell is going on?*

As the crowd thinned, I saw him. A man wearing a motorcycle helmet about forty yards away was pacing in front of the High Topper sneaker store and waving a rifle.

Holy shit, an active shooter.

Bam. He fired a shot in the air.

People hit the ground and crawled for cover. More crying.

Without thinking, I crouched down, turned my camera toward him, and hit "record" before dropping behind the concrete planter. I hooked my foot around one leg of the camera's tripod.

A few people seemed to like my planter idea and crammed in next to me. A girl in a UGA tank top whimpered beside me, curled in a fetal position.

A drunk man in Gator attire crouched behind me and slurred, "Is this for real, is this for real? What the fuck, man?"

"Stay down, bro," I whispered.

Do I run? Stay put?

I don't own a gun, and I wouldn't have been carrying it even if I did. The only weapon I had on me was one of my

Buck pocketknives, which wouldn't do much against a rifle.

I peeked over the planter and watched in horror as a man wearing a blue baseball cap quickly shuffled toward the shooter. He was holding a pistol with two hands, his arms extended out like he knew what he was doing. Maybe a cop but in street clothes. Dressed like any other fan.

Blue Baseball Cap slowed to a deliberate and methodical pace, just to the right of me and about thirty yards from the shooter, who was then holding the rifle flatly against his chest.

Bam, bam, bam. Three shots. The guy with the rifle crumbled to the ground, his gun hitting the concrete with a loud clack.

Blue Baseball Cap then bent down and gently set his pistol on the ground before he raised his hands in the air.

"Holy shit, he got 'em," I said to the drunk Gator fan.

Jacksonville sheriff's deputies seemed to come out of nowhere and quickly surrounded Blue Baseball Cap.

All the cops had their guns drawn, some looking around the shops and up at the rooftops.

They told everyone to stay down. A few seemed to attend to the shooter.

The crowd of police grew even bigger, and I couldn't see much anymore.

Loud cries, unmistakably from a woman, pierced through the shattered window of the High Topper.

I stayed down but lay prone to stretch out and see if I could pull the tripod to me without knocking it over.

While I was still shaking and seeing people running and

screaming—and grown men in tears—I thought the danger was over.

Holy shit. Holy fucking shit! I think I've just filmed some dude take down an active shooter in high def.

After a few deep breaths, I got to my feet only to hear a cop yell at everyone to stay down.

I slid down to one knee behind the planter and saw the number of police and security guards at the Waterfront growing exponentially. Again, my gut said this thing was over, but survival instincts and guys with guns were enough to keep me low to the ground. This would be a stupid moment to be killed by the good guys.

Cops started to talk to witnesses and move some folks away from the body.

After another moment, I started to lower the legs on the tripod so I could reach the camera. I finally retrieved it and sat on the ground with my back to the crime scene, still behind my concrete planter.

I stopped the recording and watched the camera go blank. I still had my lapel mic on, my earpiece dangling behind me.

More cops and security guards were coming into the Waterfront, but I was focused on my camera. *This could be big. Career-changing big.*

I put in my earpiece, pressed play, and watched the screen.

0:01 The shooter paces and waves the rifle in the air. He's wearing a motorcycle helmet with the shield down, a gray sweatshirt, and jeans.

0:03 Screams. Crowds of fans running. Screaming throughout.

0:05 Mumbling by the UGA girl, the drunk guy, and me.

0:07 Drunk guy: "Is this for real, is this for real? What the fuck, man?"

0:11 Me: "Stay down, bro."

0:15 Blue Baseball Cap approaches the shooter. He looks like any other fan. Jeans, T-shirt but clearly armed.

0:18 Shooter turns toward Blue Baseball Cap.

0:20 Bam, bam, bam! Bullets hit the shooter.

0:21 The shooter falls to the ground.

0:24 Me: "Holy shit, he got 'em."

0:30 More screams, and Blue Baseball Cap puts down his gun and raises his arms in the air.

0:32 Police start to converge.

Thirty seconds of journalistic gold. I had it, and a lot of people were gonna want it.

I immediately called my colleague, Ted Stone, at the newsroom.

He didn't even say hello, just, "Pete, they're saying shots fired at the Waterfront. Where are you? Did you see anything?"

"I got it all."

"What do you mean?"

"Holy shit, you're not gonna believe it," I said. "I have footage of the shooting."

"Okay, okay," Ted said. "But what the hell happened?"

"A Good Samaritan just took down an active shooter. I have the whole thing," I said between breaths.

"Are you fucking kidding me? An active shooter on Florida-Georgia weekend, and *you* got it on camera?" As a former newspaper crime reporter and investigative producer, Ted immediately knew how big this was.

"Yep, tell the brass," I said.

"I will," Ted said. "But Pete, listen to me. You need to send that footage over right away and then see what else you can find out. The cops are gonna want to see it, but send it to us first. Got it?"

"Yeah, yeah," I said. "I'll send it to you right now. Ted, the shooting is the big headline. But the subtext here is that this guy got dropped by somebody in the crowd. This is gonna get nuts."

"The cops are gonna want it, probably in the next few minutes," Ted said. "And we should give it to them, but let's get it saved to our server and talk to Rod about getting it on the air."

"Sending it now," I said. "Then I'm gonna go see what else I can find out."

"Keep your phone close," Ted said as he hung up.

I knew jaws would be dropping all over WJAX. This was big.

It took a couple of minutes to upload the video clip to the station's server, which gave me a chance to collect my thoughts. I took a bunch of deep breaths, which I'd learned in yoga classes, and exhaled slowly after each one.

Upload done.

I grabbed the camera and the tripod and started to walk through the crowd, now a confused mix of law enforcement officers and fans, some clearly stunned and upset, others gawking. Police were tightly packed near the body, but I was able to see the shooter lying on his side. Bloody and definitely dead. The police had taken the helmet off. He looked Anglo, probably in his late twenties, clean-shaven, and hair trimmed above his ears. He had on jeans, running shoes, and the gray sweatshirt. From my viewpoint, I could see only three letters on the sweatshirt: *USN*. I'd been around this town long enough to know the fourth letter was an *A*. United States Naval Academy.

Oh man, the plot thickens if this guy's Navy.

I tried to get closer, but a Jacksonville sheriff's deputy saw my gear and told me to back up. "The media guys will probably set up an area for reporters in a few minutes, but right now, this is an active crime scene," he said. He didn't ask if I had any footage.

"Is Rebecca Dawes coming?" I asked.

"You know Rebecca?" he asked.

"Yep."

Know her? Worship her might be more fitting.

The officer said he imagined she'd arrive soon.

I'd covered a few crime scenes in Jacksonville, and only the big ones drew out major players like Rebecca. She was smart, fair, conscientious, and incredibly nice. And easily the prettiest cop you will ever meet.

She'd attended UF, like me, but we didn't overlap. I met

her a year ago at a press conference, and a few days later, I asked her out. She politely said that she was dating a marketing executive for the Jacksonville Jaguars. I still flirt with her whenever I see her, and she humors me.

I sent Rebecca a text. I could have called her, but I guessed a call during the biggest local crime of the year from a guy who had unsuccessfully asked her out nine times would get pushed to voicemail.

I let my thumbs do the talking: "This is Pete Lemaster from WJAX. I'm at the Waterfront. I have the whole thing. Call me."

Thirty seconds later, my phone rang. It was Rebecca.

"Hey, I'm at the Waterfront. Are you on your way?" I asked.

"Yes, of course. What do you mean you have the whole thing?"

"I was filming a package about the cocktail party and did my standup right before the guy was shot," I said. "I spun my camera around and got the whole thing."

"Holy crap, we're gonna need that footage, Pete."

"I know," I said. "We want you guys to have it, but I don't need one of your lunkheads seizing my gear. It's already in the cloud on our server. Anyway, what I'm saying is, your people and the feds can get it from the station, but I can show it to you when you get here so it doesn't catch you off-guard."

"Are you okay?" she asked.

Wait, is she concerned? About me?

"Yeah, I'm fine. It was nuts, but I'm okay."

"That's good," she said. "Now tell me exactly what you saw."

I hustled through the details of the clip. "One more thing. You're going to be good to me, right?"

"What does *that* mean?"

"Ha, nothing inappropriate." I laughed. "No, listen, I need you to help me stay a step ahead of the *Evening Star* and anyone else who comes sniffing around down here. Deal?"

"Sounds like you're already ahead, but 'deal,'" she said and hung up.

The *Florida Evening Star* was the only local daily newspaper still in business in Jacksonville. It had been the paper of record in the area for decades, and they were our main competition for reporting real news.

I saw a small crowd gathering around a woman in a UF hoodie. A young guy with a reporter's notebook was asking her questions. I leaned in and saw his ID badge.

Dammit, Evening Star.

The woman was explaining that Blue Baseball Cap was her boyfriend and they'd come to the Waterfront for an alumni happy hour and barbecue.

I overheard her say they ran for cover and then her boyfriend took out his gun and fired two, or maybe three, shots at the shooter. The reporter took this down, and then another eyewitness started rattling her version of the incident, at which point the *Evening Star* reporter turned away from the girlfriend. Hack move.

I approached the girlfriend and asked her name.

"I'm Hailey Marsh," she said, wringing her hands and wide-eyed.

I told her I was with WJAX and that, at some point, I'd love to speak with her on camera, but first I had a few questions.

Almost triumphantly, she said, "There have been so many horrible shootings in America, I think I'm just happy this one ended the right way. The only person who died was the bad guy himself, ya know."

I said I couldn't agree more and asked, "What's your boyfriend's name?"

"Walter Swanson."

"Do you know what kind of gun he used?"

"I think it was his nine-millimeter, and maybe it was a Glock," she said. "No, wait, it was the Smith & Wesson."

"Thank you. So you're pretty sure it was a Smith & Wesson nine-millimeter?"

"Yes."

At that moment, a woman wearing an orange UF hoodie and a stern gaze approached and wrapped her arm around Hailey, who started to crumble into her arms. I could see this interview was going to be over very soon.

"Hailey, one last question. Does your boyfriend have a concealed carry permit?" I asked.

"Oh, yeah, he's all about it," she answered, nodding her head. "He teaches classes and everything."

"We're lucky he was here," I said as she was led away by Orange Hoodie.

I scrambled to write it all down.

Samaritan is Walter Swanson
Works in Jacksonville
Concealed carry permit
Smith & Wesson 9
GF is Hailey Marsh

Take that Evening Star *hack.*

I felt a tap on my shoulder, and there stood Rebecca Dawes, rocking the full police uniform, standing about five foot five with a slim, athletic build and olive skin. Her straight dark brown hair was in a ponytail and her piercing, expressive brown eyes bore into me.

Be still my heart.

"Let me see it," she said.

Rebecca led me under the yellow crime scene tape and past the High Topper to a little alcove. I pulled out my phone and cued up the tape. I offered her one of my earbuds, suppressing my desire to crack a "meet-cute story for our future children" joke. I held out my phone, and her brow furrowed as she focused on the footage. At the moment the shooter dropped to the ground, she squeezed my arm, sending a jolt through me, almost to my toes. Another surreal moment; for the first time, I had her complete attention, and it felt good.

"That's incredible. Can you send it to me?" Rebecca asked.

"Like I said, you guys need to go through the station, but I wanted you to see it before we go to air or it leaks."

"I already called the station about it, so I hope it's on its way to my assistant at headquarters." She smiled. "But wow, amazing footage."

"Right place, right time, make your own luck, et cetera, et cetera," I said.

She hooked a stray lock of hair behind her ear. *Oh my god, with the hair. Is this woman trying to kill me?* Then she said, "We may not have our act together on this footage by the time the sheriff gets here, hopefully in a few minutes. He was at the Quarterback Club party."

I cleared my throat and tried not to think about her hair. "I'll show it to him if he gives me a short interview and you keep him away from the *Evening Star*." Fully expecting heavy pushback that didn't come.

"Ah, I see how this is going to work." Rebecca's lips turned up ever so slightly, suppressing a smile. "Make it quick, but yes."

Her voice trailed off, and those brown eyes grew bigger as she looked at something behind me. I turned to watch several EMTs wheel a stretcher out of the High Topper store—one tech holding an IV bag in the air like they do in medical dramas. The woman on the stretcher looked like a stereotypical Southern grandma but with a bloodstained shirt. The victim of the third bullet.

Chapter Two

7 p.m., Friday, Jacksonville Waterfront

MY PHONE BUZZED. It was Ted, and I had already declined him twice while talking to Rebecca. I picked up this time and, again, no pleasantries.

"We're still working on the footage," he said. "We have about five versions of it so far, and Rod is talking to the lawyers and the network. The usual pain-in-the-ass back and forth."

"Network?" I said.

"Yeah, network, big shot," Ted snarked.

"Wow, okay, any idea when it will get on the air?"

"I think soon," he said. "We're editing out the profanity, but the big question is, do we actually show a guy getting shot and killed? How much do we blur it, that kind of stuff. They know it's great and don't want to fuck it up, but they also don't want to be insensitive."

"Makes sense."

Ted cleared his throat again. "Right now, we're live outside but no talent. The anchors are discussing what we have so far but clamoring for more. Jill is on her way, but she's stuck in traffic. So many cop cars. Total chaos."

Jill Thompson was a solid young reporter, a fairly recent

addition to the station who started her career in sports but covered pretty much anything they threw at her.

Here's the thing about the TV news business: It's nothing like it was even ten years ago. Streaming and social media ate the audience, which sent stations into cost-cutting panic. Older reporters got "surplussed," and younger ones had to become generalists. I'm a one-man band, sports reporters have to do news, anchors do weather, and so on. It's not very glamorous anymore.

"They want you to do a standup as soon as possible," Ted continued. "Are you on the way to the tent?"

I told him I was walking out and looking for our live truck and pop-up tent—the tent keeps us out of the sun and rain. The viewers never see it.

"After your hit, you can trade off with Jill as we figure things out," he said, "but they want your eyewitness stuff right now."

"I got it, Ted, but listen, I have a lot more. Can I do a quick data dump?"

"Go."

"Okay, so Rebecca Dawes said she'll do a briefing around eight o'clock." I pulled my notes out of my coat pocket. "Figure that will happen closer to nine. In the interim, I'm going to try to get two minutes with the sheriff. Rebecca promised me. And we're gonna need a couple more reporters."

"That will be me and Olivia," he said. "The boss gave me to you. Be gentle." Olivia Marquez was one of our best and a whip-smart digital journalist.

"Perfect," I said as I looked over my now sweat-stained notepad. "Here we go, can you take this down?"

"Yes, Pete, go."

"A few minutes after five p.m. today, a gunman with a long rifle entered the center courtyard area of the Jacksonville Waterfront. He waved the rifle aggressively, and thousands of people, mainly fans in town for the Florida-Georgia football game, ran screaming. The gunman fired one shot in the air, which further scattered the crowd and sent many diving for cover. He continued to stalk around the crowd. An armed bystander approached him and fired three shots. Two hit the gunman, and the third…"

I paused, trying to read my notes. "This is where I need your help. I'm pretty sure the third bullet hit somebody in the High Topper, but that hasn't been confirmed. Maybe, for now, we say the third shot missed? Or we say the third shot may have hit a bystander? Anyway, Olivia can fact-check. Now, here's what we need to confirm: Spoke to a woman who says her name is Hailey Marsh and that she works near the Waterfront. She says her boyfriend Walter Swanson is the Samaritan. She thinks her boyfriend's gun is a Smith & Wesson nine-millimeter and says he has a concealed carry permit—says he's big on the right to carry."

Ted jumped in, "I figure we're gonna have to wait on the identities, but nobody else has this, right? Maybe we get Olivia to start checking the social media feeds. Swanson and the girlfriend are both UF fans, so they might be alums."

"Perfect. There's more: The dead shooter was a white male, late twenties, maybe military. I think he was wearing a

Naval Academy sweatshirt."

Another voice came on the line. It was Rod Kirby, the news director and acting general manager of the station.

"Are you okay?" Rod asked.

"It was insane, but I'm fine."

"Pete, the footage is fantastic, and we're trying to figure out how to present it," Rod said. "But we're hoping to get it on the air in some form tonight. We're already getting calls from the sheriff's office, the FBI, and, for some reason, the governor's office."

"The governor's office? Weird." I knew there was a "political football" joke in there somewhere, but I kept it to myself.

"Well, we have Legal figuring it out, and we probably have to give them whatever they ask for, but we want it on our air first," he said.

"Rod, I know this isn't what I normally cover, but I'm way ahead of everyone on this," I said. "And I'm telling you, this story is way bigger than my lucky day. Did you hear the other stuff I got?"

"I did," he said. "That's great stuff, and the video separates us from the other media outlets for the next day or so, and we're gonna want you on the front line to get the story out and promote the station."

Promote the station? Fuck all the way off, Rod. For a second, I panicked, thinking that I might have said that out loud. But the line stayed quiet. I'm safe. For now. *Fucking suits. Focus, Peter.*

"The footage may go up for the first time on *Nightly*

News," he said.

Whoa. National. Now we're getting somewhere.

"You better plan on getting back here after the standup and be up early tomorrow because *The Morning Show* already called and is slotting you as we speak."

Double whoa.

"Okay, sounds good," I said coolly, even though I was trying to figure out how to high-five myself. "I'm headed to the truck. Anything else?"

"No, I'll leave you with Teddy," Rod said. "Stay safe."

Stay safe? That's funny. "Will do."

"Okay, Ted, please get on the research," I said. "I guess start by confirming our Samaritan—is that what we should call him? Nothing else is coming to me."

"Armed bystander?" Ted offered.

"That works better. Okay. Talk soon, dear," I said and hung up.

The Morning Show. Shut the front door.

I stepped away from the Waterfront. The race was now on. I was no longer on the inside, so all the journo hacks would be nipping at my chinos. But I was good with the team concept, and Ted was perfect for this.

I saw our satellite truck and Bobby Rodriguez, an old-school camera operator, pacing like the caged animal that he probably was in a prior life.

"We're going live in five minutes, man," Bobby said.

"I know. Let's go inside, and I'll bring you up to speed." I gave Bobby the basics, and he reacted with the expected run of expletives.

Bobby went outside to get the gear set and check in with the station. I think he could tell I needed a moment.

I had just watched a person get killed. I saw another victim who might not make it. And I'm in the middle of the story of the year—at least here in Jacksonville.

Why did the shooter come here today? Why fire only one shot? Who is Walter Swanson?

I looked at my phone and saw about a million missed calls and texts, including a bunch from my mom.

Oh crap, I had told my brother I was gonna interview the drunks at the Waterfront today, so my whole family was probably freaking out.

I texted my mom that I was okay and then called my brother, Dave, a former paratrooper and now lawyer. I just hit him with the quick facts—he would call the rest of the family and let them know I was fine. The call was quick and expedient, just what I needed.

"Got it, Slappy," Dave said. "Be safe and keep us posted." And he hung up.

Yes, on occasion, my older brother called me "Slappy." I have no idea why. I don't know when it started, but whenever I tried to get him to stop, it only got worse.

Brothers. Can't live with 'em; can't drink without 'em.

Jacksonville Waterfront, 7:30 p.m.

AND I'M BACK on the air...

Standing under our tent in front of the Waterfront, I

recounted my story with the same two anchors in my ear and wearing the same coat and tie I had on two hours earlier. The station was promoting our coverage as "Shooting at the Waterfront."

The anchors were both real pros, and they floated easy questions and coaxed me along—stretching things out, even. They actually pulled more details out of me than I had been using to frame the story in my head. I'd become so accustomed to aligning facts in short and clever sound bites that it was an interesting exercise to try to remember the expressions on the faces of the fans, the sounds and overall feelings, both before and after. I did my best to recall as much as I could and was live with them for about six minutes, which is an eternity in the television game. This was interesting perhaps only to me because the whole incident went down in about a minute's time. *Man, so quick.*

After the live shot, I sat in the truck and debriefed with Jill, who had arrived with another photographer. While sitting in traffic on her way, Jill had done a lot of fact-gathering and had the general gist of the story down, and I felt pretty comfortable handing things off to her at the live truck with Bobby.

I took the other photographer with me to Rebecca's press briefing—which, as I figured, did not start anywhere near on time. At about 8:30 p.m., with police lights flashing in the background, she stepped in front of a pool of dozens of microphones and cameras. Behind her stood at least five other official-looking, heavy-hitter types, along with a bunch of folks from the Jacksonville Sheriff's Office, the FBI, the

Florida Department of Law Enforcement, and, I think, the Federal Bureau of Alcohol, Tobacco, Firearms and Explosives. And in the background, Governor Jim McManus.

The circus is definitely in town now.

Jim McManus, Florida's firebrand Republican governor, was elected on the president's midterm coattails. Some believed him to be a near-perfect facsimile of the president, just without the baggage.

By most objective measures, he'd done a pretty good job running the state. During the COVID-19 pandemic, he locked down nursing homes to protect the elderly but kept schools open and was far friendlier to businesses than governors in blue states. Many folks believed it was an inevitability he would run for president. The question was when and who would challenge him for the nomination.

One issue with the governor was not his politics but his operating style and his attitude toward reporters. He'd been incredibly hostile and dismissive to the media, and he infamously excommunicated several daily newspapers from his press briefings. He was more likely to be on a national, conservative-leaning cable network than a local Florida station. I rarely even tried to get interviews with him anymore. And his staff were all jerks to us—I think they had to pass a special anti-media test or something.

The governor learned, from watching the president, to play to his conservative base, which responds consistently when it comes to shootings and the liberal backlash from shootings.

My brother-in-law owns a gun shop, and he explained

the philosophy like this: The heavily pro-Second Amendment "rights" folks always come out in force after a shooting. They buy up all the ammo, and weapon sales are brisk. They will say, he explained, that they are arming themselves in case they come across an active shooter, but they are actually afraid of the backlash. Gun lovers are upset that people have been killed, but what makes them even more worried is that the anti-gun "left" may try to pass laws to take away their guns. So, what do they do? They buy even more guns.

And when an armed bystander takes down an active shooter, which also happened at a mall in Indiana last year, the pro-gun lobby comes out with an "I told you so" attitude, saying that more armed people will make our country safer. My gut says I really don't want the whole population armed, with everyone carrying a gun like in the old Wild West. But that's just my take, which I usually keep to myself. Frankly, I think the subject is better discussed over a pitcher of beer than in a voting booth.

Rebecca gave her briefing, offering a rundown of what happened without disclosing names or any further details of any of the parties involved. She artfully said that one bystander was wounded and was taken to the medical center. She added that she did not have any details on her condition but was told she was conscious when she was transported from the Waterfront. She said the coroner and the CSI teams would continue working through the night and that we were fortunate as a community that there were only four shots fired in total.

And then she went through a list of the injured. About a

dozen people were taken to the hospital, mainly out of an abundance of caution. Several seniors were shaken up with scrapes and bruises, one fan broke her leg, and another fractured his wrist. Three Lambda Chi fraternity members had severe cuts and scrapes after they jumped into the river and then tried to crawl out over a barnacle-covered pylon. That line drew a few muted chuckles.

She said she would take a couple of questions before handing the briefing over to the FBI and Florida Department of Law Enforcement. And then, the governor wanted to say a few words once the briefing was completed.

I raised my hand. "Just to be clear, at this time, you are not releasing any stats or background on the shooter, the armed bystander, or the woman who was sent to the hospital? If so, when do you think you might release that?"

"We are still holding back on releasing those details because we want to notify the families, and we are still interviewing the armed bystander, so hopefully soon," she said.

Several reporters asked some other questions, mostly benign and a few silly. A guy from the *Evening Star* asked if the game was still on tomorrow.

"I'm not sure who makes that decision," she said, quickly looking for the next hand. "But I haven't heard otherwise."

Cancel the game? I get that it's a question reporters think they have to ask, but seriously, no way they would cancel the game.

After a couple more questions, Rebecca turned the floor over to the FBI Special Agent, who basically ran through the same set of facts. He took no questions. Then a representative from the FDLE gave the perfunctory schtick about how the Jacksonville Sheriff's Office and the FBI would have the full cooperation of the State of Florida, etcetera, etcetera. And then he kicked it back to Rebecca.

She thanked everyone for their patience on a difficult day and promised more information tomorrow, probably midmorning. She then introduced Governor Jim McManus.

With his trademark tightly groomed goatee and a dark, double-breasted suit, he stood before the group looking—well, let's just say it—"presidential," because we know that's what this is all about, right?

McManus praised the actions of the JSO, FBI, and FDLE. He said that the law enforcement officers at the Waterfront saved lives and repeated what the FDLE guy said about cooperation.

He then took an extended pause, clearly framing his next statement.

Here it comes.

"I'm in town for the game tomorrow, and I was speaking at the Quarterback Club earlier, but I chose to come to the Waterfront because of the incredibly heroic and patriotic actions of one man.

"Since the beginning of our nation, our citizens have codified in our Constitution that we have the right to bear arms and the right to self-defense. We will not be terrorized in our communities, in our homes, or at our football games. We will protect our families, our loved ones, our fellow citizens, and ourselves from anyone who menaces us and infringes on our way of life and our liberty. I came down here this evening to personally thank Walter Swanson, the armed bystander who risked his own life to save the lives of many others by fearlessly approaching, suppressing, and killing the active shooter. Mr. Swanson is a hero."

Whoa, the gov just uncloaked the Samaritan. I guess scripts are for suckers.

Rebecca's jaw dropped, and the FBI guy looked absolutely pissed.

"I had a moment to speak with him just a few minutes ago," McManus continued. "He's a humble, everyday citizen, a hero, and a patriot. Very soon, we will have Mr. Swanson as a guest at the governor's mansion in Tallahassee, and it's my hope he will stand as an example of how our country will not be held hostage by mentally ill people who misuse firearms.

"I also want to reaffirm what was said earlier about the game. I've spoken to the president and athletic director of the University of Florida and the president of the University of Georgia as well as the managers of the stadium. The game will be played tomorrow. You have my promise."

He turned away, taking no questions.

I called Ted.

"I'm assuming you saw that," I said. "The governor just uncloaked Swanson."

"Yeah," Ted said. "Let's run everything we've collected on him. We have a few hours' head start."

"Yep, good call," I said and hung up.

I was convinced we should be able to report some good

information on Swanson before anyone else had much to say. And, if we were lucky, he would make his social media accounts private or start sanitizing his feeds.

I left my gear with the photographer and worked my way toward Rebecca.

"Good job juggling all that," I said.

"Thanks, I don't really have much more to say," she said. "You are probably ahead of all these guys already."

"Can you get me an interview with Mr. Swanson?"

"No chance."

"He's not doing any media?"

"I didn't say that." She smiled and stepped closer to me. "I'm saying you have 'no chance.' I think you are familiar with that concept, right?"

I smiled at the zinger and then collected myself.

"What are you talking about?"

"An FBI public information officer and I met with him, and we strongly discouraged him from doing any media right now," she explained. "But then Swanson said he would only speak to First America Network affiliate stations and only after he does a national interview with Skip Kennedy."

"No way." My resentment was building.

"It gets better," she said, leaning in closer and almost whispering. "He told McManus he doesn't want to talk to anyone until after the game, and I think the governor is running point with Kennedy."

"So he's going to the game tomorrow?"

Cue the shitshow.

"Yep, and the governor invited him to sit in a skybox and

be recognized at the game, but Swanson said he would only do it on two conditions."

"You're making this up?"

Is she messing with me?

"I am not. He wants to bring his girlfriend and," she paused, "he wants to be Mr. Two Bits. During the game."

Her words hung in the air as she displayed a devilish smile I had never seen on her before.

"Get outta town," I said. I couldn't get the questions out fast enough. "The athletic director agreed to it? Won't the Georgia fans eat him alive?"

She leaned in and whispered, "Stand up and holler."

And then, she was gone.

Chapter Three

10:15 p.m., Friday, WJAX

I RETURNED TO the newsroom and found my footage on every screen imaginable in the building, seemingly running on a loop throughout the whole place. Some clips had sound, others not, and it wasn't just on our air. TVs and screens all over the station were tuned to national feeds, other stations, and online outlets. *Wow.*

I heard a bunch of comments as I walked to my desk:

"Way to go."

"Are you okay?"

"Glad to see you are still alive."

"This is why we own guns."

I gave Ted a quick high-five and a slap on the back. He had a broad smile.

"Holy crap, Stone, what a day," I said. "I'll be right back."

I worked my way over to Rod's office and leaned into his doorway.

"Good to see you," he said, smiling broadly. "I think we've licensed this footage to every station in America and most of the civilized world."

"I hope my holiday bonus will reflect that," I said. No

reaction.

"Listen, Pete, as I said on the phone, we want to work this story and make sure we cover every aspect of it that we can. And we want you to quarterback it."

An appropriate term, given the weekend.

"Sounds great to me," I said. "I'll debrief with the guys and figure out what we're gonna do for tomorrow. Looks like Mr. Swanson is going to be at the game."

"Can you confirm that?" he asked.

"I have a good source," I said with what had to be a smirk.

"Your girlfriend?" he asked, eyebrows raised.

"From your mouth to God's ear," I joked.

I guess it's that obvious.

"As if the game needs any further craziness," Rod said. "Well, we only have the morning newscast and one evening newscast tomorrow, as you know, and it would normally be your day off. But I think I can find some overtime budget for you, so you should take a crew to the game and see what you can figure out."

Overtime? Ha! The crew gets overtime. I'm on a salary, and I'm sure I will find myself begging for an additional comp day in six months. Have I mentioned I deplore business guys?

"Let's keep digging," he said. "We have nothing on the deceased shooter, and we're just starting to get Swanson's unfiltered politics."

I told him I would be sitting down with Ted and Olivia and confirmed my interview on *The Morning Show* would be a little after nine a.m.

"Try to get some rest after you frame out your day," he suggested.

"I'm on it. Thanks for your help today, Rod."

"No, thank *you*," he said. "Let me know what else you need."

I sat down in a small conference room with Ted and Olivia. She had downloaded a ton of information on Swanson; he was prolific on social media compared to the average guy.

"We started with Insta, and it goes back about five years," she said. "Lots of hunting pictures. Dead deer. Guns, knives, camping equipment. Lots of boring pictures documenting his trips in the woods. It looks like he went out west and shot an elk a couple of years ago too.

"He then appears to have embraced bow hunting. Many pictures of deceased hoofed creatures. A PETA man he is not. Hailey enters the picture, literally, about two years ago. Looks like a few weekend jaunts to Savannah, Charleston, and Helen, Georgia. Really normal stuff. His content seems a little less gory at this point too. Maybe she mellowed him out.

"Then he discovered video. He's done a bunch of gun safety videos on TikTok. Here's how you handle a shotgun. Here's how you handle a rifle. Here's how you handle a—wait for it—handgun. Cue a nine-millimeter Smith & Wesson."

"Nice," I said. "So, we have him with the gun he used today or at least a similar one?"

"Yep," Olivia confirmed. "We are already editing all this, so you can calm down. We were super excited too, and it's now in the works."

"Oh, and he also talks about Second Amendment stuff sometimes," she continued. "But he's not hardcore, at least in my opinion. He's pro-gun, but I don't think he's a gun nut or someone who would raise any concerns. He also recently launched an online course on gun safety. I can't quite tell if it's meant to be a master class sort of thing or a 'gun safety for dummies' kind of thing."

"We should see what else we can find out about the course," I said. "I wonder if people are signing up now that he's been uncloaked by the gov?"

"We will work on that," Ted said.

"What about Facebook or message boards?" I asked.

"Well, it's hard to be prolific on multiple platforms and still hold down a real job," Olivia said. "He has a bunch of duplicate posts and a few things kissing the president's butt around the election, but nothing crazy. And we *are* in one of the president's strongholds, after all."

"He works as a technician of some kind for a contractor that runs cable and stuff," Ted explained. "Hailey works in HR at a car dealership."

"Swanson grew up north of town," Olivia continued. "According to LinkedIn, he went to the University of North Florida but is probably a Gator fan by geography and because Hailey went there. All in all, he seems like a fairly normal North Florida native."

"We're putting together the background package and

will only need a voice-over for it," Ted said. "We want you to do it, assuming the fame hasn't put you out of our price range."

"Ha! I need the work and the job security," I said.

"We will let you know," said Ted. "They are looking at this for tomorrow night, so you can do the voice-over anytime before that."

"Do we have anything on the deceased shooter?" I asked Ted.

"Well, as you saw, the authorities didn't want to release anything, but they couldn't do anything about the governor. They are keeping things close to the vest, and it's only been about five hours since the incident, so I'm not completely surprised. At the same time, I made a few calls, and every agency is tight as a drum on this. Nobody's saying anything, and it's a little weird we have nothing."

"I agree, we've gotta figure out who this guy was, but I guess all we can do is keep pushing," I said.

I thanked them both and made a wisecrack about needing my beauty sleep for *The Morning Show*, and then I headed home. What a day.

MY APARTMENT WAS only about a ten-minute drive from the station at this hour, and I was anxious to take a shower and get out of my work clothes.

At home, I pulled on jeans and a T-shirt. In the refrigerator, I found a chicken Caesar salad kit and my beloved: a tall can of Guinness draft. Come to Papa.

Here are a few of the great things about Guinness in the big can: First, it's Guinness—why mess with perfection? Second, it's about fifteen ounces versus a typical twelve-ounce beer. So that means there's more beer. Third, a tall boy is only 160 calories. Fourth, it has this cool nitrogen thing that simultaneously improves the taste and provides entertainment.

After popping the top on the can, I waited a moment to give the magic nitrogen plastic thing time to release its nitrogen goodness. Then I poured the beer into a glass at an angle. They say forty-five degrees, but I haven't owned a protractor in a long time. If done correctly, and it's tough to mess up, the nitrogen-bolstered, caramel-colored bubbles cascade down the inside of the glass, looking almost alive. A delectable yet not-too-thick layer of foam accumulates at the top of your glass, and if you're lucky, it rises slightly above the lip of the glass, but gravity or friction or whatever won't quite have the power to make it overflow. Enjoy and repeat as required.

I took my salad and beer to the kitchen table and started going through my phone. Text messages from friends and family, but nothing I needed to worry about. A bunch of voicemails from numbers I didn't recognize, but I was about ready to put my phone away.

I started to feel the numbing impact of the malt beverage, and a final waning of adrenaline after six hours of nonstop activity. During my career in journalism, I had never seen anyone get killed. Yes, I covered plenty of stories involving death, but I always showed up after any violence was over. I'd interviewed people who witnessed killings or lost loved ones, but that was long after the danger. Today, I saw a person exit this earth in an instant and right in front of me. Crazy. Scratch that. In retrospect, it was terrifying.

"Numb" was looking pretty good right then, but I still needed answers.

But first—*damn!*—I forgot to call my mom.

I knew she would be concerned, but make no mistake, Evelyn Lemaster never coddled any of her children. Yes, she was a loving and compassionate parent, but while I spent part of my youth kicking balls around the pitch, call her a "soccer mom" at your peril. She was formerly an investment banker and now seemed busier than ever even though she claimed to be semi-retired. She made a ton of money identifying successful tech startups, and lately, she'd become an influential angel investor. Almost goes without saying that she was dumbfounded when I told her I wanted to study journalism, but she grew to accept my passion, particularly after job offers started coming in months before I received my master's degree.

Lately, she'd been focusing her maternal instincts on how to leverage my talents to become a brand ambassador, or an influencer, or whatever—probably because she wasn't seeing any grandchildren coming from my direction anytime soon. She wanted her youngest to be a player on the national news scene, not a regular reporter in what she considered a "backwater outpost," meaning Jacksonville. Whenever I defended my adopted town, she would always say, "It's a nice city, but it could use a little more Southern charm and a little less, well, Florida."

Today, she was mainly concerned about my overall safety and state of mind. I told her I was fine and gave her an abbreviated recap of what happened. When I told her I was appearing on *The Morning Show* the next day, she transformed into her more comfortable role as mentor and adviser.

"This is the type of opportunity we've been looking for, Peter," she said. "I know you have to continue paying your dues, but you are as talented and as good-looking as any of those people at the network."

"Thanks, Mom, I'm excited. Tired but excited."

"You know I can always call the guys I know at the network," she offered.

"I know, but I earned this. And you know I don't want your help."

"I'm gonna call my friend at the network and let him know you will be on tomorrow morning."

"Mom, no, you're not. I really wish you wouldn't," I said, trying not to get upset. She did this constantly. Grown man and I still had a snowplow mom.

"Make sure you let them know you are willing to come back," she said.

"They are all really smart people, Mom. Pretty sure they know every local reporter wants to be a national reporter."

"Okay, I'll behave," she said, and after a pause, "I saw your friend Rebecca Dawes on TV. Did you talk to her?"

I know where this is going. Different type of misbehavior.

"Of course I talked to her. This is a huge story, Mom. And I told you, she has a boyfriend, remember?"

"Boyfriends come and go, Pete."

I heard a knock at my door, and I was pretty sure I knew who it was.

"Someone's at the door, Mom. I think it's Denise. Gotta go."

"Who's Denise?" she said, but I hung up and left her hanging.

My neighbor Denise was a lawyer with one of the big downtown firms. She moved into the apartment two doors down a month or so ago. We'd chatted a few times and became friends. Denise was single, attractive, and really nice, but I wasn't sure if there was any chemistry between us.

As she stood at the door, five-foot-six with shoulder-length blonde hair and green eyes, wearing jeans and a sweatshirt, all I could think was: *She looks good in jeans.*

I then saw she was wearing a UGA sweatshirt.

"Oh my god, Denise, were you at the Waterfront today?" I asked suddenly. The adrenaline was back.

"No, no," she replied with a look of surprise. "I went to an alumni happy hour downtown, but I saw you all over the place on TV."

"Okay, good. Yeah, it's been a day and a half."

"Are you okay?"

"I'm fine, just exhausted. Honestly, any other time I would invite you in or see if you wanted to hang out, but I am…just done."

"On no, don't worry, I saw your light on and was curious."

"I'm gonna be on this story pretty hard for the next few days, but I will catch you up when I can."

"Sounds good. Have a good night."

I closed the door but snuck in a "Go Gators" before it latched shut. There was still a game tomorrow, and they were our rivals, after all. I heard a muffled "Go Bulldogs" through the door.

I switched my phone to "do not disturb" and turned on the TV, thumbing through the channels.

Something classic, familiar, or funny would be nice right now.

I landed on *Star Wars: The Phantom Menace*. Perfect. I'd seen it at least five times. *Can't they tell the emperor and the senator are the same guy?* I thought just before I drifted off to sleep.

Chapter Four

7 a.m., Saturday, Pete's Apartment

I WOKE UP a few minutes before seven and checked my phone. It didn't look too bad, only a couple of missed calls from local numbers and one from Santa Barbara, California. I knew no one in Santa Barbara.

I figured anyone who really needed me would call back or try the station if it was super urgent. I also had a bunch of texts, mainly saying congratulations or asking if I was okay.

Maybe I could program my phone to send an auto-reply that said: "I'm fine, and thanks for the kind words about my story." How obnoxious would that be?

My phone rang just then and the name on the screen was Cole Nathan, one of my college friends. Seven a.m. on a Saturday. *This should be good.* I answered.

"Buddy," Cole said, "how's it going?"

"I'm fine, man," I said. "Craziest day of my life yesterday, but I'm fine. Can I catch up with you later?"

"Yeah, yeah, real quick…" Guys like Cole are not easily denied. "Do you know you're a meme?"

"I am?"

"Yeah, your 'he got 'em' line is breaking the fucking internet right now," he said. "Dude, you should be doing all the late-night shows. This is gonna take off."

"Well, I'm doing *The Morning Show* in an hour or so if I can get you off the phone," I said.

"See what I mean, you are blowing up," he said with a laugh. "I think this is the next 'Let's go Brandon,' and we should capitalize on it."

Just to be clear, Cole was probably onto something. He was a very successful contractor, and I often said he was one of those guys who could just smell money. Every house he'd ever bought he'd sold at a profit. Every business deal he'd made had worked in his favor. The king of timing, he always knew when to jump in and when to cash out.

While we were in college, he partnered up with a guy who had launched a "Send a Brick to Your Congressman" campaign. This was years before the issue had national traction. Cole coordinated the logistics of shipping the bricks to representatives and senators. They sent a few thousand bricks to Washington, and Cole made something like $30,000. So, I knew his words were worth listening to.

"I want to sell the 'He got 'em' merchandise with your blessing," he said. "Hats, shirts, flags, coffee mugs. I have a guy working on designs already."

"Slow your roll, dude," I said. "If you want to do that, knock yourself out, but I can't help you."

"You're always telling me you could use some extra cash," he said.

"The station won't do it, even though they are greedy bastards, and I signed an eighty-page contract that prohibits practically everything. And a guy did get killed, by the way."

"Screw that guy, and he can't really complain, can he?" Cole said.

"Because he's no longer with us. I get it." I paused. "I can't do it this time, dude, but I can't stop you from making a mint or sending me some merch."

"Well, I wanted to talk to you first," he said. "But I understand. That Walter Swanson is a fucking hero, by the way, and this is gonna be big."

"Swanson will be at the game today, so keep an eye out," I said. "And I am doing *The Morning Show*. But I really have to go."

"See, you could be selling shirts for us already," he said with a laugh, and we hung up. I spent about thirty minutes walking on my treadmill before getting dressed and heading to the station. On the way, I picked up a strawberry smoothie with extra protein—nothing green goes in my drinks, thank you very much.

I SAT DOWN in the chair a few minutes before nine a.m., and an instantly recognizable voice came in my ear—Cathy Merrick, the legendary host of *The Morning Show*, working on a Saturday, no less.

So, here's what I learned about Cathy. While she was a great journalist and had the image of America's sweetheart on the air, in a one-on-one situation, she cursed like a truck driver.

"Good morning, Pete, we're looking forward to having

you on in a few minutes, but I have a couple questions for you," she said, as friendly as she could be. You could almost hear her electric smile.

"Good morning, Ms. Merrick, and fire away," I said.

"Please, call me Cathy. So, what's going on with this Swanson guy? We want to interview him but can't get anywhere with him. What the fuck is going on down there in Jacksonville?"

"We can't get him either, and word on the street is he only wants to speak with affiliates in the FAN Network."

"You've got to be fucking kidding me."

"Cathy." I paused to emphasize our new first-name-basis relationship. "He's not doing any media until after the football game today."

"No way."

"And he's not doing anything until after he does a face-to-face with Skip Kennedy."

"Un-fucking-believable."

"I agree with you if that helps," I added.

"He's really stretching his fifteen minutes of fame, that little shit."

"We're trying to find his friends, and we're doing the best we can, but it's a hectic weekend in Jacksonville, and his demands aren't helping. Sorry."

"That's okay, I appreciate the intel," she said, shifting to her trademark chipper tone. "So, we will do our live bit in a few minutes. Still nothing on the identity of the shooter? Weird we don't have that yet."

"We don't, and I agree again that it's weird."

She said, "Talk to you in five," and was gone.

The Morning Show interview went great. Cathy went through the footage and asked me how I kept my composure and if I was scared. I told her I was in the right place at the right time—and behind the right concrete planter. And then I followed up that the whole thing was over shortly after I figured out what was going on. Luckily, the shooter didn't take more shots, and he was alone. She then asked one of the unanswered questions: Why hadn't the names of the shooter and the hospitalized bystander been released? I explained there was a briefing scheduled for later in the morning, and we hoped to know more by then. She thanked me and said they would have me on again if they needed an update. And then it was over.

America's "fucking" sweetheart.

One of the funny things about the news business is that there's often a ton of buildup even for segments that last only four minutes. And I was just one small part of Cathy's morning. She was probably talking with someone else right now, with equal enthusiasm, about next year's fashions or how to make the perfect daiquiri.

As I exited our station's in-house studio, Ted and Olivia each gave me a thumbs-up and then I headed down to the Waterfront for the briefing. It was forty-five minutes from now, and I was probably forty-five minutes away with game traffic. I was cutting it close but pretty confident it wouldn't start on time.

WHEN I ARRIVED at the Waterfront, I had a minute or two to spare and tried to find Rebecca, but I had no luck.

A few minutes later, she arrived with another large phalanx of law enforcement types, and I was expecting to hear from more politicians and maybe the mayor. But Rebecca approached the microphone and said rather brusquely that the FBI was going to handle today's briefing and she would not be taking any questions on behalf of the sheriff's office.

I made eye contact with several other local reporters, and we all exchanged glances of disbelief.

Did Rebecca get pushed aside by the FBI, or did she not agree with how they wanted to handle it?

Special Agent Jerry Howard approached the microphones and said he would be brief.

The FBI had confirmed the active shooter was, in fact, killed by two shots from the gun of armed bystander Walter Swanson, and Mr. Swanson was thoroughly questioned by authorities and went home last night. He also confirmed that the third bullet struck High Topper patron Stephanie Singleton, who was transported to Jacksonville Memorial Medical Center in serious condition.

That's new. Mrs. Singleton wasn't in "serious" condition yesterday.

He went on to say that authorities had several conversations with members of her family, who wished to thank everyone in Jacksonville and around the world who had expressed their concern and offered their prayers for Mrs. Singleton.

The FBI would not be releasing any further information on the active shooter. Agent Howard took no questions and stepped back.

Rebecca approached the mics and said, "That's all for today," and the officials dispersed.

"Agent Howard, nothing new at all. Are you stonewalling us?" one reporter yelled.

Agent Howard turned at the sound of his name but didn't respond and then stepped into an SUV and left the Waterfront.

No news makes it news!

What is going on? The guy is dead. Is the shooter like James Bond or something?

Angie Irwin, another local reporter, came up to me and said, "I know you won't tell me if you know, but do you know anything?"

I told her I was just as surprised as everyone else.

"We're all standing here with our dicks in our hands," she said.

I laughed.

She could be the next Cathy Merrick.

I called Ted.

"When does the briefing start?" Ted asked.

"It's over," I said.

"What do you mean, it's over? You're kidding."

"Dude, it was the shortest briefing in the history of fatal

shootings," I said. "Only the FBI guy, Agent Howard, spoke. He confirmed it was Walter Swanson who shot the gunman and said they met with him and sent him home. They released the name of the High Topper customer, Stephanie Singleton, and said she remains in serious condition. Nothing else. Nothing on the shooter. No idea who and certainly no idea why. We are still completely in the dark. Maybe they think that it's game day in Southeastern Conference football country and we're just gonna move on?"

"He might be right," Ted said.

Rod decided there was no reason to keep a live truck at the Waterfront as it was no longer an active crime scene. It was unclear whether the restaurants would reopen, but game fans were milling around anyway.

Any additional official information on the case was going to come from the FBI field office or the sheriff's office and Rebecca. I wasn't sure, though, as her lack of participation in the press conference was a head-scratcher.

Chapter Five

3 p.m., Saturday, The Stadium

IT WAS STILL two hours from kickoff, so Bobby and I went to the stadium to get some footage of the tailgating and cocktail party. It's such an intense rivalry that the schools can't even agree on how many times the game was played. UGA counts a win in 1904 in a game that was played in Lake City, Florida. UF disputes this. Such are rivalries, and for UGA, I guess a win is a win. That's what is so great about college football in the South—the stories are almost as good as the games themselves.

I entered the press box but wasn't exactly sure what I was covering. I had the tip from Rebecca that Walter Swanson was going to be there, along with her "Mr. Two Bits" suggestion. Was she just messing with me?

I had seen enough pictures of Swanson in the past eighteen hours to know what he looked like, but I didn't know where he would be sitting. Plus, the FAN thing. This guy wouldn't be talking to me unless I found a Skip Kennedy mask.

After wandering around the luxury mezzanine for a bit, I recognized Kamari Small, one of the governor's aides, a smarmy little guy who excelled at being annoying to reporters. I asked him if McManus had any media availability today, and he told me, "The governor is a football fan, too, ya know. Sometimes he just wants to enjoy the game like everybody else."

I pressed, "So no availability?"

"You will hear from him at halftime," he said.

What does that mean?

"He's doing interviews at halftime?" I asked in vain.

"No, you're not listening," he further smarmed. "You will hear from him at the half."

"Okay, I got it," I said. "I'm just doing my job here, ya know. It's not like he spends a ton of time in Jacksonville."

"What you're missing, Pete, is that you aren't helping me do my job." He was getting ready to pontificate, so I just looked at him like I didn't know what he was talking about. "My job is to build the governor's national profile and get him elected to higher office, not make him a local hero or the king of Jackass-ville."

"Ouch," I said, feeling the sting for my adopted home. "I get it. Not sure you need to be quite that blunt. We *are* in the 'bless your heart' South and all."

"Pete, here's my card. Help me do my job, and then we will talk about how we might help you."

"Fair enough."

He then slithered off.

So, the gov had something up his sleeve for halftime and an eye on the Oval.

I returned to the press box and found a comfortable seat with a decent view of the field. I didn't want to take a prime seat away from a reporter who was actually covering the game. The press box was on the fifty-yard line, but it was fairly high up, so it wasn't a great seat—but, hey, I was in the building.

I splurged on some chicken wings and a diet soda, steering clear of the French fries and beer. I was technically still working.

It turned out to be a decent first half. My Gators were a bit overmatched by the Bulldogs, but a timely UGA turnover on the two-yard line right before the half kept it close. When I was in school, we'd beaten Georgia something like ten years in a row, and it had taken them a long time to rebound. Right now, the Bulldogs were very talented, and while my guys were in this game, it was just barely as the half ended. Of course, there was always hope.

Rebecca then entered the press box wearing a UF polo shirt and jeans but with her hair down and blown out straight. By the looks of her, you would never imagine she was a cop.

She came right over to me and immediately said the shitshow this morning was not her idea. I said I was sure it wasn't and mentioned that we all have to toe the line sometimes.

I also learned that her seat was in the Jaguars' box.

"With the boyfriend?" I asked.

"Yes," she sighed. "As usual, he's schmoozing around looking for sponsorship customers. Doesn't seem to stop working even when my team's playing, not his. I told him I was going to visit my media buddies."

So, I'm a buddy. Alas.

"And I thought it might be interesting to check out these halftime extracurriculars with you," she added.

Hope flickers.

The UF and UGA bands were oddly on the field at the same time, simultaneously playing alternating Florida- and Georgia-themed medleys, which we both agreed was a strange sign of unity for this rivalry. They quickly cleared the field.

Then the public address announcer directed the fans to midfield for a special message from Florida Governor Jim McManus. He stood at midfield wearing a light-blue dress shirt, slacks, and, likely, fancy Italian loafers. He was holding a microphone.

Next to him stood a white male, approximately the same height as the governor, wearing jeans and a University of Florida baseball jacket. While it was late October in Jacksonville, it wasn't quite cold enough for that jacket.

"You see the jacket, right?" I said.

"Mm-hmm." Rebecca smiled.

I could practically hear "Don't Stand So Close to Me" by The Police playing in my head. *Does she have any idea?*

McManus lifted the microphone and did his thing.

"On behalf of the great State of Florida, I want to welcome you to one of the greatest college football games in America. We are here today to cheer on the Florida Gators and the Georgia Bulldogs."

Cue the big hoots and applause.

"As many of you know, this game was nearly marked by

tragedy. Last night, we had an active shooter incident just up the street at the Waterfront, but thanks to the bravery of one man, this tragedy was averted. I have already thanked him personally, but I also wanted you, the fans, to recognize him for his incredible bravery and patriotism. Florida and Georgia, please stand and let a great American…"

The place was already going nuts. McManus had them eating out of his hands.

"Let a great American, Walter Swanson, know how much you appreciate his bravery."

Sure, three-quarters of the fans were pretty well-lubricated, but the stadium was as loud as I had ever heard it. Bedlam.

Swanson put his hands in the air and waved like a conquering hero. He turned to each section of the stadium and waved. The roars increased.

Then McManus took it up a notch: "USA! USA! USA!"

And the crowd joined in.

Deafening.

When that cheer subsided, McManus said that Swanson had a request.

"Take it away, Walter," he said.

Rebecca bumped me.

Swanson took off the baseball jacket to reveal he was wearing a long-sleeved yellow dress shirt and an orange-and-blue tie. It was absolutely clear to every UF fan that he had donned the outfit of an iconic University of Florida fan known as "Mr. Two Bits." He had a whistle around his neck, and he produced a small placard that had been tucked under the jacket. In orange lettering on top of a blue background, it read: "TWO BITS."

As the fans started to figure it out, the Florida fans went nuts. The astute among the Georgia fans, not so much.

In the 1950s, a UF fan started his own tradition at Gator football games. Wearing his aforementioned signature outfit, he would move between sections in the stands at UF home games and rally the crowd with what became an iconic cheer, called "Two Bits." He would blow his whistle to get the attention of fans, wave his placard, and then start the cheer. He did this at every home game for nearly sixty years. Today, UF honored the tradition by having a well-known alum lead the cheer before home games—usually an athlete who donned the signature costume.

"I can't believe what I'm watching," I said to Rebecca. "And he's not a graduate, so the AD had to approve this, right?"

"Shh. Too many questions. Let's just enjoy this," she said, touching my arm.

I could hear Sting: "Please don't stand so close to me."

So, there stood Walter Swanson among eighty thousand fans who had just given him the loudest ovation I had ever heard—and he was about to royally piss off half of them.

He held up the sign. Blew his whistle repeatedly. Showed the sign to each side of the stadium and then slowly lowered his hands and got into a slight crouch.

The UF faithful did the rest.

Swanson jumped in the air, and the crowd—well, half of them—yelled, "Two Bits! Four Bits! Six Bits! A Dollar—*All for the Gators, stand up and holler!"*

Half of the stadium's fans rose in unison, cheering madly.

As for the other half, let's just say the Georgia fans were a bit more muted.

As the governor and Swanson left the field, I turned to Rebecca and saw an electric "I told you so" smile on her face.

"One for the ages," I said.

"Indeed," she said. "After the game, he and the girlfriend hop on the FAN News jet for New York, and he's slated to do Skip Kennedy in prime time on Monday."

"And then every FAN affiliate in the country on Tuesday." I groaned.

"Probably, but you still have the best source on the inside," she said with a smile.

"So, Swanson goes from sipping beers at the Waterfront on Friday night to the Four Seasons and a shopping spree in New York on Sunday," I mused. "What does he tell his boss? Can you call in sick for that?"

"The guy's a hero, remember?" At that moment, her phone buzzed, and she stepped away.

A guy I'm assuming was her ad man boyfriend met her outside the press box and put his arm around her.

Alas. I wonder where my neighbor Denise is sitting.

Chapter Six

7 p.m., Saturday, The Stadium

TO AN OBJECTIVE sports fan, the rest of the game was fun and competitive, which means it was agony for both Florida and Georgia fans who were far too invested in the outcome. It went back and forth until about midway through the fourth quarter when a Georgia defensive back intercepted an errant Gator pass, returning it for a touchdown and a fourteen-point lead. The dreaded "pick six" had done us in.

Though one never likes to lose to a rival, I was pleased we kept the game close and it wasn't embarrassing.

Even though I mainly spent the day watching football, I was pretty tired and decided to cut out and avoid some traffic as well as the happy-yet-obnoxious Bulldog fans, who would be primed to party.

When I got home, I texted Denise to see if she wanted to hang out. She replied a moment later with an enthusiastic "Yes!" and a Bulldog emoji followed by a V for victory emoji.

Didn't even know there was a such thing as a Bulldog emoji. But why would I?

A moment later, my phone buzzed again with another text. I thought Denise might be trying to rub the win in further, but it was from a number I didn't recognize.

"This is Rebecca, my private phone. Call me on this line."

So, she has a business and a personal phone. *Not sure I'll ever be busy enough or important enough to have two phones.*

I added the new number to her contact info and called her.

She answered in a very quiet tone. "Kyle Charles Newberry."

"Who is that?" I asked.

"The deceased shooter—I gotta go," she said and hung up.

Wow.

I texted her back: "Thank you." No emojis.

"You're welcome," she replied. "I had fun at halftime."

Cue heart palpitations.

I wrote it down: "Kyle Charles Newberry" and then immediately typed it into Google.

Nothing. How could it be nothing? Nobody has nothing. I know I'm not the greatest Google searcher, but nothing?

Facebook: Nothing.

LinkedIn: Nothing.

Instagram: Nothing, but nobody uses their real name anyway.

I called the desk, hoping to get Olivia. She answered, clearly not happy to be working on a Saturday and particularly this weekend, even though she went to UCLA.

"How bored are you?" I asked.

"You know, it's not boredom. It just sucks having to work tonight," she said, her usual fun edge clearly worn down.

"Write this down," I said, and then I caught myself. "Please. Kyle Charles Newberry. I have it that he's the deceased shooter."

"I think Rebecca has a crush on you."

I didn't take the bait, maybe because I hoped it was true. I said nothing.

Finally, Olivia cracked and asked, "What do we know so far?"

"Not much. I did a quick search and found nothing, so I decided to call in the cavalry. See what your magic fingers can find."

"I'm on it. When do you want the info? Or should I just email what I find as I dig it up?"

"That works, but I have a feeling it's not going to be much beyond the government databases, and we can't go on air until we get confirmation."

I flipped on the TV and saw there was a little more than five minutes to go in the Mississippi State-Alabama game, and it was close.

Ted wouldn't take my call until after the game, so I settled in to watch. Aside from college football, the most popular sport in the South is hating the University of Alabama. Ted is a Mississippi State grad, and even though the Bulldogs were within a field goal, 'Bama has the ball, and they were driving. We were both going to be unhappy tonight.

When I was in college, I lived in a fraternity house, and we were famous for having big parties on Saturday nights in the fall. Bands, DJs, big stage, lights, super loud. But our social chairman would always make the announcement in the weekly chapter meeting: "We will have a party on game day only if we win." Saturday night energy would get sucked out of our college town if the Gators lost. What's funny is that I remember we threw a lot of parties but also seemed to lose plenty of football games.

Ted had been a star tennis player in high school in Virginia, with scholarship offers from dozens of big-name universities, but he blew out his shoulder playing dodgeball during his senior year. His dominating serve never returned to his surgically repaired shoulder, and every school rescinded their scholarship offer except one: Mississippi State. The coach still saw promise in the young man from Richmond and chose not to go back on his word. Ted played four years for Mississippi State, mainly second-team doubles. He earned a journalism degree and was the most loyal Mississippi State Bulldog I've ever met.

A few minutes after the game ended, I called Ted, and he immediately went into an extended rant about play calling, clock management, a lack of commitment to the run, and the evils of the Alabama coaching staff.

I listened intently and empathetically. I'd had the same conversation dozens of times, just with a change of a few names and uniform colors.

When he finally calmed down, I told him I got a lead on the name of the shooter, but we were unlikely to get much from the internet about Kyle Charles Newberry.

"Do you want to join me in some old-school door-knocking tomorrow morning so we can preserve our lead?" I asked. "Assuming Olivia gets us an address."

"Ah, the lost art of shoe leather journalism—and off-the-clock, no less," he said. "I'm in; pick you up at nine?"

"Sounds good. And I promise not to talk about your game if you don't talk about mine."

"Deal," he said and hung up.

Chapter Seven

7 a.m., Sunday, Pete's Apartment

DAY THREE OF the biggest story of my life started with pounding, both on my door and in my head. I'd had a couple too many glasses of wine after I got home, and I was feeling, in the words of one of my college fraternity brothers, "overserved."

And then there was the door.

I checked my phone, saw it was eight a.m., and then went to the door, wearing boxers and a T-shirt, to find Ted Stone's smiling face through my peephole. He was holding two large coffees.

I opened the door. "We definitely said nine a.m., dude."

"We did," he replied. "But there's some actual news going down. The police breached Newberry's apartment out by Bay Meadows, and Kirby wants us out there."

My aching head. Fucking Kirby.

"Wow," I said as I slowly, very slowly, started to process the urgency. "Okay, gimme a moment to get my act together."

I took a deep breath and then reached for my wallet and pulled out $20.

"Can I have *both* of these coffees?" I asked. "And can you

maybe go back and get a third along with some breakfast for yourself?"

I handed him the money and asked him to return in about twenty minutes.

He had a look of surprise on his face and then peeked around me to see my bedroom door was closed. He then got it.

"Rebecca?" he asked.

"No, no," I whispered. "My neighbor. Just give me a chance to shower and try to defog."

"Got it," he said. "See you in twenty."

I retreated to my bedroom, where Denise was still under the covers.

"The cops found the shooter's house, so I have to go."

"Okay," she said.

"I finagled a coffee from Ted, and you can stay here as long as you want," I said plaintively as I rested the coffee on the night table. "Just not sure when I'll be back."

"How am I gonna get home?" she asked with a smile. "You're making me walk two doors down by myself?" She giggled.

"Yeah, I'm sorry, want me to call you an Uber?" I joked. "Just lock the bottom lock, I guess."

Denise grabbed my arm and pulled me down toward her, and we shared a light kiss. I took a shower, shaved, and then scarfed down three Tylenols and two big glasses of water before starting to nurse the coffee. My head was still throbbing, and I wished I had a Coke, which was my college go-to hangover cure, but I didn't keep any in the house—

empty calories, alas. I was just gonna have to tough it out.

I got dressed and made sure I had a pad and pen. And for the first time in a long while, I appreciated that there was a woman in my bed.

Denise was sitting up, nursing her coffee and scrolling through her phone when Ted sent me a text that he was downstairs.

"That's my ride," I said.

She waved me over and again pulled me toward her and kissed my cheek.

"Who's Rebecca?" she asked.

My phone rang and I saw it was Ted, clearly concerned I might have gone back to bed. I scooted out without answering her question.

Saved by the bell.

TED KNEW NOT to ask me anything about Denise. My scowl was more powerful than telepathy. He handed me a blueberry scone, which I essentially inhaled, my body quickly absorbing the sugar and carbs.

Staying camera-ready fucking sucks. And I should have known better than to open a second bottle of California cab.

About twenty minutes later, we pulled into an apartment complex in the Bay Meadows area, not far from I-95. It was a typical suburban neighborhood with the traditional mix of ranch homes and low-rise apartment buildings, surrounded by strip malls, doctor's offices, hotels, and chain restaurants.

THE BYSTANDER

You could pick up the Bay Meadows neighborhood and drop it outside any medium-sized city in America.

Newberry's apartment complex was small, about thirty nondescript units. Lots of brown. The parking lot was full, mostly with economy cars—Hondas, Toyotas, Fords, and Hyundais. Yellow police tape encircled part of the southernmost section of the complex. Residents were milling around in the parking lot, some in lawn chairs, others sitting in their cars.

"Should have brought these people coffee and donuts," I said to Ted.

We noticed some other reporters, but even with their hangover-free head start, we were confident we could get some valuable information quickly and efficiently.

For me, the adrenaline rush helped with my aching skull.

Ted and I went in different directions to gather as much information as possible before the residents started to go back indoors.

After about two hours of interviews, we compared notes:

At about three a.m., police started knocking on doors and clearing out apartments in the building.

- Residents were told the shooter from the Waterfront was their neighbor.
- Police seemed confident the apartment would be empty, but they were wary of possible booby traps.
- Just before four a.m., a SWAT team breached the unit through a window.
- Lots of noise, and a large group of officers were going

in and out of the unit.
- Things calmed down pretty fast after that.
- Police took a bunch of stuff from the apartment, but no one could tell exactly what.
- Most neighbors didn't know Newberry.
- Once shown his picture by the cops, they confirmed he lived there.
- Nobody claimed to be his friend.
- A few neighbors talked to him at the mailbox, emptying trash or going in/out. Once chatted about the Jaguars game.
- He seemed like a nice enough guy.
- Landlord said his rent was always paid on time.
- He seemed to work a late shift as he left for work in the afternoon and came back at night.
- Was gone on a lot of weekends, packed a roll-on suitcase, and would leave on Saturday mornings.
- No one saw any guns.
- A few visitors, maybe a girlfriend.
- Kept to himself.
- Cops asked all the same questions we were asking.
- Nobody offered coffee, donuts, or jack crap for the inconvenience.

I turned to Ted and said, "So, we got a normal guy with a regular schedule. No one saw any guns. And the 'donut eaters' didn't share."

Ted laughed. "Yep. Regular guy. Talked about the

THE BYSTANDER

weather and the Jags on the way to the dumpster. But the cops have flipped his place and are probably dissecting his laptop and electronics as we sit here."

By 11:30 a.m., it was a full-fledged scene in Bay Meadows as Jacksonville was waking up to hear the name of the shooter and learn of the raid on his apartment.

Next came Rebecca, who quickly began to organize a briefing with her team.

Not quite as much media but a lot of neighbors and onlookers in the crowd. Plenty of law enforcement standing behind the bank of microphones.

As we were waiting for the briefing to start, Ted and I called Olivia. She confirmed Newberry's name was out, and the internet was firing up with all kinds of theories. She said it was already getting hard to tell which statements were facts from people who actually knew him versus conspiracies. But she was monitoring and digging.

A few minutes earlier, our truck showed up, and Bobby set up to tape the statement. We weren't going live, so my job was to pay attention and, well, be a reporter.

I caught Rebecca's attention, and she gave me an acknowledging half-smile. She was back in uniform and all business.

She read the following statement with the now-familiar crew of law enforcement folks standing behind her:

> "At approximately four a.m. today, the Jacksonville Sheriff's SWAT team and the FBI breached the Bay Meadows apartment of Kyle Charles Newberry, who we have identified as the active shooter who was killed at the

Waterfront on Friday night. As far as we have been able to determine, he lived alone.

"Law enforcement agents took great care clearing out the residents of the complex and entering the unit. It was possible Newberry may have booby-trapped his apartment, so we took appropriate steps to enter the unit through the side window. We quickly determined there were no explosives or anything else that could endanger the residents or our officers.

"Over the next several hours, law enforcement methodically went through Mr. Newberry's apartment, collecting evidence and further information on him.

"Here is what we are prepared to release and confirm at this time: Kyle Charles Newberry, age twenty-nine, was born in Jacksonville and worked as a customer service representative for a large healthcare provider in town. He was a Navy veteran who was honorably discharged four years ago.

"We confiscated a number of weapons from the apartment, including nine handguns of various calibers, four shotguns, and one hunting rifle, which would not be—again, not be—considered an assault rifle. We also confiscated several boxes of ammunition, again of various calibers. In addition, we removed twenty-two fixed-blade, sheath-style knives and approximately seventy-five pocketknives, including several automatic switchblade-style knives.

"We also confiscated a laptop computer, an Xbox console, two cellular phones, and some paper records. There was nothing in his apartment that is illegal. Aside from the knives, guns, and ammunition, it was a fairly typical-looking apartment, according to our team.

"We want to thank the residents of the complex for their cooperation as we work to keep our streets safe.

THE BYSTANDER

Most are now able to return to their apartments.

"We also have some additional information on Mr. Newberry. When he entered the Waterfront on Friday night, he had no identification, and he was alone, as verified by surveillance footage. It took us some time to determine his identity and locate his residence.

"We believe Mr. Newberry acted alone, and the evidence gathered this morning continues to back up that belief. We are reviewing phone and electronic records, and if anyone aided Mr. Newberry, they will be prosecuted to the full extent.

"That concludes the official statement, and I will take a few questions."

Angie Irwin was quicker than me and asked the first question. Ted gave a look suggesting I receive a mental demerit.

But how many glasses of wine did Angie have last night?

"You said several boxes of ammunition," Angie said. "Do you know how many rounds he had?"

"More than two thousand rounds." Rebecca had clearly anticipated the question.

"Thanks. And just to confirm, fourteen guns, nearly one hundred knives, and more than two thousand rounds?"

"That's correct," Rebecca confirmed.

"Plus, the gun he had at the Waterfront, so fifteen guns," Angie said. It was more of a statement than a question.

"We confiscated fourteen guns here, Angie," Rebecca said, slightly annoyed.

I jumped in. "Mr. Newberry was wearing a U.S. Naval Academy sweatshirt on Friday night. You confirmed he was in the Navy, but was he a midshipman?"

"The Navy has confirmed he was in the service and was not an Academy graduate," she said. "We don't believe he ever attended the Academy."

"Anything on motive? And how do you know he acted alone?" I asked as deferentially as I could to counterbalance Angie's hard edge.

"We have no comment on his motive at this time, and nothing we have seen or found indicates he had any accomplices," she said. "That's all for now. Thank you, and please note that any further information will be distributed by the JSO or the FBI field office directly."

Ted and I hopped in the truck with Bobby and quickly edited the footage into a short package for that evening's newscast. I recorded a short voice-over, and then Bobby uploaded it to the station's server. A three-man band does the one-man band's job in one-third of the time.

I had a feeling I was going, once again, to be editing my own footage real soon.

REPORTERS HAD BEEN sniffing around and, like us, had the name but couldn't confirm it.

Even TMZ had it on the air a few minutes before the briefing. I didn't know how they did it, but I'd noticed that while they were good at breaking these types of news updates, they never dug much deeper.

Once his name was broadcast, all hell broke loose across

the media landscape.

- Talking heads on cable news networks called Newberry a coward.
- Right-wing commentators said he was a domestic terrorist.
- Members of Congress from around the country said this was yet another sign of the mental health crisis in America.
- Others said we weren't doing enough for our veterans.
- One radio host said the fact that another mass shooting was prevented by an armed bystander proved, unequivocally, that the gun control movement was nonsense.
- The conservative consensus: We need more Swansons to prevent the next Newberry.

Back at the station, Ted and I sat with Olivia, who had been trying to find out more about Newberry. She wasn't looking optimistic when she gave us the download.

"The guy has no online profile," she explained. "No Twitter, Facebook, Instagram, or LinkedIn, and this isn't just me talking. The internet message boards are full of people who knew him and even say they were friends with him. Everyone is looking for his social feeds, and his friends are basically confirming we aren't going to find anything.

"He worked at Southern Regal Insurance downtown, according to several posts. As we suspected, everyone was shocked and said he was a nice guy. The Navy confirmed he was honorably discharged but nothing else. It's Sunday, remember.

"The conspiracy theorists are looking for connections to anything overseas, but the chatter is that he mainly served stateside. There is nothing to suggest he has ever even been to the Middle East, but we can't fully confirm either way."

"So, more questions than answers yet again," I said.

"Yep. So far, no online screed. No posts on right- or left-wing sites. Nothing anti-anything. No white supremacy, nothing anti-white, black, or brown. Nothing anti-LGBTQIA or plus! There are a few things on the public record aggregation sites, but mainly they confirm, in a half-assed way, most of the info we already have, like his age and address."

"When you said no online profile, you were not kidding." Ted sighed.

"It wouldn't surprise me if he had a flip phone," Olivia said with a straight face. "I'm totally serious. I bet the electronic record on this guy is gonna be zilch. If you tell me he didn't even text, I wouldn't be surprised. But even my grandmother texts. I wish I had more, but this guy is like vapor in today's online world."

"Gotta be something to do with the Navy, right?" Ted suggested.

"I don't know," I said. "There has to be some small percentage of the population who are not online at all. We all have childhood friends who are basically unaccounted for online, right? So, Newberry was one of them."

Olivia continued, "There's a current groundswell online that this guy's emblematic of what's wrong with the United States military right now—that we're training guys who are out of whack. He's getting vilified like crazy everywhere, and the conspiracy theorists and the folks on the right are saying thank God for the Second Amendment and that we need more mental health protection for our soldiers, sailors, and marines. A lot of people have gone to the scene and gone to his apartment and talked to his neighbors. And they've largely toed the line that they don't know very much about him. That and lots of doors slamming, as far as I can tell. I think you guys got the neighbors at the right moment. They're already tired of it."

Olivia had clearly dug deep.

"I even did a dark web search," she added. "Prior to the shooting, there was nothing. Since the shooting, lots of conspiracy stuff. And that's the bulk of what I have on Newberry."

"What about Swanson?" Ted asked.

"He's the other side of the spectrum," she replied. "I'm already sick of his online persona."

"Let's have it," I said.

"He has active profiles like we discussed the other day. And the internet sleuths have been pulling up all kinds of miscellaneous stuff on him. His online videos about gun safety and gun handling are the big drivers. If you look at the reviews before his name was made public, you see he largely gets positive feedback. He's a decent-looking guy who speaks in clear terms with a nice, educational, and even fun tone.

He was trying to build his personal brand as an expert and was getting some traction. His TikToks, for example, would get a mixed bag: 500 views, 1,100 views, 12,000, 18,000 for one about assault rifles where he shoots up some stuff afterward, and some that only got a handful. On the whole, before his name went public, he had a total of one hundred thousand views, or in that neighborhood. But just so you know, a good TED Talk can easily get fifty million views, and the cute girls in bikinis on TikTok were totally trouncing him.

"Now, since his name came out, he's been getting a ton of traffic, and many media outlets have talked about his online course. Frankly, the production value of those videos is much higher and probably looks better on regular TV."

"Can we see?" I asked.

She cued up one of his videos:

"Hi, I'm Walter Swanson, your local gunsmith, and I'm here today to talk to you about my online course about gun safety for every man and woman. In this course, we will review several different types of handguns and how to properly handle, load, unload, and store them safely. We will discuss different types of gun locks, how they work, as well as different gun safes and where to take in-person courses to learn how to fire your weapon and improve your marksmanship. You can also purchase my guide with my top ten key points so that you will absolutely, without fail, earn your concealed carry permit. Our full course includes four parts and is available for $39.99. I look forward to helping you become a safe, properly armed citizen of our great country."

"This video, along with Pete's footage, has been edited together in hundreds of different ways," Olivia said. "Many without giving Pete or the station any credit."

Trolls are fucking with my retirement fund.

"Not sure if you saw the *New York Post*," she said, "but its page-one headline was 'He Got 'Em.' Don't worry, the guys in New York are mailing us some copies. Your footage, parts of *The Morning Show* interview, and some of Swanson's info are everywhere, and I mean everywhere. The shooting at the Waterfront has its own underground economy. You can find computer-generated click-bait stories that are pretty funny. You click on the story, and it drives you to pages filled with ads for supplements and ED medications. I also saw a site selling 'He Got 'Em' shirts and mugs."

Go get 'em, Cole.

Rod Kirby entered the conference room and told us he wanted the three of us to keep working on the story for the next several days, saying the station's website was getting tremendous traffic because of the footage and because we'd been a bit ahead of everyone else. He wanted me to take tomorrow off, and then Ted and Olivia could get a break later in the week.

We needed to find out more about Newberry in the next day or so and then catch the Kennedy interview to see if that elevated the story.

We decided to divide the duty—Olivia again focusing on the online developments, the internet sleuths, the conspiracy theorists, and any actual news interviews. Ted would focus on the Southern Regal Insurance angle, while I would reach out to his family.

We didn't think we would get much officially out of Southern Regal, but the good news was that it was one of the few large companies in Florida that still had a decent-sized public relations department, with plenty of former local journalists. I'm sure they mobilized their crisis team on Friday and were on alert this weekend, knowing we would eventually start calling. Ted and I each knew several folks there. We could also reach out to possible coworkers. Most would have already been muzzled by the company's media relations policy, but it couldn't hurt to try to get some insight.

My task was to try to find family members and individuals who knew him personally. First obstacle: Olivia informed me he was an only child and both of his parents had passed away a couple of years ago. She did, however, field a call from one of Newberry's friends; she thought he would be the best place to start.

His name was Kevin, and it turned out he barely knew Newberry, having only met him once or twice, which I think meant once. He said he was a nice guy and that he was surprised to hear the news. But Kevin knew Newberry's girlfriend and gave me her number.

Okay, now I'm moving.

I called Tina Carson and quickly learned she could best be described as a girl Newberry dated a few times. According to Tina, he was *not* her boyfriend, though she said he was a good guy.

She met Newberry at a party, and he was a normal guy

but one who could be moody. They went out a few times, but there was no real spark. She said he was a decent-looking guy who was in good shape. She thought he might work out, but he wasn't ripped or super athletic.

When I asked about his politics and guns, she said that sort of thing rarely came up. She never felt unsafe or intimidated by him. Part of the problem, aside from the overall chemistry, was that he worked nights and then had some kind of part-time job at the convention center on many weekends. Tina had an office job and liked to go out on weekends.

She said he was often stressed because he had been injured when he was in the Navy and was still dealing with some chronic health issues. She said he didn't like to go to movies, for example, because it was hard on his back to sit through them.

She had not spoken to him in several months, and he didn't text, which she thought was weird. He didn't have a smartphone.

And yes, Olivia kicks ass.

Tina had heard about the shooting the same way as everyone else—from the news. And she had no idea he was the shooter until this morning. Luckily, she had not spoken to any other reporters.

I will never hate hearing those words.

She gave me the names and numbers of a few other people who knew him, and the responses were very consistent:

"Completely shocked."

"Wasn't a gun nut as far as I know."

"Did not have any mental health issues as far as I could tell."

"Shocked to hear about the guns, knives, and ammo."

I went over my notes with Ted and Olivia, and then Ted shared what he'd learned about Newberry's day job.

"I was able to confirm he was a contract employee for Southern Regal and worked in the customer service department downtown," Ted said, filtering through pages of notes. "He had been there for about a year, and as far as I could tell, he was a good employee. I talked to a couple of his coworkers, and like everyone, they are stunned that this happened. The problem was the injury from the Navy. The people I talked to said he had some type of injury that forced him out of the Navy, and he was pretty much in constant pain and discomfort. Again, with the sitting. Tough to have a job sitting in front of a screen all day when you can't sit for very long without pain. One guy said Newberry was often the only person who was standing in a office with fifty people. They actually moved him to a corner so that it wasn't so conspicuous. He was a good guy. Good at his job. Stood and stretched a lot. He was close to a girl named Cindi Meadows. She's out of town, and I haven't been able to track her down. But the intelligence-gathering from the employment front is that nobody had a clue. Shock."

"So, we basically have no motive," I said. "We have a guy with a gun but no reason as to why he would want to shoot up the Waterfront."

"That's about right," Ted said. Olivia concurred.

"Well, I'm exhausted from today's early wake-up call

from Ted, and tomorrow's now my day off, so I'm gonna hit it." I sighed.

"Oh, why are you exhausted?" Ted asked, one eyebrow raised and a silly grin on his face.

"Am I missing something?" Olivia asked.

"Nope, no one is missing anything," I said. "Good luck tomorrow. Call me if anything crazy happens."

ON MY WAY home, I picked up a small bouquet and a quickie meal from the supermarket. I returned to my apartment and found my bed neatly made and the wineglasses and dishes from the night before washed and on the drying rack. I felt pleasantly surprised, though I shouldn't have been.

She's a really nice lady.

After my keto meal, I walked down the hallway and knocked a couple of times on Denise's door. She opened it with a big smile, which grew to a blush when she saw the flowers.

"Last night was great," I said. "Sorry I had to cut out. And thanks for doing the dishes."

"Thank you for the flowers," she said as she gave them the obligatory sniff. "I had a good time, too, and you are welcome."

Cue the awkward pause.

"I actually have an early meeting tomorrow," she said. "And I was a bit hungover too. Text me tomorrow?"

"Of course," I said, not really sure what I was expecting her to say or do. I wished her goodnight and received a kiss on the cheek in return.

Did I just dodge the Rebecca followup bullet? Feels like it.

I walked back to my apartment and got a text from my mom.

Mom: "Forgot to say you did very well on *The Morning Show* yesterday. Cathy Merrick is sooo sweet."

Me: "Thank you."

Mom: "You should be interviewing Swanson instead of Skip Kennedy! You're smarter and better looking."

Me: "But I have a soul."

Mom: "What does your soul have to do with it? Does your soul have a house in the Hamptons like Skip?"

Me: "Goodnight, Mom."

I tossed my phone on the night table. My mom. She wants me to have it all. Or the appearance of having it all for her cosmo klatsch. Even if it is all her doing.

My body needed sleep.

Chapter Eight

7 a.m, Monday, Pete's Apartment

I WOKE UP on Monday morning feeling a thousand times better. It was supposed to be my day off, but I couldn't seem to get my mind off the story.

I spent about thirty minutes on the treadmill, watching TV and switching channels.

I flipped on *The Morning Show* and saw my new BFF Cathy Merrick interviewing an expert on active shooter incidents.

With so much extraneous crap on the screen—weather, news scroll, traffic report, etc.—I couldn't figure out what her name was.

She said Swanson's action to shoot at Newberry was an extremely rare occurrence. From 2000 to 2021, fewer than three percent of 433 active attacks in the U.S. ended with a civilian firing back, according to a study from Texas State University. *Huh.*

It was far more common for the police or a group of unarmed bystanders to take down an attacker—or for the police to kill the shooter. In twenty-five percent of the cases, the attacker stopped firing due to leaving the scene.

"The only thing that stops a bad guy with a gun is a good

guy with a gun," the expert pointed out, is an inaccurate statement because of the word "only." But that hasn't stopped gun rights groups and social media trolls from jumping all over it.

Interesting.

The expert, whose name I still did not know, closed out by saying it was undeniable Swanson acted heroically, but she also made clear it would be a mistake to think armed civilians can be relied upon to regularly stop mass shootings.

I switched over to FAN News, which was heavily promoting Skip Kennedy's interview with Swanson in what they were calling the "Hero at the Waterfront."

The FAN anchors gushed about Swanson, and then they played a short teaser clip:

Swanson: "I teach gun safety, and many of my students are concerned about active shooter incidents. They are worried about themselves and mainly about their kids, and that's why they take my course. So, I've been through the active shooter scenario a thousand times in my head, and on Friday, I was just in the right place at the right time."

Kennedy: "And with the right, legal weapon."

Swanson: "Yes, sir."

Voice-over: "Tune in tonight for Skip Kennedy's exclusive interview with the 'Hero at the Waterfront.'"

They are milking the crap out of this exclusive. Sucks so bad.

I turned on Bo Rodgers' *Bo Time* conservative podcast. He was slamming Newberry as a terrorist—maybe international or maybe domestic, didn't seem to matter.

Rodgers: "We have no idea where this guy was for four

years while he was in the Navy. Those ships go all over the world, and these guys hop off the ships and take shore leave who knows where. What's it to say this guy didn't get recruited by the next radical cell, the next Al-Qaeda? Or maybe he's a crazed white supremacist. For the past fifty years, we've been focusing on people who come to our country like the 9/11 bombers and the guys who hit the *USS Cole* and the World Trade Center the first time. Now we have to also focus on the people around us who were in our own military. And we are training these guys to be killers, but who knows if one of them has a screw loose and shows up trying to shoot up the next big game or your kid's piano recital.

"We need to get Walter Swanson on our show, and I'm glad he's teaching people how to use guns because from where I sit, we need thousands of guys like him to keep our country safe. When some nutjob threatens us, we are gonna need an armed citizen like Swanson to take him down."

I was sitting in my living room, listening to these multi-millionaire commentators who'd tapped into this far-right base, and I realized that while I didn't consider myself to be in an ivory tower, I did know I was not at all in tune with the conservative culture of the South. I grew up in Miami, among many of the "coastal elites," and even though I went to school in North-Central Florida, Gainesville was a university town and far more liberal than the rest of North Florida. And let's not even talk about my eighteen months in New York City at Columbia.

The people I surround myself with are like-minded and

generally believe in our constitutional right to bear arms, but most of my friends believe in gun control and the need to get assault rifles off the street. This thinking is reinforced when we watch CNN and MSNBC, which embrace the liberal side of the political spectrum. We also get entranced by celebrities and influencers who agree with us.

I may not live in an ivory tower, but I work on one of the lower floors.

The other half of the political spectrum doesn't agree with me. They fear if liberals get their way, everyone's guns will be taken away, and we will be in even deeper shit as a country.

The polarizing split made it tougher to cover this story objectively; everyone seemed to want you to go one way or the other.

LATER THAT MORNING, I invited myself for lunch with my brother-in-law, the one who owns a gun shop. If anyone could educate me about guns and the far right, it was Craig.

Craig Evans opened Patriot Guns more than twenty years ago in a small shopping center in northern Duval County. He quickly learned there was money to be made in the gun trade. He eventually bought his building and then acquired the entire shopping center. A big part of his success is his indoor firing range, and he leases the rest of the center to a nail salon, a tattoo parlor, a CBD shop, and Dixie Chicken. I always knew that even if I didn't enjoy Craig's company, which was basically never, I could always get a few bites of the best fried chicken in Florida.

Patriot Guns sat in a thirty-thousand-square-foot space, most of it used for the firing range, and Craig had built up a loyal client base that included men and women, young and old, and from all walks of life. Law enforcement types brushing up on their skills, hunters, gun lovers, you name it. Black, white, brown, gay, straight, yoga moms, and CEO types. He serves the rainbow, and his customers arrive in beat-up old pickup trucks, Mercedes sedans, and Teslas.

He rented range time and sold ammunition, earplugs, headphones, gun-cleaning equipment, tactical gear, all manner of political and commercial messaging T-shirts, and, of course, lots of guns and knives.

Craig liked to remind me that in World War II, Japan was deterred from invading the U.S. mainland by a fear of American citizens with guns in their closets. Japan's Admiral Isoroku Yamamoto said, "You cannot invade mainland United States. There would be a rifle behind each blade of grass."

The authenticity of this quote is widely disputed, but the point is well made. Americans have a lot of guns.

When I entered Craig's shop, he greeted me with a big smile and then reached under the counter to hand me a pair of noise-canceling headphones. He knew I liked to check out the range because it's always such a scene, but I hated the noise. This time, he handed the headphones to me instead of making me ask.

Craig married my older sister Penny about ten years ago,

and they have an eight-year-old daughter who was flirting at the time with being a vegetarian and looking for ways to save the planet. At a very young age, she'd already developed the opposite politics of her father.

"Heard you've been busy," he said. "What's going on?"

"Well, today is officially my day off," I said. "But I have some nagging questions about what I've seen and heard over the past two days about the active shooter and his arsenal. I'm sure you've seen some of the news coverage."

"People have sent me clips, and Penny has been filling me in," he said. "But you know I don't watch the news."

I knew it well but fell into the trap anyway. Many a holiday dinner had been interrupted and punctuated over my work for the "fake news" media.

"Regardless, you know I will help you in any way I can." He smiled.

"Well, I'm trying to understand as much as I can about the active shooter, a guy named Kyle Newberry, and the guy who shot him, Walter Swanson. He seems to be a big gun enthusiast. He's all over the internet, with classes and all this other stuff. He's pushing his safety and concealed-carry classes. I guess he's trying to become some kind of gun industry and firearm advocacy influencer."

"Okay." Craig nodded.

"And then yesterday, we learned Newberry owned something like fifteen guns."

"That's not a lot."

"He also had something like two thousand rounds of ammunition."

"Listen, I have many customers who have bought more than fifteen guns just from me. They also buy them at other shops and from dealers, and two thousand rounds is not that much ammo for a lot of guys. I know doctors and lawyers who have twice as many guns and way more ammo—and it's sitting in their gun safe in the garage right next to their fishing rods."

"And he had more than one hundred knives," I added.

"Well, that's a lot of knives for the average guy, I'll give you that. What kind of knives?"

"About twenty-five fixed blades and about seventy-five pocketknives, some of them switchblades."

I could feel one of Craig's dissertations coming.

"Automatics are legal in many states, including Florida. The switchblade stigma is long gone. All the big manufacturers make automatics. The ones that shoot out the front are a bit crazy, but what you would probably call a switchblade is pretty common these days. What you are describing to me is the inventory of a small-scale operator at the gun show. The amount of stuff would just about fill up a table."

"What are the odds?" I asked.

"Really good. Because half of my friends on Facebook are talking about Newberry because he has, or used to have, a table at the gun show."

"Why the fuck didn't you tell me?"

"Because this way was more fun, and you never asked me." He gave me an all-knowing look. "You just did your smart-guy, big-brain reporter thing and assumed you knew more than me. And I knew you were coming over here and we were gonna get chicken. More fun to mess with you."

"So, your friends knew Newberry. Did he ever come in here?"

"I don't think so. I'm pretty good with faces, and I don't remember him. It's possible he could have been here when I wasn't working, but I don't know the guy."

"Who runs the gun show?"

"That would be Lenny. He's a friend of mine. You want to talk to him?"

"If he knows Newberry, yeah."

"Give me a minute."

Craig went into his office, and I decided to check out the range. I put on the headphones and opened the heavy steel door. The faint popping noises I'd heard while chatting in the lobby grew significantly louder, even with headphones on. Craig had room for twenty people to shoot at any given time. As it was a Monday and still early, he only had a handful of customers shooting, almost all with handguns.

I'll admit I don't like handguns. I'm intimidated by them, which probably has as much to do with my lack of knowledge about them as my personal politics. I believe in the Second Amendment, and I will defend our right to bear arms with anyone, but I personally don't get handguns. In my opinion, which I know is not widely held, the only reasons to have a handgun are to intimidate or inflict damage on another human being. You never hear of a guy bagging an elk or musk ox with a nine-millimeter.

My brother Dave is a bow hunter. He has traveled the world killing animals with his compound bow—or bows, plural, as he probably has ten of them. He doesn't use a rifle because I guess he likes the challenge of trying to kill a moose or whatever at closer range with a well-placed arrow to the heart or lungs. But he's not trouncing through the woods with a Glock trying to take down a ten-point buck. Again, I don't have an issue with anyone owning a handgun. They just aren't for me.

I casually observed a middle-aged guy take target practice.

I uncovered one ear to hear the shots without the benefit of noise cancellation.

Bam! Bam!

I immediately felt like I was back at the Waterfront. That distinctive crack, followed by the sound of a shell casing bouncing off the floor. I got a chill, and that unsettled feeling returned.

Another shot. *Bam!*

Another chill.

Handguns. Not for me.

I returned to the lobby, and Craig informed me that his friend, Lenny, would be joining us for chicken.

I DON'T KNOW how Dixie Chicken got its name. Perhaps it was first opened by a woman named Dixie or named for the nickname for the South that falls below the Mason-Dixon Line. I do know that the name may one day come under fire. Country music band The Dixie Chicks became The Chicks after some folks complained that the word *Dixie* connoted the pre-Civil War, pro-slavery South. It's interesting here in Jacksonville because the city is home to the grocery chain Winn-Dixie, which caught some heat a few years ago for the Dixie in its name, but the chain stuck with it.

Seems like these things are cyclical, so I could see a day when some folks might knock on the door of a great chicken joint in Jacksonville and say, "Either produce a lady named Dixie as your proprietor or get canceled." More barstool conversation.

Entering Dixie Chicken, you are greeted by Elvis—actually multiple Elvises. Aside from the two nearly full-sized Elvis Presley mannequins that guard the door, the restaurant sports another twenty or so photos of the King. They have the young Elvis, the old Elvis, Hawaii Elvis, jumpsuit Elvis. Elvis, in various stages of his gyrating glory, keeps watch over my chicken "Graceland."

It's a small place, seating around thirty people, but it also has a brisk takeout business. The menu consists of all the Southern staples: fried catfish, hush puppies, mashed potatoes and gravy, collard greens, mac and cheese, and about five different kinds of pie, mainly cream pies, spinning in an old-fashioned glass case.

The star of the place, of course, is the Southern fried chicken. I go back and forth on differing theories on what makes Dixie Chicken so good. One is that it is simply made with tremendous love and care with great ingredients and no shortcuts. The other is that they put drugs in the chicken. I generally lean toward the first theory, but it's weird that a few hours after you have eaten at Dixie Chicken, you somehow want more Dixie Chicken.

I have spoken with the waitresses a few times, and from what I gathered, they marinate the chicken in a buttermilk mixture overnight and then double-dip it in seasoned flour and some amount of cornmeal. I think they let it stand for a while before dropping it in hot oil. Might be lard, but if you ask too many questions, they clam up like you're casing the place or trying to steal their tips.

The end result is a glorious piece of chicken with a hardened, flavorful crust and skin that melts in your mouth and lights up your taste buds. It's never more than perfectly golden brown, and they know exactly when to replace the oil because I have eaten their chicken a dozen times and never once had a piece that tasted the least bit burned. It always tastes like the freshest, newest batch. And once you break through the crust, you are greeted by a steamy, juicy, flavorful bird that will make your head spin.

I understand that there are other great chicken joints around the country. I have watched more than my share of shows on the Food Network, but Dixie Chicken is the best I've ever had, and it might be the best in the country. Then again, it might be the drugs.

Lenny Aronberg was old-school Jacksonville, in his late sixties, and had been running the gun show at the convention center for as long as Craig could remember. He joined us in a booth and was clearly looking forward to lunch. He and Craig each ordered sweet tea, and I asked for a diet soda, which immediately drew looks from them.

"The camera adds ten pounds," I said, "and I'm not good enough at this job to risk not looking thin on the air."

"Pretty boy problems," Craig joked.

"I'm definitely eating chicken," I said.

I took out my phone and showed Lenny a photo of Kyle Newberry.

"That's him," Lenny said. "That's Chip."

"Chip?" I asked.

"Yes, he went by Chip at the gun show," Lenny explained. "Short for Charles, which was his middle name, I guess. Before coming over here, I went through my records, and Chip has had a table at the gun show most Saturdays over the past year and a half. I didn't know him very well, but he was always fine with me and paid his fees on time. He had a rolling suitcase with most of his stuff. He had one skirted table, and he usually wore a Navy hat or a Navy shirt of some kind, so customers would know he was a vet, I guess. One of the tricks of working the show is knowing how to engage with people, and most gun-show customers are patriotic and respect the military."

"Was he a licensed dealer?" I asked. "We didn't find anything about him being licensed in our searches."

"I have no idea," Lenny said.

"How do you sell guns without a license?" I asked. "I don't understand."

"This is America, Pete—read your Constitution," Lenny replied. "And pay your NRA dues. You don't need a license to sell guns."

I was feeling utterly confused and could only nod as I

figured a lesson was on its way.

"Let's start with this," Lenny continued. "He had a really good eye for knives, and I think that's where he made most of his money. But, okay, ninety-nine percent of the guys at the gun show are basically working as resellers of guns. They have Colts and Smith & Wessons and Glocks, stuff like that, and they are all basically competing with one another on price. Chip was mainly selling knives, so he had less competition. He probably ordered them from the manufacturers or the wholesalers. He got his hands on a dealer account and then bought a bunch of automatics and cool tactical knives and sold them for a nice markup. Now, you don't make as much selling a $40 or $50 or $100 knife as you do on a $300 or $1,500 gun or rifle, but you can still make money. If a guy has a regular job where he's making $30 an hour, he can supplement his income by buying five-dollar knives and selling them for twenty bucks at the gun show to a kid with a hard-on for switchblades."

"Interesting," I said, realizing I knew nothing of this business or subculture, or however you might describe it.

"I'm not saying that was exactly what he was doing, but that's what I imagine he was doing," Lenny said.

"But he also had guns," I said.

"Yeah, everybody who knows about knives also knows about guns, and I'm guessing he dabbled in guns. He would always arrive early at the show while guys were setting up, and that's how he found more knives, even rare knives."

"What do you mean? What does getting there early have to do with it?"

"Have you ever bought and sold anything in your whole life?" Craig asked me incredulously.

"I'm just a dumb reporter," I said. "Help a guy out."

"The money is made on the buy," Craig said. "If you buy low and buy right, then you can always make a decent profit. Buy too high and buy wrong, and you're screwed. What he did, as far as Lenny seems to be able to tell, is to show up early at the show and see if any of the gun dealers had interesting knives, and then he'd make his buys. He would basically take advantage of the fact that the gun dealers didn't know as much about knives as he did. He would buy cheap from the dealers in the morning and sell them at a profit later in the day or the following week." Then, deferentially, Craig added, "Is that about right, Lenny?"

"Exactly." Lenny agreed. "And a guy like Newberry probably knew a bit about older guns or certain guns, so while he wasn't the guy to see for a 'normal' gun, he would buy older guns, antiques, or guns he knew were rare. Find something interesting, put it on your table, and see if you can find a buyer."

"Okay, so I'm still trying to wrap my head around this," I said. "He wasn't a licensed gun dealer, but he was still buying and selling guns?"

"Again, I don't know where you went to school or why you don't understand how our country works." Lenny laughed. "But you don't have to have a license to sell a gun to someone. Just like you don't need a license to sell a knife, or a car, or a watch, or a pen, or a television, or a laptop."

"Or chicken?" I said.

"Exactly. If Newberry was buying and selling guns but not a bunch of them, he would fall into the category of a hobbyist." Lenny pulled out his phone. "Craig told me what we were going to be talking about, so I did some of your legwork—that's what you call it, right?" He showed me the web page from the U.S. Bureau of Alcohol, Tobacco, Firearms and Explosives.

"Yes," I said. "Let's have a look."

The first highlighted excerpt read: "Federal law requires that persons who are engaged in the business of dealing in firearms be licensed by ATF. The penalty for dealing in firearms without a license is up to five years in prison, a fine up to $250,000, or both."

Okay, so you did need a license to buy and sell guns.

The second highlighted excerpt read: "As a general rule, you will need a license if you repetitively buy and sell firearms with the principal motive of making a profit. In contrast, if you only make occasional sales of firearms from your personal collection, you do not need to be licensed."

Maybe not.

"So, you're saying Newberry was only making occasional sales from his personal collection?" I asked.

"My guess is that he falls into that latter hobbyist category, so yes," Lenny said. "It's a gray area."

"So, he could sell any gun to anybody?"

"No," Craig and Lenny replied in unison.

"Let's say he has a gun on his table and someone wants to buy it," Craig explained. "The buyer has to show his identification and be over eighteen and produce his concealed-carry permit. Check those two things, get your cash, hand over the gun, and Bob's your uncle."

"Craig, nobody on this continent says, 'Bob's your uncle,'" I quipped. "There's something just wrong about using a British turn of phrase while talking about American gun laws, or lack of gun laws. But either way, is this what they call the gun show loophole?"

"Ha!" Craig said. "If you don't like what we just said, you're gonna hate this: Federal law does not require unlicensed private sellers to perform background checks on gun purchasers. *That's* the gun show loophole."

"The guy was a hobbyist," Lenny said. "And I really think he made most of his money selling knives, which are almost totally unregulated in Florida. You can buy and sell automatics and assisted opens and all sorts of stuff. Now, the knives that actually launch out, like a little harpoon—those are illegal."

"He was a small-scale operator," Craig said. "So, why should he have to deal with all the paperwork and stuff I need to do if he's mainly selling knives and, every once in a while, an antique or rare gun to a guy who may never even fire it?"

"Understood," I said. "Lenny, what else do you know about Newberry?"

"Obviously, he was a lot younger than me, so I didn't have much in common with him." He paused, collecting his thoughts. "On show days, I'm going at a thousand miles an hour, so I didn't talk to him very much. I know he had some medical complaints. He didn't like to sit because he had back issues, so he was constantly standing and stretching and doing exercises for his back. I think he dealt with some regular back pain or discomfort of some kind. He was a nice guy who paid his eighty dollars each week and never caused me any grief."

So now I have a nice, seemingly regular guy who happens to sell guns and knives as a side hustle. And there's that bad back—the injury issue again.

"Do you know anything about Walter Swanson?" I asked.

"I don't know anything beyond what I've seen online," he said. "Some guys online said they think he came to the show, but you can't believe what you read on the internet. He may have come to the show, but I have no way of knowing."

"You don't track who comes to the show or anything like that?" I asked, quickly wishing I could take the question back.

"Are you fucking kidding me? Have you not been paying attention at all? My people do not want to be tracked by the *effing* government or by me. And even if I kept track, I wouldn't share any info with anyone. Whenever anyone in the country goes postal, for whatever reason, people want to shut me down. How would you feel if the actions of a crazy person completely imperiled your livelihood?"

A rhetorical question.

"Listen, I'm a nosy person by nature, and sometimes I ask the wrong question," I said. "Not trying to upset you.

You have been super helpful."

I moved an untouched chicken thigh over to Craig's plate. His eyes lit up.

"You barely ate anything," Lenny said. "One piece of chicken and half your mashed potatoes. You did make short work of the greens. What's the name of that skinny model? Kate Moss."

"Lenny, I have no idea who you are talking about," I lied. "And, by the way, I would enjoy nothing more than eating that whole chocolate cream pie over there."

Of course I knew who Kate Moss was, but I couldn't let these guys screw with me all day long. Kate Moss allegedly once said, "Nothing tastes as good as skinny feels."

"Can I buy you guys lunch?" I asked, looking for the waitress with the intent of intercepting the check.

The next battle was joined: the quest to pay the check in a move of dominance and machismo. Who can argue the best to pay the bill is the human equivalent of rutting elephants or bighorn sheep ramming each other.

"You are not buying me lunch," Lenny said.

"No way," Craig chimed in. "This was my invite." Which was a lie.

"Both of you need to respect your elders," Lenny said.

It was exhausting to watch, and they were getting absolutely nowhere.

"I can expense it, so lunch will be courtesy of the fake news media," I finally suggested.

For the first time all day, there was silence. Neither had a snappy retort. They smiled as I handed my credit card to the waitress.

"You guys can fight over the tip," I said. No reason to let the show end just yet.

Chapter Nine

2 p.m., Monday, Outside Patriot Guns

I WAS SITTING in my car in the parking lot of Craig's gun shop, ready to head home, and my phone rang. It was Rod Kirby.

"Sorry to bother you on your day off, Pete, but do you have a minute?"

"Sure," I said.

"I just got off the phone with Jason Wheeler."

"Jason Wheeler of the Wheeler brothers?"

"That's the one."

The Wheelers were two of the most successful and opportunistic operatives in the blurry political, public relations, and media landscape. Jason had always been a private-sector political campaign guy, while Stephen made a name for himself working in the White House.

Stephen was an incredibly polarizing figure because he was the architect of some of the most controversial policies that came out of the White House. He had been an aide to Senator Ed Garcia of Texas, but sometime during his first campaign, the president tapped him for a senior policy role, and he ran with it all the way to the West Wing. If I was only allowed one word to describe the Wheeler brothers, it would only take me a millisecond to settle on *smarmy*.

Since he left the White House, Stephen had joined his brother's consulting firm, and the family business was raking it in. They represented candidates, causes, foundations, diet pill companies, direct-response pillow salesmen, pushers of low-testosterone meds, you name it. If you could promote it with an 800 number, a website, some cheap TV commercials, and a boatload of social-media ads, the Wheelers could be in on it—and they always took a big cut. They had been accused of all manner of deceptive trade practices but were never convicted. They had good lawyers and a knack for staying one step ahead of regulators.

Knowing what I did, the next thing out of Rod's mouth shouldn't have surprised me, but it still did.

"The Wheelers are representing Walter Swanson," he said.

"Okay, that's nutty." It took me a moment to process it. "But what does that have to do with me?"

"Well, as far as I can tell, they have a three-part plan for Swanson. The short-term plan is that they are going to help him crank up his online courses. They see dollar signs in promoting the courses, making them more professional, and then promoting the heck out of them using their marketing machinery. The Wheelers will take a big slice but probably make Swanson a millionaire in short order. So, that's the short-term.

"The long-term is that Swanson is going to be on Bo Rodgers' podcast today, and Rodgers is going to suggest that Swanson run against Democratic Congresswoman Debbie

Rodriguez next fall. He lives in her district. Rodgers will probably open his campaign account. They are going to make him a congressman!"

"The Wheelers make him rich, then Rodgers gets him elected to Congress," I said, clenching my teeth. "Wow. And the medium-term?"

"That's why I'm calling. They are already developing a limited miniseries about Swanson, calling it the *Armed Samaritan* or something like that, for Netflix or Hulu or Amazon—you know, the highest bidder. They called me because without our footage, it's much less interesting, and they want you."

"They want me?"

"The station owns the footage, you know that, but we don't control you. And I'll be honest with you, Pete, you can work with them as long as it's in a journalistic capacity that doesn't conflict with the station and your day-to-day work. It's in your contract just for these types of situations where a story becomes a book or a movie, etcetera. We don't own you, Pete. We own most of you but not all. So, you can do books or documentaries and get compensated, but it has to be properly negotiated with the station's consent and in compliance with your contract. If you do work outside the normal scope, you should get paid for it.

"Most of the time, we just want to be sure it's aboveboard. I don't give a shit if you're the master of ceremonies for a charity and they give you a room night in a nice hotel. Who cares? But this could be worth big bucks for the station and for you personally, so it needs to be handled properly.

THE BYSTANDER

They could do this without you, but they saw you on *The Morning Show* and think you are an interesting, easygoing guy who can turn a phrase. Frankly, they'd be stupid to do this without you. You were on the scene and had the presence of mind to film it. Everyone's seen the footage, and I think Swanson's fifteen minutes of fame would already be up without it. You should be in the documentary. So, to summarize, call your agent. I'll give you Jason Wheeler's number."

"Well, that's a lot to unpack," I said, my head now swirling with thoughts of some extra income. "Any idea how much cheese we're talking about?"

"These guys know how to make money, Pete, so I don't think they're going through all this effort to put a few hundred bucks in your pocket. But one more thing: I can't tell you what to do on this, but these guys are really aggressive, and plenty of people think they are shady. So, be careful. Call your agent."

"Thank you, Rod. I appreciate it and will absolutely keep you apprised. I don't know jack shit about how this stuff works."

"That's generally how I like it," he said with a laugh.

I jotted down the number, said thanks, and hung up.

I called my agent, Evan Lieberman. We first met when I was in graduate school and he was in law school at Columbia. We were drinking buddies and became fast friends when I figured out how smart he was and realized he was the easiest laugh on the planet. He has a great sense of humor, but he laughs at nearly all of my jokes. He's perfect for my ego. We also share a very similar worldview, which I attribute to my belief that he and I watched all the same television shows, went to the same movies, and listened to the same music when we were kids, even though we lived on different sides of the country and didn't yet know each other.

In law school, he clerked for an entertainment law firm that hired him after graduation. When I got my offer to work in Ohio, I called him and became the first client he ever landed on his own. He has since signed many more and negotiated a ton of TV reporter contracts.

"What's happenin', man?" he answered the phone with typical enthusiasm. "I haven't called you because I figured you've been busy."

"Oh good, then that means I haven't forgotten to call you back." I paused. "I haven't returned many calls for the past several days, to be honest. But I did have an interesting conversation with Rod Kirby this morning."

"About your contract? He'd be crazy to want to renegotiate right now with a year left, and you're red-hot." Typical Evan, always seeing the big picture.

"No, the Wheeler brothers called him, and they want me to be part of a documentary."

"Get the fuck outta here. That's crazy. I mean, a good crazy. I think."

"I think so too. So, you know the details of the shooting, right?"

"The guy got shot at the Waterfront, and you filmed it. I live in New York, the media capital of the world, not under a rock."

"Okay, sorry, but my ego gets in the way, and I've been checked a few times over the past couple days."

"You are supposed to have an ego, Pete, but tell me what's going on with the Wheelers."

"Well, they are now representing the armed bystander, Walter Swanson. Apparently, he's been busy in New York for the past couple of days because he's already working with the Wheelers on a whole boatload of crap. I mean, they're talking about running this guy for Congress at some point. And the Wheelers are going to put Swanson's online courses on steroids and really cash in. And—this is my part—they are already working on a documentary of some sort for Netflix or some other major streaming platform. They want me to participate. And you know how much I know about this stuff—like nothing."

"Gotcha. Now I understand," Evan said.

"I'm going to give you Jason Wheeler's number so you can call him and figure out what's going on, okay? I guess we need a meeting or a call or whatever. I don't even know what to do next."

"This is exciting, Pete. You can make money from this."

"That's basically what Rod said."

"Okay, I will call them and call you back."

I headed back toward home but made a few day-off stops: haircut, groceries, light bulbs, car wash.

And then Evan called back.

"This looks real to me," he said. "The Wheelers have brought on a guy to produce the series. They are putting a package together to sell to one of the streaming services, and they know enough people that they think it will get bought. The producer has a track record, and they have some writers who are turning this into a three-act story, kind of framing it like act one is Swanson's background and early life, act two is the shooting, which would be where they want you, and act three is the aftermath—and his ascension."

Damn, the only thing that moves faster than a bullet is the media's response to a shooting.

"So, they've already kind of got this whole thing laid out?" I asked. "That's super quick."

"Yep. And apparently, they even have some budget numbers."

"What kind of numbers?" I was getting excited.

"Well, they wouldn't give me anything specific, but I told them that we weren't going to take a meeting without high-five figures guaranteed up front and a piece of the back end."

"And what did they say? You're killing me."

"They said okay."

"They said okay?" I asked, knowing I sounded like an idiot.

"They said okay, Pete. That's how this works. They are willing to pay to lock you in and then share the profits if it's successful. I think we can negotiate something good, but I wouldn't jump right into bed with these guys. I think you should meet them."

Never thought about this sort of thing when I started writing for my high school paper. These guys were a bit sketchy, but it was a lot of money. No harm in "taking a meeting," as

I think they say in Hollywood.

"Pete, are you there?" Evan snapped me back to reality.

"Yeah. Yeah, let's meet them."

"Good, because they want to send their jet to pick you up Wednesday morning. And we'll meet them at their offices on Fifth Avenue and hear the pitch."

"You're shitting me! A private jet to New York?"

"I shit you not, Pete."

"Wow, I need to process this."

This is the big time.

"They will either put you up at the Marriott Marquis Wednesday night or fly you back. If you stay, we can eat our way around the city like the good old days."

"Holy cannoli, okay, let me think about this for a second. I can't just take Wednesday off and go to New York in the middle of this story. And then be sitting with the guys who are shaping it and not report on it. That doesn't make a ton of sense."

I paused to think, and Evan respected my silence.

"Well, you always say that a negotiation is a give-and-take, right?" I said.

"Yep. So, you want something. What do you want, Pete?"

"I want an interview with Walter Swanson," I said. "I hate to make you do more work, but can you tell them that I will come to New York Wednesday if I can get an on-camera interview with Swanson?"

"Of course. That might squirrel the deal and my commission." He laughed. "But hey, why not? Go big or go home."

"Yeah, I know. But I think I can sell a trip to New York on the Wheelers' dime to Rod if I come back with an interview with the guy of the moment."

"I get it. You're not such a bad negotiator after all," he said, followed by his characteristic laugh.

"Thanks, Evan. Let me know."

I ended the call. I really had nothing to lose.

I probably shouldn't take the free flight from the Wheelers from an ethics standpoint, I thought. But no way Rod would pay for me to go up there. And he couldn't stop me from taking the free flight for personal business. *Not a bad play, unless it doesn't work.*

Chapter Ten

4 p.m., Monday, Pete's Apartment

WHEN I GOT home, I tuned to our station in time to see Jill's update on the victim of the third bullet:

"This is Jill Thompson reporting from Jacksonville Memorial Medical Center with an update on Stephanie Singleton, who was shot at the Waterfront on Friday. We are learning that the grandmother of three was taking her grandson to the High Topper for a new pair of sneakers, and then they were planning to meet the family for dinner.

"The errant bullet has caused significant internal injuries and was at one point lodged near her lungs. She has been in and out of consciousness, according to doctors and her family members. She's seventy-two, so you can imagine that her family is extremely concerned. The hospital has her listed in serious condition. This means that her vitals may be unstable and not within normal limits and the patient is acutely ill, and indicators are questionable. She could be upgraded to fair condition, but doctors also warn that if things worsen, she could be downgraded to critical condition. According to one doctor, it's a bit dicey because of her age and the damage.

"I had an opportunity to speak to her family members

today, and her daughter said that her mom is a fighter who worked really hard her whole life. She has been volunteering part-time at the local elementary school even after retiring from the public school system. She enjoys spending time with her grandkids, traveling, going to the movies, doing jigsaw puzzles, and baking. So, she's really a person who loves life, a lot of fun to be around. And they're just hopeful that, you know, things will improve.

"Doctors said that she is responding to medication, but regardless, she will have a long road to recovery.

"Jill Thompson, WJAX, reporting from Downtown Jacksonville."

MY PHONE RANG. It was Evan. He told me that they would give me a half-hour with Swanson in their conference room, but they wanted me there only with my one-man-band camera setup. I told him to agree to it. He said he would organize the rest with them by email and have them send me the itinerary.

I wanted to fly back that night, so Evan and I would have to choose just one of our favorite hangouts for the post-meeting meal. Corned beef, pizza, or Chinese? Just one. I hate adulting.

My phone rang again. My mother.

"I'm kinda busy," I said. "I just negotiated an interview with the shooter, and the Wheeler brothers want to talk to me about a documentary."

"The political Wheeler brothers?" she asked.

"That's them."

"Interesting. How did they get in touch with you?"

"They're working with Swanson. They called the station, and the station put them in touch with me. I had Evan speak with them."

"That's the way to do it. They are very slick. I'm not sure I like how they make money."

She paused. Something was up. I know my mother. Long pauses are never good.

"The more I think about it, the more I don't like it." Then, she repeated herself: "I don't like it."

"What are you talking about? You're always telling me I need to build my brand, leverage my influence, and all that crap. They're talking about paying me a lot of money. Like down-payment-on-a-house money."

"Pete, you don't need to be so involved in something so controversial and political. These guys politicize everything, and that's not the type of reporting you should be doing. You don't want them screwing up an opportunity for you to do something bigger."

"What are you talking about, Mom? This is the biggest story I have ever seen. It's real news."

"If you want to become a real influencer with staying power, stay away from politics."

And if I don't want to be an influencer? I paused, needing to think, and then I got practical.

"But I've already scheduled it, and I'm getting the interview basically in exchange for the meeting," I explained.

Man, she drives me crazy sometimes. "I worked hard to get this done, and even Evan was impressed with my negotiation skills."

"So, Evan's going with you?"

"Yes."

"Okay, good," she said. "You know I've always liked Evan."

"Everyone likes Evan."

"He understands all the stuff that you don't pay attention to."

"I know, Mom, that's why he's my agent."

"Just be careful," she said. "These guys play in a cesspool. You don't want to get their stink all over you."

"Lovely way to describe it," I said. She could be so exhausting.

Another pause, and she asked, "Now tell me, who's Denise?"

"My neighbor. She's a lawyer with Winchell & Watson. We've been hanging out."

"Can I meet her next time I'm in town?"

"No promises. I have to go. Love you, Mom." I hung up.

A FEW MINUTES before eight p.m., I heard a knock and found Denise outside my door holding a plate of homemade brownies and a six-pack of one-hundred-calorie IPAs, a brand I had mentioned I liked.

I smiled at her. "Are you wooing me?"

"Pretty sure I don't need to," she said. "Can I come in?"

"Of course," I said. "I'm getting ready to watch the big Kennedy interview if you want to join me."

"Sure," she said.

"I'm giving you fair warning that I may yell at the TV," I said. "Seeing a guy scoop me just because of his political agenda is maddening. Kind of like watching your rival team play for the national title. I want to watch, but I don't plan on enjoying it."

"I completely understand," she said with a kind, empathetic look.

I stared longingly at the brownies covered with plastic wrap. *Do I make the first move?*

I popped open two beers. Denise declined a glass, so we clinked cans. Something to be said about a woman who will drink straight from a can. Friendly, approachable, girl next door—or the girl two doors down.

"Everyone at work was talking about the shooting," Denise said as she removed the plastic wrap and offered me a brownie, which I accepted. "Thankfully, no one from our firm was there, but everyone has an opinion about it."

"Lawyers with opinions?" I mock questioned. "Who would imagine?"

"I know, right?" She laughed. "My colleagues were all chiming in as if it were billable time."

That's funny.

"Anything interesting?" I asked.

"Well," she continued, "several people had friends of friends who said they were at the Waterfront, but I couldn't pin anyone down who actually seemed to be there. I was figuring I might want to connect you with them."

"That's sweet of you," I said. "We are still digging and talking to a lot of folks who were involved. Any legal issues jump out at you, counselor?"

"Well, we are a business firm, so we don't do criminal, not even white-collar," she explained. "But we had a spirited conversation about the Good Samaritan law and how it might apply to Swanson. The law is intended to cover police, first responders, and others who try to help during a crisis, like doctors or nurses. The lady in the High Topper, what was her name?"

"Stephanie Singleton," I said.

"Yes, Stephanie Singleton has to recover from a gunshot wound, so who is responsible for that—her medical bills? Does the Good Samaritan law cover her? What if she has a permanent injury from the gunshot? And what if she dies? It's open for debate because Swanson's not law enforcement. And if the law doesn't cover him, it's super ironic because he's almost the classic, non-legal definition of a Good Samaritan."

"So, if Swanson's not a Good Samaritan, then who is?" I asked. My legal knowledge came from one mass communication law class in college and binge-watching *Law & Order*.

"Typically, it's doctors, like when they say in the movies, 'Is there a doctor here?' in a restaurant or onboard a plane or something like that." She started to talk me through it as I imagined she would describe it to a client. "The law exists so that a Samaritan won't be afraid of getting sued if he, or she, treats someone they don't know. In a crisis, the injured party might be unconscious or incapable of telling the doctor or first responder about allergies or preexisting issues. And they might just not be a very good doctor, but they are trying to help. The law shields the Samaritan from liabilities if something goes wrong."

"Okay, but given all that, do you think the law covers Swanson?"

"I think it does, and most of the other lawyers agreed," she said. "They think it should be interpreted broadly. Where it doesn't apply is when the person giving aid also committed the crime. You can't be the criminal *and* the Good Samaritan."

"No protection for the bad guys?"

"Exactly," she said.

"Why were you guys discussing this?" I asked.

"That's what lawyers do," she said. "Lawyers are always going to look at the law. I'm sure the people who are into guns are talking about the guns, and the PR agents are worried about the reputation of the Waterfront. People talk about what they know. View things through their particular lens."

We sat on the couch, and she snuggled up next to me. I grabbed the remote and tuned the TV to FAN News just as the show was starting.

Kennedy came on wearing his signature blue suit and bow tie, and went right into it:

"Tonight is a rare opportunity on Kennedy, my friends. A little bit later, we will air my exclusive interview with an

American hero, Walter Swanson, the patriotic citizen from Florida who took down an active shooter at the Jacksonville Waterfront, likely saving dozens of lives and quite possibly changing every anti-gun argument we have heard from the radical left for the past thirty years. We will air the complete interview in a few minutes.

"I want you to know that I have had a chance to talk to Mr. Swanson. He is a salt-of-the-earth individual, a gentleman, and a patriot who saw an opportunity to help his fellow citizens and, with great bravery and incredibly steady hands, took down active shooter Kyle Charles Newberry.

"For those of you who haven't heard, law enforcement officials in Jacksonville breached Newberry's home, fearing booby traps yesterday. Thankfully, there were none, which would have been a final act of cowardice. The SWAT team emerged with a small arsenal of fourteen guns, more than one hundred knives, and more than two thousand rounds of ammunition. The scene of Newberry terrorizing college football fans at the Waterfront is one that we will never forget."

I made a mental note that my footage was being shown with a small "Courtesy of WJAX" in the corner. No mention of me, but that's probably the closest I would ever get to being on Kennedy's show.

Video from yesterday's press conference was then shown on the screen, and they aired one of Rebecca's sound bites about Newberry and her answer to my question about motive. And right in the middle of the screen was a caption: "Rebecca Dawes, Jacksonville Sheriff's Office PIO."

I strained not to glance at Denise. I felt her shift a little next to me. I should be focusing on *Kennedy,* I knew, but my brain was trying to find my "guy relationship guidebook" to figure out what to do in a situation like this. I don't think there's anything I could have said. I certainly didn't have any words at that moment.

I decided to let it ride and be a coward like most men.

Kennedy continued: "Before we air the interview, I want to bring in Florida Governor Jim McManus, joining us from Tallahassee, who can tell us the latest on what's been going on down there in the Sunshine State. Governor, welcome to *Kennedy*.

McManus: "Great to be here, Skip. Always a pleasure."

"That guy drives me crazy," I said to Denise.

No response.

Kennedy: "What's the latest?"

McManus: "As you just reported, law enforcement officers breached Newberry's apartment yesterday and confiscated a large cache of weapons. The investigation is still ongoing, and we don't yet have a motive."

Kennedy: "Wait, excuse me. With all due respect, Governor, the guy enters a crowded retail area waiving an assault rifle and you have no motive? His motive was to terrorize Americans and our country. Guys like Newberry are trying to shake the bedrock of democracy. His motivation is to engender fear. Now, I don't know if he had a bad breakup or other issues with his own inadequacy, but to me, his motivations were clear."

McManus: "Well, of course, Skip. What we're saying is

that we have not seen signs of any ongoing issues with the government or anything overt. This guy never wrote a manifesto, as far as we could determine, but we're scouring the internet and his background, and we're talking to people. And, you know, we're confident that we're going to uncover the truth about what was going on with him.

Kennedy: "It's domestic terrorism, Governor, but I know we all appreciate the hard work that your team is doing down there."

The pandering is unmatched.

McManus: "The more we can learn, Skip, the better off we are. We want to prevent this sort of thing from happening before shots are fired."

Kennedy: "I think guys like Walter Swanson are your best source of prevention. You've met him, Governor. You even took him to a football game. What do you think of Mr. Swanson?"

McManus: "I have been truly impressed with the way Walter has comported himself during this entire situation. He seized on a moment and performed a purely altruistic act. When you think about it, Skip, how many altruists are really out there? I'm a politician. I'm not one. You're a journalist who believes in justice, but you have your motivations too. We all try to do the right thing, but this guy entered the fray courageously and without fear for his own safety and then saved countless lives. I took philosophy classes in college, but I've rarely seen true, bona fide altruism. Standing for the greater good. The needs of the many. You get my point.

As you said, I have had a chance to talk with Walter and

his girlfriend. He's an extremely nice, grounded guy, as you have learned. And he's someone who has a passion for gun safety. Aside from his actions already kind of lighting a fire of political change in America, I think he has an opportunity to really expand his platform of gun safety and find ways to arm our citizens safely and properly because, unfortunately, even though I oversee an incredible group of law enforcement agencies in Florida, we have ten million people in our great state, and if one-hundredth of one percent of them are as crazy as Mr. Newberry, then we will have a real problem on our hands.

Kennedy: "That's well said, Governor. Thank you. And we appreciate all your help in getting Mr. Swanson here today. I know he told you that he wanted his first interview to be on *Kennedy*, and you helped make the connection. I appreciate it.

McManus: "You're welcome, Skip. Be well, God bless you, God bless the great state of Florida, and God bless America.

Kennedy: "Thank you, Governor. After this break, we'll show the interview.

As the station cut to a commercial, I turned to Denise and said, "That's a lot to unpack."

"She's pretty," Denise said.

I'm dead.

"Who's pretty?" I asked. I knew that wasn't going to work, so I recalibrated quickly. "Oh, Rebecca?"

Don't agree that she's pretty.

"She's a friend I know from work," I said, "who I think

might be engaged to a guy who works for the Jaguars. I know her, but I'm not seeing her."

I think I'm still dead.

"Ah, okay," Denise said. "That's actually none of my business. I was just saying she's pretty."

Women are so much better at this than men, or at least me. Pretty sure I'm still toast, but I was glad that I tried being honest—with some omissions.

"I'm glad you're here," I said. "I like having you here."

"And I like being here with you."

The oxygen was back in the room.

"Well, isn't that half the battle?" I suggested. "Finding someone you like being around?"

"Well, yes and no," she said. "I just got out of a relationship where I felt like he was stringing me along. I always felt like I was in competition with other women for his attention. I realize we are just getting to know each other, but I'm looking for someone who just wants to be with me. I hope you can respect that."

"I do," I said.

"Good," she affirmed. "Where are my brownies?"

Whew. She changed the subject. Back in the land of the living. *Not sure I'm clear of this issue, but I'm okay for the moment.*

The show came back on, and Kennedy said that he had recorded the Swanson interview earlier and invited his audience to watch.

Walter Swanson was medium height with a full head of light-brown hair. He was clean-shaven for the interview,

THE BYSTANDER

though he typically wore stubble in his videos. He was wearing what looked like nice jeans, a pressed button-down shirt, and what was likely a new sports coat. He sat up straight in his chair across from Kennedy, looking uncomfortable. No matter how many times you film a selfie video, nothing prepares you for the intimidation of big-time television. He looked a little scared, but who wouldn't be? No amount of prep in two days could really get you ready for something like this.

I turned to Denise. "I hope they cranked down the A/C in there for the poor guy. I'm predicting a lot of sweat."

"That's mean," she said.

"That's television," I said. "But Kennedy knows what he has. Here come the softballs."

Kennedy: "Walter, thank you for being here and for granting your first interview to *Kennedy*. I know you make a lot of videos, but I also know our studio can be overwhelming, so let's begin with some basics before we get into what happened on Friday. Tell me about yourself and what you do for a living."

Swanson: "Thank you, Mr. Kennedy. I'm a big fan of your show, and when this happened, I felt that you would be the best person for me to talk to about it."

Kennedy: "We appreciate that, Walter. We are happy to have you in New York."

Swanson: "I work for a technology and security company in Jacksonville. I'm a supervisor, and we do everything that keeps buildings and businesses safe and secure, like cameras, security systems, keycard systems, and computer firewalls.

We keep the bad guys out of business. I work all over the Jacksonville area.

Kennedy: "You were born in Jacksonville?"

Kennedy probably isn't this nice to his own mother, I thought.

Swanson: "Yes, I was born there and have lived there my whole life. I like to hunt and fish, and I'm a big believer in gun safety and education."

Kennedy: "Tell me more about that."

He would definitely be telling his mom to hurry up by now.

Swanson: "Well, I noticed that there were lots of videos online about people shooting guns and blowing things up. I feel like, mainly, people just want guns for safety and to protect themselves. I always worry that people will be careless with their firearms and do something unsafe or dangerous. Some of these newer guns don't even have safeties on them. There's a Glock that is designed for law enforcement, and they removed the safety because it could slow down a police officer. The problem is that it makes the gun more dangerous. I heard a story of a young cop who picked up his gun while he was getting ready to walk his dog and the dog yanked on the leash and the officer ended up shooting part of his thumb off. If a trained law enforcement officer can nearly lose a thumb by being just a little careless, imagine what could happen to a regular person?"

Kennedy: "That's fascinating."

Gag me.

Swanson: "I started making videos because I enjoy fire-

THE BYSTANDER

arms, but I believe in using them responsibly. I practice my marksmanship on a regular basis and have taken some field courses, kind of like the way they train police officers. I was never in law enforcement or the military, but I really respect the work they do, and I kind of feel obligated to be a well-trained civilian."

Kennedy: "Take us back to Friday night at the Waterfront. Why were you there?"

Swanson: "Well, I'm a big football fan. My girlfriend went to the University of Florida, and I have been a Gator fan my whole life. Both of my parents and my brothers went there, and it is a family thing as much as anything else. I was working on a job downtown, and when I finished, I decided to meet my girlfriend down at the Waterfront. A lot of her friends were coming into town for the game, and that's where everybody was meeting."

Kennedy: "You were at an outdoor bar?"

Swanson: "Yes, the place transforms for the Florida-Georgia weekend because there are so many people there."

"Did you notice that Swanson put Florida first?" I said to Denise.

"He's misguided," she replied.

Swanson: "It was a little after five p.m., and we had just sat down and ordered drinks. I literally had one sip of my beer when the commotion started. I had my back to it, but I could see the look of panic in people's eyes, and my girlfriend said something was going on. Then people started running and screaming and saying, 'There's a guy with a gun!' Lots of screaming and profanity. By now, you have seen the footage. We all froze for a second and agreed that we should get out of there. We tried to get inside the restaurant, but there were so many people. And then I heard the shot. People really started to freak out, cramming through the door. It was chaos, and I was worried that we would get trampled. I wasn't moving, so I decided to turn around, and I saw the guy. He was walking back and forth, and then he turned his back to me. I had my gun, and I'd thought it through a million times. My best chance of survival and the best chance of survival for my girlfriend and all these people was for me to try to take this guy down. So, I pulled my gun out of my ankle holster and aimed it at him. I took a few steps toward him, with both hands on my weapon. A lot of people had scattered. When he turned toward me, I had a clear shot, and I took it. Thank God I hit him.

Kennedy: "You showed incredible poise and marksmanship.

Swanson: "A lot of people I know in law enforcement and at the gun range would have done the same thing."

Kennedy: "Were you afraid?"

Swanson: "Hell yeah. But it happened so fast. I saw the opportunity, and I took it. I'm not happy the guy died, but I also didn't want him to keep shooting or be sitting there wounded with an assault rifle. Some people have said I should have shot him in the leg or something. Honestly, that's more for cops and the movies. I was in fear for my life."

Kennedy: "We think you did the right thing. So, what's

next for you?"

Swanson: "Well, I don't know for sure. A lot of people are telling me that I now have a platform, but I don't really know what that means. I want to keep educating people, and I think gun safety and gun rights are important issues. I don't know exactly what will happen next, but I will probably be back to work next week."

Kennedy: "Have you seen the GoFundMe page that was set up for you? Looks like some folks have made sizable donations as a thank-you."

Swanson: "Honestly, I don't know anything about it. No offense, but I'm skeptical of the media industrial complex, so who knows how that stuff works and if I will ever see any of that money or if it will go toward gun safety and education."

Kennedy: "Well, I think you should get the money. We want you to keep doing what you're doing. How can people take your online courses?"

Swanson delivered the URL of his courses to the audience of the highest-rated news show in America. A marketing bull's-eye.

Kennedy: "On behalf of the football fans at the Waterfront last week and all of our FAN audience, thank you for your bravery, Walter.

Swanson: "Thank you, Skip.

And they went to commercial.

"Sorry they didn't give you any credit for filming it," Denise said, rubbing my shoulder.

"Ah, that's okay. What did you think?" I asked.

"I think the guy acted heroically," she said. "He saved a

lot of lives at great risk to himself."

"I agree."

"Can we watch something else now?" she asked. I opened Netflix and handed her the remote. She found a romantic comedy, and we relaxed and hung out for the rest of the night. I walked her back to her door just before eleven p.m.

Chapter Eleven

8 a.m., Tuesday, Pete's Apartment

HOW DOES THE phone know to ring just as you are stepping out of the shower? Trying not to slip and kill myself, I reached it in time to see, yet again, the number from Santa Barbara. Whoever this guy was, he was persistent. It was five a.m. in California.

"This is Pete," I said.

"You're a tough man to get ahold of, Mr. Lemaster," said the voice.

"It's been a busy couple of days. Who's this?"

"My name is Barry Petroff, and I'm an attorney in Santa Barbara, California."

"Okay, if you have a legal question, you're probably better off calling the station and our lawyers because I don't have any legal authority over much of anything except for my own personal affairs."

"This isn't necessarily a legal matter for you. It's about my client, Kyle Newberry."

"Again, if this is some sort of wrongful death thing, you need to talk to somebody else. And your guy was shot waving a rifle around a crowded mall on the busiest day of the year."

"There's more to this story, Mr. Lemaster, if I could have a few minutes of your time."

"Go ahead," I said, continuing to towel off and hunting for my clothes.

"There's more to Kyle Newberry than what people are saying and what is being reported."

This guy sounded pretty serious.

"Kyle was my client, and our conversations are protected by attorney-client privilege, even though he is deceased," he continued. "But I will tell you this: Kyle Newberry was not a terrorist, neither international nor domestic. And he was not mentally ill. He was troubled, without question, and anyone who knew him was aware that his life was difficult and very painful."

I wasn't sure what to make of this guy.

"I want to stop you there, Mr. Petroff. Can we switch to Zoom? I would like to see who I'm speaking with, and it's easier for me to take notes."

He agreed and within a couple of minutes, I was face-to-face with Barry Petroff. I turned on my dictation app so I could record the conversation and automatically transcribe it. He had no issue with it.

"Okay, so what kind of law do you practice?" I asked.

"I'm a civil attorney, and I represent many military veterans. I have filed federal cases on behalf of former soldiers, sailors, and airmen all over the country. Many have been injured in some way and need legal assistance. I'm a vet myself."

"You're in California. Are you licensed in Florida too?

How does a guy in Jacksonville end up being your client?"

"Federal cases can be tried by out-of-state lawyers. Happens all the time. Takes a little paperwork, but it's fairly common."

"So, Newberry was filing a lawsuit?" I prodded.

"I was helping him with some issues with the VA," Petroff answered. "But I can't get into the specifics."

"You're not making this easy, Mr. Petroff. Did you ever meet Newberry in person?"

"We talked on the phone and through video calls like this."

"Okay, what else can you tell me? We are all trying to figure out why this seemingly normal guy went to the Waterfront with an assault rifle."

"I had known him for about a year, and he was always in complete control of his mental faculties. He was a smart, methodical guy, and as you have probably already figured out, he was a throwback, an old soul. He came from a military family, and he didn't embrace a lot of things that young people his age were into. He hung out with older guys."

"I heard about that," I said, thinking back to my conversation with Craig and Lenny.

"So, you probably also learned that he didn't have a smartphone, didn't text," he said. "The guy actually wrote and mailed letters. After being in the Navy and getting injured, he had a fairly common skepticism of the government, but he wasn't militant. Pretty sure he was a registered Democrat."

I cut him off.

"So, you have said he was 'in pain' and 'troubled,' but you also said he was in complete control of his faculties. All seems kind of cryptic. Have you filed a lawsuit or something?"

"No we haven't," he answered.

I was cueing up the kill shot. In TV news, we have a really narrow window for stories. So many people call with crazy angles, and we just don't have the airtime or the desire to cover everything. I was preparing to cut attorney Petroff loose.

I explained, "Unfortunately, a lot of times in the news business, people talk and get upset, but unless there's a legal filing, it's tough to report on it. People argue all the time, but the filed lawsuit makes it real. I appreciate your call, and if there is ever a need to provide a character witness for Newberry, then I guess you are it. But he did threaten a lot of football fans a few days ago. Nobody seems to be too upset that he's dead."

There was a long pause. Mr. Petroff was used to getting his way.

I've dealt with a lot of people like that. He reminded me of my brother Dave. He's built a successful law practice and is a really good lawyer, so he has kind of gotten used to people being deferential and kissing his ass. I get the same long pause from him when I catch him off-guard with a "brotherly" insult. Then again, he still calls me Slappy.

"Okay, Mr. Lemaster," he said. "I'm going to email you some documents. They do not specifically involve Kyle

Newberry, but I can assure you that he was fully aware of these documents and the legal matters they cover. I know I'm being cryptic, and I'm sorry if this feels cloak-and-dagger, but I believe there's another story to be told here, and you will be well served to check it out. Perhaps we can talk tomorrow after you have had a chance to look them over."

I couldn't believe he just said "cloak-and-dagger." I replied, "I can't make any promises, but I will run it by our team and see if we can carve out the time. I have to be honest, I'm busier than a one-armed paper hanger with the hives."

He laughed.

I told him to send the files to my personal Gmail account because the station's spam filters often send emails with attachments into oblivion. We ended the call.

I can't even begin to tell you how many "great stories" have been pitched to me when the documents that were supposed to back them up were utter crap. I'm guessing it was less than even money that Petroff's documents would help my story. We will see. But I do give him credit for being persistent, and I guess old habits die hard with these military guys, getting up at the butt-crack of dawn. Reminded me of those old Army commercials: "We do more before nine a.m. than most people do all day."

I finally got dressed and headed to work.

ONCE AT THE station, I immediately went to Rod's office and told him about my Faustian bargain with the Wheelers. He seemed genuinely impressed and said, "I'm looking the other way about the plane ride" as I left his office.

I sat down with Ted and Olivia in the conference room. Ted was anxious to give me the rundown on what he had learned about Kyle Newberry the day before.

"While you were getting your beauty rest, some of us were doing real reporting," he said.

"My reporting might surprise you, but let's hear what you got first."

"By all accounts, Newberry had a normal childhood," Ted began. "He was born in Norfolk, Virginia; his father was in the Navy. His mother worked part-time and was the 'room mom' type. He was an okay student. Played T-ball and soccer. A Cub Scout for some period of time. Family moved around a bit to other Navy towns.

"He went to high school in San Diego, and then his parents moved here. He enrolled at Florida State College here in Jacksonville. He joined ROTC, and after two years had an associate's degree and decided to join the Navy. He was in supply and logistics. He was deployed at sea a few times, but it's hard to tell if he ever saw combat. Unclear if he ever saw a foreign port. My guess is yes, but it is pure speculation that he was ever anywhere outside of NATO or other closely allied countries. These guys want their time off in San Diego, New York, or Hawaii, not Cairo or Cambodia or whatever."

"I hear the beaches in Cambodia are amazing," I interjected.

"Not my point, but getting back to it, he was stationed at a base on the West Coast, again in some sort of supply or logistics type of position—you know, a desk job. One day, he's in a car accident on the base. Nothing horrific. Nobody died. But he got bounced around really good, and he ends up with a pretty severe back injury. He's only something like twenty-five at this point, nearing the end of his enlistment. He heals pretty well, but his doctors tell him that the injuries will likely be worse as he gets older. And that turned out to be true."

"What about his parents?" I asked.

"Well, we thought he lost both of his parents, but we have since learned that his father died of cancer while he was in the Navy and his mother is in a nursing home in southern Duval County. Apparently, dementia, pretty bad."

"Oh gosh, so sad," I said.

"Yeah, he moved back to Jacksonville, gets a job at Southern Regal, the health insurance company, and starts working on getting his bachelor's degree, again from the state college, which is super flexible with him because he's a vet and he's got some medical dispensations. Anyway, he's no charity case, but he's regularly in a lot of pain. We heard the stories that he was always standing up and stretching and that sort of thing, but I found out a lot more when I finally reached his friend, the previously elusive Cindi Meadows. She was out of town at her sister's wedding and had last seen Newberry last Wednesday. She and all of her coworkers are devastated. They can't believe it. She said that his back injury got progressively more difficult to deal with, just as the Navy doctors had predicted. She said he couldn't really function without his meds. Off the medication, he could barely walk, couldn't sleep, and he certainly couldn't work effectively."

"Couldn't he see doctors through Southern Regal?" I asked.

"That's what I was thinking," Ted said. "But he was only part-time, so even though he worked for an insurance company, he didn't have benefits. Ridiculous, right? So many companies these days are hiring people for part-time positions to avoid paying for medical or retirement benefits, even big healthcare companies. But Newberry did have health coverage through the VA. The problem, according to Cindi, was that it was a royal pain in the ass."

"Good grief," I said.

"Yeah, no picnic whatsoever. Apparently, he confided a lot in her, but she also said he was a friendly guy who talked to a lot of people. He mainly complained about the bureaucracy at the VA from what I can gather. She wasn't the only friend who knew he was in pain."

"So, we need to try to find more friends," I suggested.

"Yeah, we do," Ted continued. "Anyway, Cindi says that things got worse a few months ago when he was assigned a new doctor. His first doctor really understood his case, but a few months back, Newberry goes to see him to get his prescriptions refilled and the doctor says that very soon he wouldn't be able to treat him anymore because it takes the VA six months to pay him, and half the time it is wrong. The doctor can't handle the messed-up cash flow and says he can make so much more money without the hassle by focusing on non-VA, private-sector clients."

"Always comes down to money, right?" I said. "But hey, that's another solid angle for a news story: financial pressures and incentives."

"Yes, but this story is also about pain," Ted said. "The doc gave Newberry a few months' warning, but then about three months ago, Newberry is assigned a new doctor. And the new doctor changed his prescription. So, he is now getting progressively worse, and the new doctor is trying to back him off the pain meds. And because they are some type of opioid, he has to get authorization each month to get them refilled."

"That's a nightmare scenario for the guy."

"Yep. Cindi said the new prescription was a problem, but Newberry tried to work through it. He would have difficult days when he would need an 'extra' pill even though it wasn't really 'extra' because it was the same dosage the previous doctor had prescribed. Does that make sense?"

"Yeah, he was under-prescribed, I guess."

"Right. So, Cindi says that he was constantly in distress about not having enough pain medications, and it would be really bad toward the end of the month because he would run out or nearly run out. And if he went more than a day or so without his meds, it was really, really bad. When she saw him last Wednesday, he said he'd been on the phone trying to get his prescription renewed. She said he was frustrated but not any more than usual. She went on her trip and thought nothing of it. She thinks he may have been in distress but had no idea why he would go shoot up the Waterfront."

"Being in pain all the time could certainly cause someone to act erratically, right?" I asked.

"But then he shoots up the Waterfront?" Olivia, who had been listening and jotting down notes, said, "Doesn't make much sense."

"I agree. And I have some further info on that. Anything else, Ted?"

"Yeah, just to close out: Cindi and his other coworkers paint the same portrait we have gotten from everyone. Newberry was a nice guy. He read a lot of books. He read a lot of military history. He followed the news. But he wasn't a member of the TikTok generation or anything like that. He didn't do social media. He may have in the past, but it just wasn't his thing. So, that's how I spent my Monday. How about you?" Ted looked as superior as ever.

"Well, I learned a heck of a lot about our gun laws yesterday," I said. "And Newberry was a regular at the gun show. My contact said he had a table at the show and mainly sold knives as a side hustle, but he also dabbled in guns, though nothing too crazy. Basically, they are saying that he sold guns and knives as a source of second income, and the cops confiscated his inventory."

"Fascinating," Olivia said. "So, perhaps not a crazed gun nut after all?"

"Perhaps," I said. "But I also had a couple of other interesting calls this morning, one from Newberry's lawyer, who is supposed to be sending me—well, us—some documents."

I recounted my talk with Barry Petroff and how his positioning, though cryptic, seemed to align with what we were learning about Newberry.

"I kind of thought Petroff would turn out to be a nut, but maybe not."

"So, no documents yet," Ted said.

"Correct." I'd checked my phone a few minutes earlier.

"How do you spell his name?" Olivia asked as her fingers flew over her keyboard.

I spelled it for her.

"Alright, I got him," she said. "Decent-looking guy, fifties, veteran? Him?" She turned her laptop.

"That's him," I concurred.

The photo showed him in a nice suit, pressed shirt, tie, pocket square, and glasses sitting behind a beautiful wooden desk with a golden retriever at his feet. If the goal was to paint him as competent yet approachable, it worked.

Olivia rattled off some details: "His practice areas are medical malpractice, catastrophic injury, wrongful death, employment law, active military malpractice—and veteran military malpractice. I'm clicking on that first. Gonna put that on the monitor."

She did some magic, and her screen was now mirrored on the big-screen monitor in the conference room.

Didn't know we could do that. Man, I am so behind the times.

The page was titled "Legal Advocacy for Military Veterans." It listed a lot of typical law firm content with long lists of different problems that were meant as much to influence search results as they were to give information to human readers.

"So much mumbo jumbo," I said.

"Lawyers are search-engine-optimization whores," Olivia said.

She worked her way down the web page and then stopped on a section that made us all gasp:

"*Veteran Suicide and the VA:* The U.S. Department of Veterans Affairs treats the mental health issues of our nation's veterans. Unfortunately, treatment for mental health conditions including PTSD, depression, anxiety, and chronic pain is often significantly delayed or essentially ignored. The resulting mental crisis can and has led to a high incidence of veteran suicide. Such occurrences should not be viewed as a failure of the veteran but rather as a preventable and treatable ailment of the veteran. We are here to assist veterans in asserting their rights."

A chill started in the back of my neck and quickly raised goosebumps on my arms.

"Holy shit," I said. "Petroff's saying Newberry committed suicide."

"No way," Olivia said.

"Active shooter, death by cop?" Ted speculated.

"Damn." I felt numb and frozen in place. A million thoughts were running through my head. *Suicide. Oh, man. How did I not see this before?*

"Is this the motive we have been looking for?" Ted asked. "Did Newberry go to the Waterfront to commit suicide?"

A moment went by as I thought it through and lost track

of the conversation.

"Pete," Ted said, staring at me, a little puzzled. "What are you thinking?"

I looked at Ted, paused, and said, "I was thinking that if Petroff is right, how do we prove it?" This was partially true.

"I just Googled 'veterans and suicide,'" Olivia said. "It's a fucking epidemic. There are a million news stories, and your man Petroff is in half of them."

"Fucking fuck fuck." I slammed my fist onto the table.

"What?" Ted asked.

"I gave him my Gmail account, and I have been checking my work email. I'm such a fucking idiot," I said.

"Your words, not mine."

Sure enough, I opened my Gmail and found an email from Petroff, sent just a few minutes after we got off the phone.

I forwarded the email to Ted and Olivia, and we all started reading.

I first opened an article from the *Washington Post*.

Olivia's right. It's an epidemic. This was intense.

The headline read: "Parking Lot Suicides: Veterans are Taking Their Own Lives as a Form of Protest."

Wow, a massive Sunday article detailing dozens of veteran suicide cases. According to the article, veterans were taking their own lives on VA hospital campuses as a form of protest against a system that wasn't helping them.

I couldn't read fast enough, and I also felt like I was gasping for air.

A thirty-three-year-old Marine, an Iraq War vet, checked

himself into a VA hospital, spent four days in a mental health unit, and then walked outside and killed himself in his pickup truck. His family was apoplectic. He did everything he was supposed to do. He went to the hospital, and they knew he had all these problems, but somehow, he ended up leaving the hospital, getting access to a firearm, and killing himself.

Great reporting. This was just one of nineteen suicides that occurred on VA campuses in a twelve-month period, seven of them in hospital parking lots.

In Florida, a Marine Corps colonel dressed in his uniform and wearing his medals, sat on top of his military and VA records and killed himself with a rifle. He left a note: "I bet if you look at the *twenty-two suicides a day,* you will see the VA screwed up in 90 percent of them."

A thirty-two-year-old former Army sergeant and Afghanistan veteran hanged himself on the grounds of a VA facility in Tennessee. He enrolled in an inpatient treatment program for PTSD, substance abuse, depression, and anxiety. He entered the program to get better but was kicked out for not following instructions, including being late to collect his medications. A few hours before he took his own life, he wrote on Facebook that he was feeling empty, adding a distressed emoji. "I dare to dream again then you showed me the door like last night's garbage," he wrote. "And now I'm homeless right before the holidays."

My chest tightened. *Breathe, Pete.*

The story went on to say that mental health experts were worried that veterans taking their own lives had become a desperate form of protest against the system that some veterans felt hadn't helped them. Veterans were one-and-a-half times more likely than civilians to die by suicide. The veteran suicide rate was 26.1 per 100,000 compared to 17.4 per 100,000 for non-veterans.

Nine million veterans depend on the VA hospital system, which was described in the article as a frustrating bureaucracy where veterans must prove their injuries are connected to their service and requires miles of paperwork.

I think I'm gonna be sick.

To close out the story, a VA spokesperson said that the VA was aware of the issues and had been working on suicide prevention issues for many years. "The agency is deeply concerned..." Blah blah blah.

The story noted that Secretary of Veterans Affairs Frank Martinez could not be reached for comment despite numerous attempts.

Olivia chimed in with online feedback about the *Post* story.

"I found an item in *Politico* that the president flew into a rage when he read this story," she said. "He called Martinez to the White House and apparently got so mad that he threw a plate of chicken tenders against the wall in his private dining room."

"If it sticks, that means it's done, right? Or is that spaghetti?" Ted joked.

I didn't laugh.

"We are talking about suicide, Ted," Olivia gave him an admonishing look.

"Yeah, you're right, but the guy gets pissed about the bad press, not the issue behind it. But yes, that was insensitive, sorry," Ted said.

"I have read a few articles about Martinez; he's a climber," I said.

"Some are saying he's eyeing the White House," Ted said.

Olivia recounted that Martinez spent some time in the George W. Bush White House as a national security analyst, but his big break came after he retired from the military and was hired by defense contractor WestStrike. In less than a decade, his personal wealth skyrocketed from just under $200,000 a year as a general to tens of millions at WestStrike.

"Ridiculous money," Ted said.

"Yep," she said. "But he left WestStrike two years ago and spent some time with a venture capital firm. He was recently tapped by the president, who aside from being constantly enamored by military professionals, saw Martinez's business acumen and ability to run a large organization as a potential match for the beleaguered Department of Veterans Affairs."

"Kind of makes sense," Ted said.

"Yes," Olivia answered, "but Martinez quickly realized that the VA was, in military parlance, a shit sandwich. What the agency needed was a drastic change of culture and a lot more money in its budget. He's been fighting for his political life in Washington, and this was before the suicide stories."

As we began to work our way through the other documents, Rod came in and said I needed to head down to the medical center for a press conference regarding Stephanie Singleton.

By then, it was late in the afternoon. Couldn't be good news.

Chapter Twelve

2 p.m., Tuesday, The Medical Center

BOBBY THE PHOTOG and I arrived at the medical center and saw a small lectern set up outside the main entrance. Best to keep the reporters outside the hospital. I had a sense of dread when I approached Angie Irwin.

"The scuttlebutt is that Stephanie Singleton passed," she said. "But we don't have confirmation."

"That's what I figured," I said. "So sad."

"Yeah. It's like your grandma just died. This could get ugly."

"We'll see."

My phone rang. Olivia. I stepped away from Angie as Bobby continued to set up.

"How's the mood?" Olivia asked.

"Ominous," I said.

"The boss wants me to have something up as soon as possible," Olivia said. "The *Evening Star* is already reporting that she passed. When do you think it will start?"

"I'm thinking in a couple minutes. Do you want me to FaceTime it?" I suggested. "So you can hear it as it's happening, and then you won't need me to report it back to you."

"That's a good deal," she said with an audible sigh. We were all tired.

"I'll call you when it starts," I said.

Television reporters spend an incredible amount of time waiting around. And it's tough in Florida because even in October, it can be incredibly hot and sticky. In the summertime, forget it. There's nothing worse than sweating on camera, so we really try to wait in a car or the truck until the last possible moment. We had some shade, and my experience with the medical center was that they generally ran on time, so I toughed it out, sweat be damned. And I needed the fresh air.

I chit-chatted a bit more with Angie Irwin, and she admitted that her station was not willing to put a lot of resources behind the Waterfront story anymore. They seemed to think that it was over. The same with the other affiliates. It seemed like the other news directors believed the story would soon slip into memory, and they would be on to the next thing.

I disagreed.

A few minutes later, a spokesperson for the hospital approached the lectern. I FaceTimed Olivia and pointed my phone toward the lectern as a woman approached.

"Thank you for coming. My name is Amanda Franklin, and I'm the director of communications for Jacksonville Memorial Hospital. With deep sorrow, we are announcing that Stephanie Singleton succumbed to her injuries and passed away about ninety minutes ago. As you know, she was the victim of a gunshot last Friday night at the Jacksonville

Waterfront. By all measures, for which you will hear more in a few minutes, she put up a gallant fight. I'm going to turn things over to our on-call surgeon, who will give some details, and we also have a representative from the family who would like to speak as well."

I noticed a well-known Black pastor from Jacksonville named Cyrus Johnson standing nearby. This might get interesting.

Franklin then introduced Dr. Stuart Weiss.

If the goal was to be boring, antiseptic, and almost completely lacking in compassion, they had the right guy.

After offering some extraneous remarks, he said the bullet had lodged precariously near her lungs, and she had preexisting conditions that hindered her recovery. While things seemed to improve on Sunday, she developed an infection that caused a buildup of fluid in her lungs, and she eventually succumbed to her injury from the gunshot.

He then took questions.

Angie jumped in. I wasn't in the mood to compete with her.

"The gunshot was the cause of death, correct?" Angie asked.

"No, the cause of death was actually sepsis," Weiss said. "The infection caused her death."

"So, the gunshot didn't cause her death?" Angie pressed.

"Well, yes, the gunshot definitely led to her death," the doctor said, sort of snidely. "It's a complication from the gunshot, I guess, is the best way of describing it for you."

"For me? What is that supposed to mean?" Angie sniped.

It was getting a little tense.

"Well, I could get into a deeply technical description, but they actually told me not to," Weiss continued. "So, I'm telling you that we are saying it was sepsis. It was from the infection from the gunshot wound. She had damage to her lungs and other organs."

"What other organs?" Angie asked.

A feeding frenzy was in the works.

"Part of her liver was severely damaged from a so-called hollow-point bullet. It did significant harm to her," said the doc.

"So, let me get this right, because, you know, I'm not too quick," Angie said, a crescendo of snarkiness building. "Singleton was shot and brought to the ER and stabilized. You performed surgery, but there was damage to her liver and her lungs. She seemed to improve, but then things took a turn. She got an infection. And today, she passed. Is that about right?"

"I would say that's correct." Dr. Weiss looked flummoxed and defeated.

Angie turned to the communications director and said, "Amanda, why couldn't you guys just say what happened? All this parsing and lingo does nobody any good." A small cheer arose from the cadre of reporters. Amanda frowned.

The problem is, there are good PR people and then there are bad PR people. And not bad as in evil, just bad as in ill-prepared. About ninety percent of PR people are young kids straight out of college who have no idea what they're doing. They spend their time promoting events and people who aren't newsworthy and usually at the direction of disengaged bosses. When you get a call from a "bad" PR person, it is painful, awkward, and eventually becomes annoying as fuck.

There's maybe ten percent of them who actually understand and respect the rules of the road of journalism. If they are smart and understand what really makes something newsworthy, then they can be the source of great stories—and fun to work with, go drinking with, and so on. Sadly, Amanda was in the ninety percent—the "bad" category—particularly today. She handed over her briefing to an untelegenic doctor with a patronizing attitude.

Weiss is probably a brilliant doctor, but he clearly had no media training, and his hospital communications staff made him look like both an idiot and an asshole at the same time. No easy feat.

With that train wreck over, she handed over the lectern to Reverend Cyrus Johnson, speaking on behalf of the family.

"I stand in front of you today with a very heavy heart," Johnson began. "I had known Stephanie Singleton for nearly twenty years as she was an active and valued member of our church. She was a wonderful person from an amazing family, and today, she returned to the Lord, having lived a full life. The family can be very proud of her. She provided for her family, sent her kids to college, and was enjoying her senior years when she was taken from us."

Man, this guy can elocute.

"She goes to a better place," he said and then took a long pause. It was noticeable. Purposeful. And then he continued:

THE BYSTANDER

"Yet we have to remain in a community where you can get shot in the mall with your grandbaby by your side. In Stephanie's case, she wasn't killed by some gang banger in a drive-by like on television. She wasn't the victim of a random occurrence by an active shooter. She was killed by a man they are calling one of the good guys. Yes, he saved other lives, but his actions also took two lives, including one of our own. It's a terribly sad day."

He again paused, collecting his thoughts. "When I heard that there was an active shooter at the Waterfront who was killed by an armed bystander, I said, 'Thank God Almighty.' But then the other facts started to slowly come out. And I mean slowly. Too slowly."

Another pause.

"Now, as a community, we have to ask if this is the way we want to police ourselves. The Singleton family is asking these questions right now. And we owe it to them to ask ourselves if regular citizens are qualified to police our community. We have to ask ourselves if any one person should be entrusted with life-and-death decisions. We have to ask ourselves if being armed at a particular moment is justification for deadly force."

He was now rolling. I could feel a full-throated climax brewing.

"We are a nation of laws," he continued, "but also one that seems to not understand whose job it is to enforce those laws. Was it Walter Swanson's job to enforce the laws? I did not see a badge on the chest of Walter Swanson. Where were the sheriffs and law enforcement officials, who are being praised by the governor, while my friend Stephanie lay bleeding in a sneaker store with her terrified grandson bearing witness to her suffering?"

He let that sink in.

Reverend Johnson then said, "This isn't right. I don't know what the answer is, but this isn't right. Over the past four days, we have spent a lot of time in prayer, but sadly, today we will grieve for our sister, Stephanie. The family asks for privacy as they grieve. They are not interested in doing any media interviews. They want to grieve with their friends and family around them."

The big finish is coming.

"Today, we pray and grieve," he said. "Tomorrow, we will celebrate her life, and soon after, very soon after, we will seek justice for Stephanie Singleton. Thank you."

Wow. Powerful stuff.

Wrongful death lawyers all over North Florida are trying to figure out how to make contact with this family. This part of the story is not over, that's for certain.

I flipped my camera setting so that Olivia could now see me. "Did you get that?" I asked.

Olivia was typing furiously. "Holy crap, that was incredible. Thanks, Pete."

I did a quick standup with Bobby, recounting the details—summarizing Angie more than the doc, if I'm being honest. The footage of the reverend was way better than anything I could have said, and the editors would decide how much of it they wanted for tonight's newscasts.

At the station, I reconvened with Ted and Olivia in the

conference room to figure out what they'd learned.

Ted was incredulous.

"I have spoken with, literally spoken with, a dozen decent contacts at the VA here and in Washington, and I have nothing," he said. "They have completely clammed up. Now, granted, I have only talked to communications people. I don't know any insiders. Everybody I have talked to has been briefed and told to keep their mouth shut."

"That's not good; we have to push harder," I said.

"Wasn't there a VA guy at one of the press conferences?" he said. "Will Rebecca help us out? And by us, I mean you."

"I can try," I offered.

"They may have clammed up because it's political," Olivia said.

"Okay, how so?" I asked.

"This is really ugly for everyone in government but particularly Republicans, who are so pro-military," she said. "Even though the president has weighed in on this issue, it's amazing that it's only now smacking us in the face. I'm reading these stories all over the place, written by well-known reporters at big papers. But this has not gotten any real traction. It looks really bad for the president and Frank Martinez, who was supposed to be the savior of the VA, based on what we have learned. He was supposed to be the turnaround guy who would use this as a stepping-stone, but instead, it's a weight around his neck."

"Not a stepping-stone but a weight around his neck... Pretty good lead-in," Ted said.

"I think there could be careers in journalism for each of

you. More behind the camera for you, Ted," I said.

He just shook his head. "Call your girlfriend. We need to pry our way into the VA."

I NEEDED A favor from Rebecca, but I wasn't sure if it was a business/journalism favor or a personal favor. Which number should I use?

I tried her business line, and after two rings, she picked up.

"Hi, Pete."

"Hey, how's it going?"

"It's going okay. A little busy since the reverend lit us up at the press conference."

"Yeah, one can only imagine what a Sunday sermon must be like."

She laughed. "I was thinking the same thing."

"So, I was wondering about a couple things," I said. "Does the death of Stephanie Singleton change anything on your end?"

"Well, that's actually going to be a question for someone like the district attorney," she said. "But I can't go on the record here telling you the district attorney is looking into this because I don't know if that's the case. Does that make sense?"

"It does."

"At this moment, we aren't charging anyone in this case. My phone has been ringing off the hook with some pretty pissed-off people. The reverend has fired up a lot of folks, so I'm happy to take a call from someone who isn't attacking me."

"Always happy to come to the rescue," I said. My words hung in the air.

Line crossed? She's certainly no damsel in distress.

"What else do you need?" she asked.

"Help with the VA. I saw someone from the Veterans Administration at one of your briefings. Are they still here, or are they based here? We're having trouble getting comments from them."

"Well, the official position is that we can't give out any contact information for them," she said. "That's the official position. Personally, I wish it was different if you catch my meaning. Personally."

"Okay, thanks, I guess. By the way, looks like I'm gonna be interviewing Swanson in New York tomorrow."

"Get outta here, good for you." She sounded genuinely happy for me. "The station's sending you up there? Didn't see that coming."

"It's a long story," I said. "Better over a drink sometime." That, too, hung in the air a little too long for my liking.

"In your dreams, Pete," she said with what appeared to be a giggle. "Gotta go."

We hung up, and I waited a moment to text her personal line: "Personally, I think it took me far too long to figure out what you wanted me to do. The VA has totally clammed up on us."

Another instance where women are so much better at

this sort of thing than most guys. Maybe it's part of the fact that they mature faster than boys. We are trying to amass testosterone while girls are learning how to communicate verbally and non-verbally. She deliberately said *personally* twice, so I thought I was on solid ground.

She replied: "You're fine. The VA is driving me crazy. So secretive. I work for the police. Not a police state. VA is freaking out about this. And they've got our whole team on edge. They have delayed evidence. Could be worse. Can't say much more. Maybe over that drink. Gotta run."

Two major breakthroughs in one text conversation, but I didn't know which one had me more excited: A possible VA cover-up or the prospect of Rebecca Dawes wanting to go out with me. That was clearly an affirmative on a drink.

I floated into the conference room, evidently with a huge smile on my face. Ted and Olivia each lit up.

"What did you find out?" Ted asked.

"You look like you just won the lottery," Olivia said.

"Well, I didn't get a contact at the VA, but Dawes basically just told me that the VA may be covering up evidence," I said, holding back the info on my possible date.

"Get outta here," Ted said. "She told you this?"

"Well, she texted me," I said.

"She texted it? Give it," Olivia insisted, reaching for my phone.

"I will read it to you," I said. "The VA is driving me crazy. So secretive. I work for the police. Not a police state. VA is freaking out about this. And they've got our whole team on edge. They have delayed evidence. Could be worse.

Can't say much more."

"Wow," Ted said. "I can't believe she put it in writing. I can't believe she trusts you with that."

"It must say something else," Olivia noted, seemingly looking right through me. "Why won't he show us?" She paused. "But, hey, that's huge."

"It's huge, no doubt," I said.

Both parts.

"I'm assuming that you haven't had time to review the other attachments from Petroff yet?" Ted asked.

"No sir," I said. "What do you make of it?"

"I should make you slog through it, but I'm in a good mood. Also, Petroff issued a press release about this case. It's a pretty good summary."

He handed it over to me. The headline read: "U.S. Government Settles Wrongful Death Lawsuit for $1 Million After Suicide Outside Georgia VA Medical Center."

The information in the news release was chilling.

Not how I was expecting to feel today.

"The family of Michael Pearson, a Navy veteran who died by suicide after he was denied medical treatment at a VA Medical Center, recently negotiated a $1 million settlement with the U.S. government as compensation for the 35 days of pain and suffering he experienced before his death. Pearson died from a self-inflicted gunshot wound in the parking lot of the VA Medical Center.

"According to the lawsuit, Pearson's referral to a pain specialist was never scheduled, and he experienced physical agony after being denied medication previously prescribed by a community pain specialist. Pearson was honorably discharged from the United States Navy with an exemplary record following a tragic car accident that left him with serious injuries to his legs, hip, pelvis, and back. His condition deteriorated because he did not receive needed prescription pain medicine. He reached a breaking point and shot himself in the chest.

"According to attorney Barry Petroff, Pearson's death was imminently preventable.

'Michael Pearson served his country admirably,' Petroff said, "and had been on a path to lead a long and happy life before the negligence brought his life to a tragic close.'"

Ted and Olivia had been silently watching me read while acknowledging my frequent gasps.

"Holy crap," I said. "It sounds just like Newberry. The accident. The problems with the doctor. The pain. And the VA."

"It's a—" said Olivia.

"Fucking epidemic," I completed her sentence.

As expected, Ted was deeply, deeply pissed that I was taking a private jet to New York without him. His only solace was that he would get to watch me tell Bobby that he wasn't going either. A Bobby Rodriguez expletive-laden tirade was more entertaining than almost anything on TV.

MY PHONE RANG as I was driving home. It was my brother-in-law, Craig.

"Listen," he said. "Do you know this Swanson guy?"

"No," I answered. "I'm supposed to interview him tomorrow, but I have never met him."

"Ah, okay." He sighed. "I have a business opportunity for him."

"I'm pretty sure I'm going to regret this, but let's hear it," I said, already regretting it.

"Have you heard about the Swanson Challenge?"

"Can't say I have."

"I'm surprised," he said. "Apparently, it's all over the internet, or at least the gun-range message boards."

"What is it?"

"Well, we set up a target at twenty-two yards, which is the distance Swanson was from Newberry. You have to start at one end of the range. We start a timer, and then you have to move as quickly as you can to the open stall, without running, and try to put the best of three bullets in the target within twenty seconds. Every gun range in the country is doing some version of this. My people are going nuts, so we're doing one on Saturday."

"So, why do you need Swanson?" I asked.

"Maybe he comes over," Craig said. "And maybe I slip him a little appearance fee and ask him to autograph some merchandise."

"I'm guessing this is not for charity," I said.

"Fuck no." He laughed. "I have mouths to feed, including my own. Listen, I'm charging twenty-five bucks and awarding cash prizes for first, second, and third. The amount of the prizes depends on how many shooters I get. With Swanson there, it could be a bonanza. He makes a few bucks. I make a few bucks. Makes sense, right?"

"I guess," I said. "Are you serious that ranges all over the country are doing this?"

"Yeah," he said. "We did something similar after the armed bystander took down that bastard in the mall in Indiana. It was a fun time. I think a guy in California came up with it originally. You want to come by?"

"Probably not," I said. "But have a good time."

"Let me know if you can put me in touch with the guy," Craig said. "I gotta go." He hung up.

I found myself driving near the Waterfront—perhaps my subconscious was messing with me. I decided to take a little detour.

I parked on the lowest floor of the garage and then exited onto the street, just a half block from the Kennesaw Bank building, where Newberry worked. I crossed the street and walked toward the building. As I approached, I saw a woman exit a door near the entrance to the building's parking lot. It looked almost like a back door.

That was interesting. If Newberry had stashed his gun and his helmet in his car, he could have easily exited the building with it, perhaps in a duffel bag or maybe even a suitcase. He could have then walked the half block or so to the Waterfront, and no one would have questioned a thing.

I then entered the Waterfront complex from the side entrance and noticed that the restrooms were only a few feet away. In the men's room was a large, wheelchair-accessible stall where he could have easily taken out his weapon, put on his helmet, and then crossed the Waterfront's courtyard. From the moment he left the bank building to the time he fired the first shot could have been less than five minutes. He probably clocked out and walked right over here.

I entered the courtyard a few moments later and reached the middle of the retail complex, looking at "my" concrete planter and the river in the background—where I had been four days earlier. To my left, I saw the outdoor terrace of the restaurant where Swanson first saw Newberry.

I walked to the approximate spot where Newberry was shot, where he looked Swanson in the eye, and where he saw death coming. He didn't try to fight it, to fire back, to even flinch. I then started pacing toward the restaurant. I stopped after twenty-two long steps.

Unbelievable.

I was standing right where Swanson took his three shots. Morbid but true. I turned toward where Newberry had stood.

Would I be up to the Swanson Challenge? I didn't think so.

I looked to the right and saw the shuttered High Topper, which I imagined was now permanently closed.

I then worked my way toward my planter. From the moment he left the bathroom to the time of the first shot to me filming Newberry getting killed was probably under two minutes. In that time, many lives, including mine, were deeply impacted. And Swanson, the Wheelers, my station, my college buddy Cole, and now my brother-in-law were making money off of it. I looked out over the St. Johns River.

Was I a bad person for earning some extra cash for my fortuitous camera work?

Chapter Thirteen

8 a.m., Wednesday, Jacksonville Jetport

A SMARTLY DRESSED woman named Donna picked me up in a late-model, pristine Cadillac Escalade for the twenty-minute ride to the Jacksonville Jetport.

"Flying private, fancy," she said.

"You only live once."

Donna dropped me off at the Air Services building, one of several fixed-based operators that managed ground services for private planes at the jetport.

The first thing I noticed was that there was almost no one inside, and it looked more like a hotel lobby or a country club than an airport. Marble floors, a wall of glass-enclosed offices, and lots of comfortable places to sit. Even a small café.

An attractive woman stood behind the only counter in the building. I approached her and told her my name and that I was flying to New York.

"Oh yes, Mr. Lemaster," she said. "We have you right here. I just need to see some ID and we'll be all set."

"Is there a security screening?" I asked.

"Not here, sir. You're flying private, and we are your hosts until you get on the plane. It looks like you are the only one on this flight."

"Ah, okay."

"You can leave your bags near the door. The plane arrived a few minutes ago, and the captain is using the restroom. He should be back after he files the flight plan. You can wait here or anywhere you like. There's complimentary coffee and some breakfast sandwiches in the café."

I could get used to this. I wandered over to the café and ordered an American coffee, though I could have had anything in the hipster coffee universe had I wanted it.

I sank into one of a dozen lounge-style chairs in the lobby and immediately felt a push of lumbar support. Does this thing vibrate?

A small table in front of my chair had copies of *Forbes, Fortune, Robb Report,* and several other glossy magazines I didn't recognize, all basically describing the world of wealth and privilege that I didn't know anything about.

As I was scrolling through my phone, a strapping man in his mid-fifties wearing a pilot's shirt approached me.

"Good morning, Mr. Lemaster," he said. "I'm Captain Jim Garland. My copilot Bill Simmons and I filed our flight plan and just completed our preflight checklist. We can take off whenever you are ready."

"So, just the three of us?" I asked.

"Yes, sir. For the flight up and the return."

"How long is the flight?"

"Approximately one hour and forty-five minutes to Teterboro."

I would have been equally impressed with a first-class

ticket if I'm being honest, but the time savings is amazing. To be in New York for a 10:30 a.m. meeting on a regular flight, I would have had to leave Jacksonville around seven a.m., which means I probably would have had to get up at 4:30 a.m. to get an Uber and go through TSA and then walk for twenty minutes to the plane. By my journalism school math, this saves something like three hours—each way.

I walked out a few hundred yards past about a half-dozen other private jets made by Honda, Gulfstream, and Lear.

The Wheelers' plane was a Cessna Citation that looked sturdy and speedy to my untrained eye. I'm not certain if they owned it or leased time or what. Captain Garland himself loaded my equipment very gingerly into the storage compartment of the plane. I was perfectly content holding my briefcase as I climbed up the gangway onto the jet.

Copilot Simmons greeted me and directed me to the cabin.

"It's all yours," he said. "Can I get you anything? Soda or some snacks?"

"I'm quite alright. Maybe some water at some point."

"We can definitely do that. If you're ready to go, just have a seat. We'll be in the air in a few minutes."

The plane featured first-class-looking leather seats, four facing forward, two facing aft, and one facing sideways toward the door. It had two cleverly designed tables and plenty of outlets to plug in a laptop or charge your phone. There was onboard Wi-Fi and a bathroom in the back of the cabin. In all, you could fly seven people with this plane, plus the crew.

But on this flight? It was only me and the two pilots.

I took a photo of the interior of the plane and texted it to my mom, figuring she might recognize it from her times flying around with her private equity and venture capital buddies.

Mom: "Going to see the Wheelers?"

Me: "Yep. Pretty plush."

Mom: "Cesspool, remember!"

Me: "Got it."

The plane took off, heading directly west before banking hard to the north. Captain Garland said we would be cruising at forty-one thousand feet and above some nasty weather near the Sea Islands, Savannah, and Charleston. Smooth sailing from there.

It was strange being the only person on a plane. I heard the low hum of the engines, but it wasn't nearly as loud as a commercial jet, and no one was fidgeting in the seat next to me.

A year earlier, I had been to the Jacksonville Jetport to interview an executive from one of the big Wall Street houses. He had flown in just to meet with reporters and talk about fraud at a local community bank his company had invested in. I'd sat in that same lobby as this one guy got off the jet, did three interviews, then hopped back on the plane and flew back to New York.

The attendant at the FBO desk told me at the time that the flight cost about $10,000 each way.

I remember thinking, *Who's that important? Whose time is that valuable?* Clearly, the Wall Street banker was important and rich enough.

Now, here I was, by myself on a jet to New York, feeling important but also a little wary.

AFTER WE TOUCHED down at Teterboro Airport in New Jersey, I collected my equipment and was met by another smartly dressed driver. This time, it was a Town Car. The equally friendly driver confirmed that we were headed to Fifth Avenue and that he would be with me for the entire day.

Interestingly, it was harder to get into the Wheelers' building than it was to get on the jet. The security guards scanned my ID, and it took them a few minutes to issue a visitor's badge. I had to open my cases so they could look at my equipment.

Piece by piece, I told the guard what each compartment contained. "This is a light. This is a microphone. This is a camera…"

Not a WMD. Jeez.

Even though I told them that I had an appointment and the Wheelers were expecting me, I felt lucky to have avoided a body cavity search.

The Wheelers' forty-fifth-floor offices had a gleaming reception area filled with contemporary art and framed magazine covers, presumably showing Wheeler clients. A pretty receptionist immediately directed me to a conference room, where my agent was staring out of a floor-to-ceiling window at the Empire State Building.

I gave Evan a big hug, and he immediately complimented me on still being skinny while he tapped on his belly.

"Regular sex and home cooking will do that," I said. Evan had gotten married a few months earlier.

"Absolutely," he said with a laugh. "How was the flight?"

"Quick, personal, impressive. The kind of thing a guy could get used to."

"I wouldn't know."

Jason Wheeler entered the office and immediately shook my hand with a big, welcoming smile. He always looked so sad and sour on television when he was playing defense for the president's campaign. Here, he appeared cheerful and optimistic, like we were all part of a happy family.

"I'm assuming everything went smoothly in the flight and transportation department?" Jason asked.

"Yep, perfect," I said.

"That's great," Jason said. "We have you and Evan here for the next couple of hours. We would like to have our meeting first, and then you'll interview Walter. We should have you on your way by early afternoon. I think they have you for a four or five o'clock departure from Teterboro. Does that work?"

"Actually, I would prefer to do the interview first," I said. "Get it out of the way and in the can and then get to the business meeting. Can we do that?"

"Yeah, we can." Jason paused for a moment. "Except Walter isn't here yet. He and his girlfriend were delayed this morning. I'm expecting him in about half an hour."

"That's fine," I said. "It will take me a few minutes to get the equipment set up."

"Okay, interview first. No worries," said a smiling Jason, and then he left.

"Well, he couldn't be nicer," Evan said.

"Yep, smooth sailing all day," I replied.

Evan ably helped me set up my gear, even serving as Walter's stand-in as I positioned the lights and reflectors. Probably the most expensive assistant I would ever have, but today, he was working for free.

THE MOMENT SWANSON walked into the conference room, I knew it was going to be a tricky interview. His body language was closed off, and he looked angry—not that I knew what a happy Walter Swanson looked like. I figured the Wheelers would have given him some media training, certainly before putting him on *Kennedy*, even if they knew he would just get softballs from FAN News.

It definitely can get intimidating under the hot lights, especially if reporters are trying to trip you up. I was excited to get started, knowing I had bagged an interview with a guy every reporter in the country, including Cathy Merrick, wanted.

Keep it cool, Peter.

I wanted to get something new and different from Swanson, something beyond what had already been reported. The last thing I wanted to do was put him on our air spouting the talking points the Wheelers trained him to say.

There's a myth that *news* comes from the combination of the ordinal directions: north, east, west, and south. Put together all your info from the four directions and you get *news*. Sorry, it's an interesting theory, but not true. The root of *news* is, in fact, *new*. So, my goal was to try to get to know a little bit more about this guy.

Once I got past the negative body language, I realized that Swanson had been given a makeover. Gone was the stubbled face and baseball cap. Today, he wore what looked like a Brooks Brothers suit, a crisp blue dress shirt, and a well-folded pocket square.

No way he folded that himself.

It was quite a departure from what I had seen in his videos and from his everyman persona. Interesting.

"It was only supposed to be you," he said, looking at Evan.

Uh-oh. Not how I wanted this to start.

"He's my agent and a friend of mine," I said. "I'm sure the Wheelers told you that we are having a meeting with them later. Right now, he's just helping out with the equipment."

"I would be more comfortable if it was just the two of us," he said, not open for negotiation.

"Okay." I paused and looked at Evan. He gave me a plaintive *whatever* sort of look.

"Thanks for your help, but hit the road," I said with a halfhearted, dismissive wave.

He laughed and exited.

I love that guy, I thought.

Swanson was definitely sizing me up and acting guarded. I didn't know why. We were connected by the Waterfront, and I honestly thought he might first thank me for having the presence of mind to film the shooting. But nope. He was assessing me. I guess he was reinforcing that I was not with FAN News.

I reminded him that this was a taped segment and that I would be taking the footage back to Jacksonville, where it would get edited down. I told him we wanted him to look and sound good, so he should just let me know if he wanted to rephrase or repeat or redo anything. No pressure. I figured I would start by trying to make friends with him, loosen him up. I knew just how to do it.

I turned on the lights and the camera and then checked his sound levels. Everything was working perfectly.

"Walter, thank you so much for taking the time to speak with me today. I would like to start with something significant."

He just stared at me.

"It's been getting a lot of play on the internet. And my question is, why?"

I paused.

He looked confused.

After a few seconds, I broke the silence. "Why Mr. Two-Bits?"

He laughed. "Did you like that?" He softened.

"Well, as a Gator fan, I loved it, but I was curious about how it came about."

"You know, I always wanted to do it. I must have said it to my girlfriend a hundred times: 'I wish I could do that.' Obviously, I never figured I would have an opportunity, but it kind of flashed into my head when I was talking to the governor."

"That's awesome," I said.

Let's become football pals.

"He had the Florida athletic director on speakerphone, and he thanked me for what I did and said that UF and UGA thanked me. And then he asked if there was anything he could do for me. And I just blurted it out. They laughed, but then the governor jumped in and pushed for it, and it happened."

"I guess if the governor says you can have anything you want, then you go big, right?" I asked.

"I was joking with my girlfriend that I should have told them I wanted to be a judge on *Chopped* on the Food Network. We love that show."

"That's a great one. It would be so much fun to be a judge on *Chopped*," I sincerely agreed with him.

"So, here's a serious question," I continued. "You went out for a night of partying at the Waterfront. Is it normal for you to be carrying a gun?"

"Well, yeah, I'm licensed. I have a concealed carry permit. And it's scary out there, you know. There are a lot of things that happen, and you worry about it. And I guess I just have a heightened awareness or something. And so, when we go to crowded places and I'm allowed to bring my gun, I bring my gun."

"Who allows you to bring your gun?" I asked.

"I mean, there are places where you are not allowed to bring your gun, so when it's legal and allowed, I bring it. I have made videos about the concealed carry rules. You can't bring your gun to a school or a university. You can't bring it to the airport, obviously. Polling places. Courthouses. Sporting events. You also aren't allowed to bring it to a bar, but we were at an outdoor restaurant that mainly sells food, so it's legal there too. I know my rights."

I nodded. Made sense.

"I still go to plenty of places without my gun. I still fly on airplanes. I still go to Disney World."

"You can't bring a gun to Disney World?" I asked. "I didn't know that, but I guess it makes sense. Happiest place on earth and all."

"Not sure I agree. It's a high-profile target for a crazy person. And I don't think they pay their fair share of taxes."

Oh man, that's how this is gonna go.

"I get that, but let me ask you something else. What's it been like for you since the incident? I mean, let's start with right after. I filmed the actual shooting, but I don't know what happened next. Did the police question you? Were they concerned that you were involved in some way?"

"Well, I was involved in that I shot the guy, but, yeah, I did spend a couple hours talking to the cops on Friday night. I just told them the truth. It was pretty straightforward. We decided to go to the Waterfront kind of as a last-minute thing. My girlfriend's a big Gator fan, and she was just absolutely down for it. It's such a scene. You know; you were there. So, we were only there for a few minutes when this thing happened."

"What time did you get there?"

"I wanted to be there before it got too crazy so we could get a table. It gets so crowded, and it's no fun waiting an hour to get a beer. It was right before five."

"How's your girlfriend? I spoke to her right after the shooting. Did she tell you?"

"She's doing well. I didn't know you talked to her." He looked at me warily again. "She decided this morning that she wanted to go home early, so she's flying back today. I'm going to be here for another few days, probably until Monday."

"Everything okay?" I asked.

He looked even more tense. "Well, this part I don't want to include, okay?"

"Yeah, sure. Like I said, no pressure."

"Okay. Well, she's pretty upset about the retired teacher from the High Topper."

Upset enough to give up a free trip to New York?

"Ah, it's certainly sad," I said. "I went to the press conference when they announced her passing. What do you think about what happened to Stephanie Singleton?"

"Well, that's another area they really don't want me to talk about," he said, less defensive this time, more sheepish.

"Okay." I wondered why.

I paused. This was not going well. I decided that I was gonna try the long pause trick. If I didn't say anything, he might fill the awkward pause with something good.

Let's give him a couple of beats and see.
One Mississipp…

"Do you want me to walk you through what happened on Friday?"

He was trying to take control of this. Didn't like my prying. The media training was kicking in, and he wanted to deliver his sound bites and be done.

I thought I'd just let him do it because this was probably what Rod and the editors wanted anyway.

"Sure," I said. "That sounds perfect."

Alas, I was now certain I was not gonna get anything new.

Here it comes.

"I realized I had trained for this my whole life."

"I knew I was the only one who could do something about it."

"Now is the moment."

"I saw my opportunity and I took it."

Sound bite followed by sound bite and then another sound bite, just as the public relations team wrote them. Frankly, to me, the interview was now boring.

"One last question," I said, "and then we can wrap things up." Another pause to make it a bit more dramatic. "Do you think you're a hero?"

I'm sure he'd already practiced this.

"People are calling me a hero, but I really think I was just in the right place at the right time. There are a lot of people who would have done the same if they had the opportunity."

And I was right. Score one for ol' Pete.

"Great, that's a nice way to close it out," I said.

I shut off my main light and turned off the camera.

"Are we done?" he asked.

"Yes, just let me take the microphone off, and you are a free man."

He shrugged.

"Hey, so I talked to a guy who runs the gun show in Jacksonville, Lenny Aronberg. He said you might have been a regular at the gun shows?" I asked.

"Hmm. He runs the gun show? I don't know him, but yeah, I have been to the gun show a few times. Good place to recruit clients for my courses."

"I bet they would love to have you there now. Probably get a lot of new customers."

"Well, I'm hoping the Wheelers can take me more national, but yeah, I should go back."

"Don't forget us little people."

It hung, and I mean, really hung, in the air. He didn't know it was a joke, and he didn't need a reason not to like me.

"It's just a joke," I said. "Just teasing. Sorry."

"Oh, okay," he said.

"I think you are doing a great job dealing with all of this stuff," I said, hoping that wasn't too patronizing. "Have you seen any of the sights? Beyond the Empire State Building?" I pointed out the window.

"We went to a show, some musical, and Times Square. It's been fun."

Okay, he's as softened as he's gonna get. Here goes nothing.

"One other thing—I was wondering, did you ever meet Chip at the gun show?" I asked, secretly clenching my teeth and trying to be stone-faced while I coiled one of the light cords.

"No, I told the cops I never met the guy."

Contain yourself, Peter. Think about old people having sex. Oh man, I wish I had my camera on.

"Yeah, makes sense," I said as coolly as I could. "Hey, listen, say hello to your girlfriend for me. She was very nice to me on Friday, and I hope she's doing okay."

"Thanks, I will," he said. "Have a safe trip back."

"And if this documentary happens, we might see more of each other," I said.

"Yeah, that's right." He shook my hand and left the conference room.

Well, that was something.

Chapter Fourteen

Noon, Wednesday, Wheelers' Office

JASON WHEELER WAS all smiles as he entered the conference room with one of his colleagues, a finance guy named Kurt. We exchanged the usual "what are you gonna do while you are in New York" pleasantries, and then Stephen came in and shook our hands, saying that he was unable to attend the meeting. Jason was clearly the frontman for this operation. In person, just like on TV, Stephen was all smarm.

Kurt launched a presentation on the conference room TV monitor, and Jason began detailing their plans. They flashed through several slides with spreadsheets that looked like a marketing plan for the online courses. I couldn't make out much but saw "email," "social," "telephone," and "text" columns. *Oh man, they are gonna text-bomb people with these courses. I hate that shit.*

I didn't see anything explicitly about him running for Congress, but then they pulled up the slides discussing the documentary series, and that's where the pitch began in earnest.

Jason essentially explained what he had told Evan two days ago. They'd already secured a screenwriter to write a three- or four-episode, Netflix-style series, and they had secured my footage from the station. They had Walter onboard, obviously, and I was the final piece of the puzzle. They made it very clear that I wasn't a required piece and that they were going to move ahead with this with or without me—but they wanted me.

It felt good to be wanted.

Evan then did his thing. He reiterated that to secure my participation, it would require a high-five-figure commitment, guaranteed and upfront, and then a percentage of the profits if it sold.

"Yep, that's what we agreed to," Jason said. "I will turn it over to Kurt with the details of what we are willing to do."

"Last year, we completed a documentary on fast-food promotion fraud," he said. "We paid our journalist narrator $45,000 upfront, and he also had a residual of two percent of profits after all expenses. That was a five-part series, and to date, his total compensation exceeds $100,000. Today, we're prepared to offer Mr. Lemaster $75,000 upon execution of the contract and the same percentage breakdown for the series. Now, it's probably only going to be three or four episodes, but we believe it has the potential to draw significantly higher viewership than the fast-food documentary. A lot of people didn't know anything about it, but it developed a strong word-of-mouth following. This project will have the full Wheeler marketing push behind it."

"We want to make you a millionaire, Pete," Jason said. "Simple as that."

"Thank you," Evan said. "Obviously, we will need to see

a written contract, but that aligns with what we discussed. However, the fast-food promo example is not as good of a comparison as the "She Thought He Was the Prince of Liechtenstein" documentary. My firm represented the journalist narrator, and he earned 2.5 percent on the back end. We think Pete deserves that."

Liechtenstein has a royal family?

Jason pushed a note toward Kurt. "We can go to 2.25 percent, but nothing more. Remember, we don't have to have Pete."

Evan looked at me. I nodded, trying to do the math in my head. The numbers wouldn't come. This is why I have an agent. And why I don't do math.

"Deal," Evan said. "We will need to know precisely what you want from him as a time commitment. We have to clear this with the station, but it shouldn't be a problem."

"Well, we will fly you up here, probably not on the private plane again—sorry," Jason said directly to me. "But a first-class ticket to New York. We have a great rate at the Marriott Marquis. We will need you here for two or three days. You will tell your side of the story and then do some narration. Again, two to three days.

"We will send you the script, and you can offer feedback. We want this to have a journalistic feel, not sensationalized. As much as we love our conservative base, there's a lot more opportunity if it's a straightforward retelling and doesn't get slanted. Years ago, someone asked Michael Jordan why he never got political, and he said, 'Republicans buy sneakers too.' Even though we are a conservative-leaning shop, we know that Democrats watch Netflix too. So, ultimately, we don't want to offend anyone."

"I think we have a deal," Evan said. "What do you think, Pete?"

"Sounds good to me," I said.

Jason then reached across the table, and we shook hands.

"Evan, I will have our lawyers send you the agreement and get your wiring instructions, and we will be in business," said Jason. "The car is downstairs at your disposal. Have a great trip back, Pete. Nice meeting you both."

Kurt shook each of our hands. And they left.

As the door to the conference room shut, I turned to Evan and whispered, "That's it. They're just gone."

"That's how business is done, Pete. When you get the deal you want, you shake on it and walk away before anyone changes their mind or decides to ask for more." But then he whispered, "Let's finish this over lunch. Sometimes conference rooms have ears."

Our driver took us straight to the Backstage Deli. I was floating on air, and not because I was getting ready to eat a massive corned beef sandwich with one of my good friends. The $75,000 would wipe out my student loan debt with more than enough for a down payment on a condo on Jacksonville Beach.

Evan could see my giddiness.

"Don't spend the money until it's in your bank account," he said. "We have a verbal agreement but not a written one—and no money yet."

"I still get to be excited," I said.

"Yeah, you can be excited. Just cool your jets a little."

The waiter delivered two Guinnesses, which are even more amazing coming out of a keg.

I toasted to Evan's negotiating acumen, which would net me thousands of dollars.

I ordered a large corned beef on rye while Evan went for half corned beef and half pastrami, and then we dove into the deli pickles.

The sandwiches were just as I remembered: corned beef piled higher than anyone can really eat unless you want to have a heart attack on the spot. The sandwich is basically the size of a soccer ball and mostly meat. And soon after it arrives, the waiter usually brings doggie bags.

"I cannot even tell you the last time I had a piece of bread," I said as I destroyed my first bite of rye, "but this is a special occasion. I'm going to ink a really good business deal. And I'm back in New York with my good friend."

We clinked our glasses together and continued to stuff our faces with glorious, fatty, juicy meat.

I adjourned to the restroom and then returned to find that Evan had paid the tab.

"You motherfucker."

He laughed. "You're my client, Pete. I made money off your last contract, and I'm gonna make money off this deal too. This one's on me."

"Yeah, but this is the first time we've come into this place when neither of us is broke, and I don't get to at least contribute? Very disheartening, Lieberman. I'm disappointed in this aspect of your negotiating."

He laughed. "Get used to it. I think a lot of people are going to be buying you meals in the future."

The Town Car dropped Evan outside his office and headed to Teterboro.

As I entered the lobby, I immediately saw Captain Garland in the lounge area. Once again, he loaded my gear into the storage compartment of the plane. He then told me that he and Simmons needed to finish some paperwork in the jetport but that I could get on board.

As I entered the cabin, I turned and saw Brigadier General Frank Martinez, Secretary of the U.S. Veterans Administration, sitting in one of the seats facing me.

"Good afternoon, Mr. Lemaster," he said.

"Am I on the wrong plane?" I asked. I must have looked astonished because I felt, well, astonished.

"You're not. I'm Frank Martinez, Secretary of the VA. I will just be a couple of minutes, and then you can be on your way. Have a seat."

"I know who you are," I said meekly.

I sat down. Shocked and a little buzzed. Two beers at lunch.

Seconds earlier, I had been mentally furnishing my condo on Jacksonville Beach, and now I'm sitting across from the VA Secretary in a private jet. Sobering.

"I understand your meeting went well today?"

"It did, thank you."

Why did I say thank you?

"Listen, you're a smart guy, so I'm just gonna be straight with you. It's my sincere hope that your investigative efforts and your colleague's repeated calls to the VA will cease from here on out. What happened to Mr. Newberry is a tragedy, but we really want to close the book on it. Do you see where I'm going with this?"

"Not really." Still buzzing.

"Let me be clear: For your overall well-being and the well-being of your mother's business, for example, I think you should cease reporting on this story. Let's let it ride off into the sunset."

I started to regain my footing. "Well, I would love to help you, General Martinez, but I'm about to sign a deal that will probably have me digging much deeper into this story."

"Yeah, about that…"

My heart sank.

Who owns this plane?

"I can assure you, Mr. Lemaster, that if you and I don't end this conversation in agreement, your participation in the documentary will be greatly diminished."

"Ah, Okay. Wow. I get it now."

"So, I don't want to get any more reports that you or your colleague, Mr. Stone, are calling my agency for further comment about the Newberry case. And I don't want to see any more stories in my daily media briefing with your byline. One other thing: Let's keep this between us. No need to involve Mr. Stone or your lawyer buddy. Are we clear?"

"What?" I couldn't believe my ears, and the only word I could get out was *what*.

"Are we clear?" he said a bit louder, with more emphasis on *clear*.

I immediately flashed to the courtroom scene in *A Few Good Men* where Jack Nicholson said the same thing to Tom Cruise, who answered, "Crystal." If I said that right now, Martinez would likely remove my kidneys with his bare hands.

"Yes, you are clear, sir," I said.

"Good." He paused for a beat. "How was the corned beef?"

Holy shit, have they been following me? What have I gotten myself into?

"What?" I said, again like an idiot.

"The corned beef. I see you went to Backstage," he said, pointing to the doggie bag I had placed on the seat next to me.

Whew...I think.

"Oh, it was delicious as always. There's still half a sandwich in there if you want it."

"No, I'm fine. I can't eat that stuff if I still want the old uniform to fit," he said, tapping his chest. "Okay, Mr. Lemaster, I'm glad we had a chance to have this chat. Have a good flight." And then he left the aircraft.

A minute later, Garland and Simmons came on board looking as though they had no knowledge of my visitor, which was complete bullshit.

Just as in the morning, Simmons asked if there was anything he could get me. "Water? Or maybe something stronger?" he asked.

"I'm fine. Just had a big lunch," I said. "Who owns this plane?"

"Most jets are owned by corporations. It's written on your itinerary and on the flight plan."

"Got it, thanks."

"We should be in the air in a few minutes and on the ground a little after five o'clock. Let me know if you need anything."

"Thanks." As he closed the cockpit door, I grabbed my briefcase and rifled through it, looking for the itinerary.

There it was: WS Jet 101, LLC. And the number on the tailfin was WS101.

Fuck me.

WestStrike 101.

Chapter Fifteen

4 p.m., Wednesday, Above New Jersey

THE PLANE LIFTED off, and I sat alone in the cabin of a jet, just me and my dumbfounded thoughts.

What the fuck just happened?

Had I just made a deal with the Secretary of Veterans Affairs to kill a story in exchange for $75,000?

How did Martinez know where I was?

The Wheelers had to be in on his whole plan.

Will there ever be a documentary?

How big was this story? The veteran suicide stuff has already been in the news, right? Does Martinez see the Newberry shooting as some kind of tipping point?

I shouldn't have accepted the free flight. Were they testing me to see if I would make a little ethical breach? Did they say, "After he takes the free flight to New York, we dangle more money in front of him"?

They knew I was a local TV news reporter who didn't cover in-depth stories. But I was also a local TV news reporter who was just on *The Morning Show*, and I can be a serious journalist. And I was uncovering some crazy shit that the cops don't know about. Walter Swanson knew Newberry, I was sure of it.

What have you gotten yourself into here, Peter?

Damn. Martinez mentioned my well-being. And my mom's business. And Evan. Is he gonna break my legs if I pursue this story? That motherfucker.

Copilot Simmons was right. I needed something stronger.

WHEN THE PLANE touched down, I turned on my phone. I probably could have used it during the flight, but it was better to be alone with my thoughts for the first time in a while—and get my shit together.

I had a couple of missed calls from Ted and a bunch of miscellaneous texts. I called Evan.

"How was the flight?" he answered without a hello.

"More smooth sailing," I said, lying. "Thanks again for lunch. I appreciate it."

"My pleasure."

"I've cleared the euphoria and the Guinness fog. Tell me the process from here again."

"Okay, well, they send us the contract and make sure it says what it's supposed to say. Then we get it blessed by the lawyers at the station. I already reached out to them and told them what the likely structure will be. They seem to think it will be okay, so that's good news. We send the station a one-page acknowledgment agreement to sign. Then you sign the contract with the Wheelers, and they wire the money. Remember, the agreement doesn't mean a thing until the money comes through. The money is the big trigger."

"That makes sense."

"Remember, these guys are very savvy. They probably set up a new corporation that we will be contracting with. The paper is really worth nothing because the company they set up will probably have no assets. So, we have to wait for the money before this becomes real."

And with that, I saw an opportunity for Evan to help me.

"Will they set up an LLC? Is that what it's called?"

"It might be a limited liability corporation, but mainly my concern is that we have a deal with a corporation that we can sue later if the deal goes south."

"So, the LLC shields them personally? And it could also be used to hide their involvement?"

"That happens, too, yes, but it's not our main concern. Again, Pete, if the money comes through, we don't have anything to worry about."

"Got it. Thanks." *And thank you for my little LLC lesson.*

"Money talks, right?"

"Yep, and bullshit rides the bus."

He laughed. Have I mentioned I love that guy?

"I want to move ahead. So, the sooner, the better," I said.

"Fair enough. I got a text from Kurt, and he said he may even send it tonight."

"Perfect, let me know. Thanks again for your help today and great seeing you. My regards to your bride."

Next, Rebecca.

I tried her on her private line. It was now about 5:30 p.m.

"Hi, Pete," she answered.

"Hey, do you have a minute?"

"Sure, are you still in New York?"

"Actually, I just got back. I was wondering if we could get that drink tonight. I know it's last-minute."

"Oh." Long pause. Caught her totally off-guard. "Um, sure, what time?"

"How about 7:30 at the Mustache?"

"Big spender," she said with a laugh.

Your Father's Mustache was a local watering hole that served good drinks and a great burger. It was a low-stress, casual choice for a drink/first date. It was certainly not a high-end place, but it was a really safe, easy choice. She knew it.

"Well, you can have anything you want under five bucks," I joked. "I actually just landed and need to hustle a bit. See you at 7:30?"

"Yes. See you then."

I called Ted and told him that I was on my way to the station to drop off the gear and the flash drive with the interview.

"How was the jet?" he asked.

"It was quite an experience. I'll give you all the details later. Any word on Petroff?"

"I sent him a text earlier today, but he never responded."

"Okay. I will call him now and see you in a few minutes."

I called Barry. I had wanted to get him on the line along with Ted and Olivia, but I needed to talk to him. One-on-

one right now might work out.

Straight to voicemail. I left a message and hung up just as I pulled into the station.

I met Ted in the conference room and handed over the flash drive.

"I tried to get Swanson to open up, but it was a nonstarter," I said. "He completely shut down any questions about Stephanie Singleton, and then he started delivering his practiced sound bites. I'm sure Rod and the editors will love it, but there's nothing new here." I held back on Swanson possibly knowing Newberry and said nothing about my confab with the general.

"I think Rod wants to promote this interview and will probably shoot for tomorrow night," Ted said. "They are going to want to drive viewership and clicks. Our friends at the FAN affiliate across the street didn't get a great interview from him either. So, I think Rod sees opportunity."

"Makes sense," I said. "Listen, I'm wiped. I know, I know. I'm not supposed to be tired after flying on a private jet, but it has been a long day."

"It's understandable," he conceded. "And the Swanson interview is a good get."

"Call me if you need me."

"See you tomorrow."

I had just enough time to get home and change my clothes. I put on jeans and a nice, casual (but not too casual) shirt.

The Mustache was only about a half-mile from my apartment. One could stumble home from there, but I will neither confirm nor deny firsthand knowledge of that. I knew it wouldn't be too busy on a Wednesday.

I arrived at about 7:25, found a table for two in a quiet corner, ordered a glass of water, and waited.

At 7:30, I got a text from Rebecca: "On my way."

About ten minutes later, she came in looking great as always. Jeans and a cute top, flattering but not too tight or overtly sexy. Her hair was blown out, and she had a little more makeup on than when I saw her at the game.

Her brown eyes sparkled as she approached. I stood, and she gave me what I could best describe as a half-hug after she hung her purse on the back of the chair. It was somewhere between a hug and a handshake.

"You're not drinking?" she asked, pointing at my water.

"Oh, no, I am," I said. "I was just waiting for you."

"Okay, because I could use one," she said.

The waitress arrived, and Rebecca ordered a Manhattan off the specialty menu. I ordered a rum and Diet Coke.

"A Manhattan, eh?"

"Yes, they're delicious. Have you had one?"

"I have, and I agree."

"Speaking of Manhattan, up and back to New York on a private jet? How was that?"

"It was wild. Have you ever been on one of those planes?"

"Well, the sheriff's office doesn't have access to a private jet, and if you're asking if I've ever been on the Jaguars' plane, the answer is no."

"I wasn't asking that. Actually, I didn't even think of

that. Don't give me too much credit," I said with a laugh.

"Some of the federal three-letter agencies have access to them, but you have to be pretty high up the food chain. The FBI shows on TV are way over the top about it. Anyway, give me all the details."

The drinks arrived. My rum and Diet Coke looked pedestrian compared to her Manhattan with an oversized square ice cube, orange slice and, I think, a cinnamon stick. She took a sip, and her eyes lit up. I didn't think they could look more alluring.

"Well, you pull into the place and basically walk right onto the plane," I said. "I was in the air for less than two hours and then took a car into Manhattan. I left my house at 7:30 a.m. and was at a meeting at 10:30. Crazy."

"How was the interview?"

"You know, it was okay. He's been trained up."

"Oh, the PR people got to him," she said with a laugh.

"I started by asking him about Mr. Two Bits."

"That's a good ice-breaker."

"Yeah, he lightened up, but in the end, I was just getting the usual sound bites, which is fine. But, you know, I would have loved to add something better."

"Something juicy?" She giggled. "Yeah, probably not gonna happen. I told you I met him. He's not a trusting sort of a guy."

"Yeah, well, that's kind of why I wanted to talk to you. Aside from just wanting to talk to you."

She smiled, but out of the corner of my eye, I noticed a lady with long blonde hair enter the front of the bar, laughing with a guy in a suit. Denise.

Must have been quite a look on my face because Rebecca turned and saw her.

"Friend of yours?" she asked.

"That's my neighbor."

She sees me. I'm dead.

She's coming over. And she's no longer giggling.

"Hey, Pete," she said.

"Hi, Denise, how are you?" I asked.

"Thought you were in New York."

"I just got back."

"You went to New York and you're back already?" Based on the look on her face, she clearly didn't believe me. "You flew on a fighter plane or something?"

Don't say private jet. You're toast. Just roll with it.

"Actually, it was a private jet."

So much for my instincts.

"Oh, private plane. Sounds extravagant."

Before I could introduce her, Rebecca tried to cut the tension.

"Hi, I'm Rebecca."

"I'm Denise, and I know who you are."

Ouch.

"We are talking about the shooting case," I said.

"I can see that," Denise said, staring at the drinks. "I will leave you to it. See you around the complex, Peter."

"Okay," I said meekly, defeated. I took an audible deep breath.

"So…not just your neighbor?" Rebecca took a sip of her

cocktail with what looked like a partial smile, but her eyes were inviting, even provocative.

"Yeah, we've hung out a few times. I'm sorry if that was uncomfortable."

"I'm not uncomfortable," she said. "I got invited for a drink, so I'm here, and I'm gonna enjoy my drink with you. So, you're fine with me." She paused. "You're in deep trouble with her though."

"Yeah, I know." I glanced over at Denise for a half-second, hoping not to catch her daggers. "She did come here with a guy," I suggested.

"You're still in trouble."

"Wait, maybe there's a double standard going here. Can't I plead my case?"

"No, no, it's not a double standard. He's gay. And you're in trouble." She took another long pull on her cocktail, clearly getting joy from watching me squirm.

"How did she know who I was, by the way?" she asked.

Oh man, not this again.

But I was a little bit quicker this time.

"They played a clip of one of your briefings on the *Kennedy* interview," I said. "We watched it together."

She seemed satisfied with the answer. It was a first date, after all. No inquisitions allowed by rule.

"So, what did you want to talk about?" she asked.

My brain flashed to saying something about her big brown eyes, but my inner editor shut it down.

"I got a call from an attorney in California who represents Kyle Newberry."

"Represents him for what?" she asked.

"Well, that's the interesting part. He represents a lot of vets who have legal problems with the VA. He literally said to me, 'All is not as it seems with this case.'"

"Mysterious," she said slyly, her eyebrows raised.

"That's what I was thinking. He actually used the term 'cloak and dagger' with me."

"It's getting more mysterious by the second." She was smiling, enjoying her drink, and seemingly enjoying the conversation.

"He's worked on a lot of cases with veterans who have committed suicide, and we've been researching it. Seems to happen a lot. I was wondering what you thought about that."

She took another sip of her drink, draining it to the sound of air pulsing through the straw.

"Here's what I think." She paused. "I think you need to order me another one of these."

"No problem." I caught the waitress's attention and signaled for another round. Mine was still half-full. I was behind but confident that I would catch up. Denise was gone.

"Like I told you before, all of the feds are taking their time releasing information on this case," she said. "You saw what happened at the FBI briefing. They're holding back on getting information out, seemingly more than usual, but what's normal with an active shooter case?"

"Feels like they're trying to cover something up," I whispered.

"I think that's dramatic, Pete. More like delaying or slow-walking. I don't think covering up is fair, but I see where you're coming from. This happens all the time for all kinds of reasons. They're just creating a million excuses to not release information in a timely manner."

The second round arrived, and she took a sip. "Just as good as the first one," she said with a devilish smile. My knees felt weak.

Good thing I was sitting down.

"I'm gonna tell you one thing. And only one thing, because I don't want to mix business and personal stuff. And I still want to hear more about your plane ride."

She's acknowledging the personal aspect. I like where this is going.

"Okay, one thing, and then we ditch the shop talk," I said.

"I can't be your primary source on this. You can't quote me or the JSO. So, this is basically deep background, okay?"

"Look who's being mysterious now."

There was that smile again and the sparkle in her eyes. She leaned in and said, "The magazine was empty."

I stared at her.

Processing.

Whose magazine? Newberry's?

"Newberry's magazine was empty?" I finally said.

"Yep," she replied.

"He went to the Waterfront with an assault rifle and one bullet."

"Yes. Remember, I said one thing, and that's the one

thing. And you will need to get at least one other source on the record to confirm it. Got it, mister?"

Holy crap. So this guy showed up at the Waterfront. Fired one shot to scare the shit out of everyone. But he had no intention of being in a shootout. He had no ammo.

I can't just let this go. I owe my mother that, at least for staying supportive. Fuck, I owe my father for this too.

Seeing that I was thinking it through, she gave me a moment. A short one.

"Got it, Pete?" she repeated and then paused. "Does anyone call you Peter?"

"I got it. That's a really good 'one thing,' I have to admit." I was still processing. "My mother calls me Peter, mainly when she's mad at me."

"Like your neighbor?"

I laughed out loud. "Oh, I walked right into that one. Touché."

"Yeah, you really did." She laughed and stirred her drink. "Where did you have lunch?"

"We went to the Backstage Deli for corned beef sandwiches."

"Those are the huge ones?"

"Yeah, the size of your head. So fatty and salty. Beers go down like water with them."

"Who did you go with? Another girl who's also not your neighbor?"

"Is that how this is gonna go?"

"Too much?"

"No, that's okay, I can take it. I went with my friend

Evan. He's a guy, in case you were wondering. I brought half of a huge sandwich home with me on what is likely my only time flying on a private jet."

"Well, sounds like you have lunch for tomorrow, or you can turn it into a hash for breakfast."

Don't make a breakfast joke, Peter. It's going so well.

"It's been a good day." I smiled at her. Hopefully, she was feeling the same way.

I figured it best not to get into my potential business deal with the Wheelers or how it might get scuttled by the general. Probably not the best of first-date topics anyway.

We laughed and told media war stories for another forty-five minutes while splitting a plate of nachos. No *Lady and the Tramp* moments.

She hailed an Uber, and it was outside the bar in moments.

I walked her to the car and said, "I would like to see you again."

"I would like that," she replied and then popped up on her tippy toes and gave me a peck on the cheek.

I reached out and took her hand. As she looked at me, I addressed the elephant in the parking lot, or at least the one in my head. "How's the adman?"

"We broke up," she said and turned to the car.

"I'm sorry to hear that," I lied.

"I'm not. Good night, Pete." And she was gone.

Pete's apartment complex, 10 p.m.

MY PHONE RANG. Mom.

"How was the trip?" she asked.

"It was interesting. Eventful. Interesting and eventful. I'm pretty tired, Mom."

"I can hear it in your voice. Is the deal moving forward?" she asked.

"Yeah, it is. Evan is working on the details, but I think things will work out...

I can't let Martinez mess with her. Scratch that. I won't let Martinez mess with her. I just need time to figure it out.

"Listen, I just had a bit of a blowup with Denise."

"What happened?"

"Let's just say I had a bad sitcom moment about an hour ago. I was having drinks at a place down the street with Rebecca Dawes, and Denise walked in and didn't take it well."

"Oh," my mom said. Another pause. She genuinely didn't seem to know what to say. A rarity.

"There's more to the story, but I don't want to get into it. Basically, Denise is very nice, but I don't think I will be seeing her anymore."

"Pete, you know I don't like to give relationship advice," she said.

"Since when?" I laughed out loud so hard that much of the pent-up stress left my body.

"Peter, if it's not going to work out with her, best to break it off sooner than later. Like a Band-Aid."

"Yeah, I know."

"If she's looking for something more than you want, you have to tell her," she said.

"I know," I said again. "She told me she's sensitive to feeling strung along."

"Oh, then even more reason to end it now."

"Yeah, I'm going to bed, Mom. I will let you know."

"What about Rebecca?"

"You are relentless, Mom. I'm sure no one has ever said that to you before."

She laughed, and we hung up.

I slumped onto my couch and kicked off my shoes.

And then it hit me. Believe it or not, Denise and my Mom had given me an idea.

Chapter Sixteen

7 a.m., Thursday, Pete's Apartment

Once out of bed, I did my morning miles on the treadmill and got ready for work. I wasn't happy with how things went sideways with Denise. She had always been super nice, and I certainly didn't intend to embarrass her by having her see me with another woman in public. It's happened to me, and I know it's no fun.

I walked down the hall and knocked on her door. Time to face the music.

"Good morning, Pete." She cracked open her door, not that I expected to be let in.

"I want to apologize for what happened last night. I'm sorry that it was awkward," I said.

Her upper lip stiffened, and she took an audible breath. "Is that what you're sorry about? That it was awkward?" She paused. "For you? Or for me? Or for her?"

"I think it was awkward for everyone," I said, trying to frame it. This conversation was also getting awkward.

"Pete, I think you are a decent guy, but are you sorry that my feelings were hurt, or are you sorry that you got caught?"

"Um, caught?" I said.

"Whatever," she said. "Would you still be sorry if I hadn't walked into that place last night?"

"Um…" I stammered. "I'm trying to apologize here."

"Seeing you there with her, it was just too many coincidences." Denise was standing taller and more confidently than ever. She was as prepared as I was unprepared for this conversation. "I know we were not exclusive, but I told you that I didn't want to feel strung along and had no interest in a competition. Do you remember that?"

"I do," I said.

I hurt her.

"Clearly, you have feelings for her. You took her on a date." She paused. "You never took me on a date." She was matter-of-fact, not emotional. Either the lawyer training had kicked in, or I was already in her rearview.

"I'm sorry that I hurt your feelings," I said. "Anything I tell you is going to sound like an excuse." Actually, this part I had rehearsed last night. "Excuses will make me feel like a jerk, but I hope you don't think I'm a jerk."

"Well, if you start to make it all about you, then you are kind of a jerk." She let that one hang in the air. "You aren't a jerk, Pete, but I also don't think we want the same things. Some people are okay with being casual. I'm not."

"I understand," I said.

"I have to get ready for work," she said.

"Okay, thanks for talking to me," I said, sheepish and defeated.

"Bye, Pete." Her door closed, and I went back to my apartment.

Could we still be friends? Can guys and women really be platonic friends, particularly after they have been intimate? More barstool conversation, but my answer is probably not.

DRIVING INTO THE station, I called Evan. He picked up right away.

"I thought of a couple things last night," I said. "Can we say that if the money doesn't arrive within a certain time, the deal is off?"

"Yeah, want to give them five business days?" he asked.

"Yes, that works. And what if I change my mind? Can I get a cooling-off period if I decide that I don't want to do it?"

"Well, we can ask for that, Pete, but they probably won't like it. You could pull out and they would have invested a lot of time for nothing in return."

Precisely. I wanted to be able to string them along.

"See what they say. It's not a deal-breaker for me, but I would like to ask."

And see how they respond.

"Okay, I'll let you know," he said. "Anything else?"

"Nope, we're good," and I hung up.

I SAT DOWN with Ted at the station, and he brought me up to speed. Rod had him working on other stories, so he had made only a couple of attempts at the VA the day before, all thankfully prior to my meeting with Martinez. Rod liked my interview and reaffirmed that he thought we would only be covering the shooting on a spot basis after it aired on Friday. I suggested that we try to get a little bit more local color on Swanson, perhaps by speaking with his employer or friends on camera. I pushed that it would add to the package he was so keen to promote.

Gotta keep my story alive.

He reluctantly agreed, acknowledging that the shooting stories were still driving traffic to the website, and the promos for the Swanson interview were starting to air. He believed it would make for a record ratings day.

We had reached out to Swanson's employer, NCIS Security, a few days earlier, and the company's publicist, Melissa Young, had been relentlessly calling us every day since the shooting. She desperately wanted us to interview her CEO on camera.

When a marketing or public relations person is that excited, it's almost an immediate turnoff for a journalist. Still, I really wanted to get some additional information on Swanson and then root around with the CEO to see what else I might find out.

Melissa squealed when I told her I wanted to do an interview at noon.

I arrived at the company's offices just outside downtown Jacksonville. The still-giddy publicist directed me to the conference room, where I set up my one-man-band equipment.

I was soon greeted by an affable and nattily dressed executive named Jeff Goldberg, who told me that he was the son of a tailor and that he purchased a locksmithing business twenty years ago that has since grown into a security and technology firm.

I wired him up, turned on my lights and camera, and we just started talking. "Let's keep this simple and straightforward and just have a conversation," I said. "Like I said to Melissa, we are looking for background on Walter. You can say a few things about the company, but I mainly need a few good sound bites. I will be sure to give you guys a good plug—deal?"

"Sounds good," Goldberg said.

"Okay, so tell me a little bit about the company—you know, the elevator pitch."

"When I bought the company, we had two trucks, and we spent our days, nights, and weekends helping people who were locked out of their homes, installing deadbolts, making keys, that sort of stuff," he said. "Today, we have more than seventy employees and a fleet of trucks and vans that we use to install alarm systems, surveillance equipment, and computer firewalls. We also have cybersecurity specialists and even a division that teaches employees at companies how to avoid phishing scams."

"That's when someone sends you a fake email, trying to get you to click on something bad?" I asked, remembering some articles I'd read about cyber threats.

"Exactly. It's amazing how some people will open an email and click on practically anything. They get fooled, and then the company's system is compromised. The bad guys are really good at it. For an hourly employee, the idea of a free pizza is too hard to pass up. Except the pizza is fake, and they end up exposing the business. So, we train them how to recognize the scams."

"Your business has really evolved."

"Yeah, there was a time when security meant locking your doors. Today, the greatest threats have to do with technological breaches and human error. The early Trojan horse email programs would usually just mess up your system, but the bad guys have figured out how to break in and then hide and wait. A little piece of code sits on your server, seemingly dormant, unless we find it and get rid of it. The bad guys love any business that moves money: law offices and real estate and businesses like that. They will watch email traffic and then create fake messages and fake wire instructions, and then some unsuspecting employee wires a million bucks to a bank in the Balkans."

"Yikes."

"Nobody breaks into a bank and tries to drill holes in a vault or crack a safe anymore. They steal electronically."

"I have to tell you, this is really fascinating." I wasn't bullshitting. "At some point, I might want to come back for a larger story. A lot of people and businesses are vulnerable to this sort of thing, I bet."

His eyes lit up. "Of course, we would love that."

I couldn't even imagine the volume of the squeal that would come from Melissa.

"But the order of the day is Walter Swanson. What can

you tell me about him?"

"Walter isn't a cyber specialist, but he is a great project manager."

"What does that job entail?"

"He's a team leader for projects that require running new cables or retrofitting buildings with new fiber optics and other hard wiring. We call it 'the last mile.' Getting the data securely from the waypoint, maybe across the street, into the building and to the computer servers and ultimately to a worker's desk. He's really good at understanding how the buildings were constructed and the best way to wire them."

"What did you think when you heard about the shooting at Waterfront?"

"Well, I was obviously shocked and couldn't believe it, but knowing him, he is definitely a guy you can trust in a stressful situation. Our business is not life-and-death. We never come face-to-face with criminals. But I was impressed though not entirely surprised that he was able to do that. I knew a little bit about his videos, but I had no idea that he was an accomplished marksman. I am so impressed with his bravery and what he did in such a crazy situation. He saved lives that day, and he's a hero in Jacksonville."

He paused and looked at me.

"Perfect, that's exactly what I need."

I turned the camera off.

"We're done?"

"Yeah, I don't want to have you keep talking and sitting under the lights when I know I already have what I need. You are clearly a busy guy."

"Thanks, I appreciate that."

"I am curious, though, why you said that you were not entirely surprised. What did you mean by that?"

"Well, between you and me, Walter had a pretty rough family life as a kid."

"Like *violent* rough?" I asked.

"I can't and shouldn't say, but he had a pretty bad temper when he first started working for me. I told him he had to calm down if we wanted to succeed. But I never had any problems with him after that, and his whole outlook and personality seemed to change when he met Hailey. She seems to level him out."

"Ah, the calming effect of a woman." I paused. "Do you expect him to come back to work?"

"Yeah, he still works here, but, between us, I'm not sure if he will be coming back. I told him to take the week off, and he seems to have a bunch of things going on since the shooting. His job is here for him, and I say that sincerely, but I'm a practical business guy. If he sees another opportunity, I think he will take it."

"Yeah, I get that."

Let's see if I can get something decent here.

"He said he was working downtown on Friday, so that was a lucky coincidence because it looks like you have clients all over."

"Yes, we are fortunate to have clients as far north as Savannah and down to St. Augustine and even Daytona. That's the beauty of Jacksonville. It's close to many different areas and lots of wealthy people and businesses who need security.

Walter could have been anywhere on Friday, but he happened to be downtown all day at the Kennesaw Bank tower.

Bingo. Guess what business is located in the Kennesaw Bank tower? Southern Regal Insurance, employer of one Kyle Charles "Chip" Newberry.

I made some more small talk with Goldberg, a really nice guy.

"Is that your Ferrari out front?" I asked.

"It is. Happy to take you for a spin if you come back."

I laughed and said I might take him up on it. I guess you can make Ferrari-level money by helping clients protect theirs.

I CONVENED A meeting in the WJAX conference room with Ted, Olivia, and Rod.

"If you will humor me for a few minutes," I began, "I want to play the footage of the shooting. Olivia, can you put it on the monitor?" She did her magic sync trick, and the footage appeared on the conference room monitor. "Play it at regular speed, and then let's focus on Newberry's reaction. Just humor me for a second." We watched the footage.

"Right there, pause it," I told Olivia as Newberry seemed to reposition his rifle. "Does that look like a reaction, like he's lowering it with purpose?"

"Maybe," Ted said.

"Eh." Olivia scrunched her face.

"It could be anything. It could be the angle. Who knows?" Rod said.

"Right. I'm not sure. I'm definitely in need of more opinions," I said. "This thing has practically become my own personal Zapruder film." I scratched my forehead. "Anyway, ever since the shooting, I've had this weird feeling about Newberry's body language when Swanson confronts him. I just haven't been able to put my finger on it. I also found it odd that Swanson immediately put his gun down. I think that contributed to my gut feeling of finality when I was there. But here's the thing: Swanson does it with such immediacy." I paused. "He doesn't know if there's another shooter. Maybe Newberry planted a bomb. Maybe there's more going on somewhere else at the Waterfront. There's no way for him to know. But he drops his weapon like it's hot."

Ted nodded in agreement, but Rod appeared to be unimpressed.

"Of course, the cops came pretty fast," I continued. "And we can't see everything Swanson sees, so maybe he's quick to figure out that if he doesn't put his gun down, he might get shot. But, for me, it's another odd bit, and this has a lot to do with my feelings because I was there. But we can't report feelings, right? That's not part of what we do. It had been lingering in the back of my brain, but I pretty much abandoned it until I got a phone call the other day from Barry Petroff, an attorney in California. Newberry was his client, but we don't really know why Newberry had an attorney. He was hired before the shooting, but he literally said to me that 'all may not be as it seems.' Like we have a mystery on our hands. I nearly hung up on him."

"Good thing you didn't," Ted said.

"Yep, because he ended up sending us a ton of documents, a big data dump. We learned that he represents veterans who have had problems with the VA, and he sent press clippings about the high incidence of veteran suicides. It turns out that it's..." I paused and turned to Olivia, extending my hand to cue her.

"A fucking epidemic," she said.

"Exactly. The suicide rate among veterans is higher than among non-veterans throughout the country, and some veterans are committing suicide in VA hospital parking lots as a form of protest. Do you believe that?" I asked rhetorically.

"I had no idea," Rod said.

"Neither did we," I said as Ted and Olivia nodded in agreement.

"And there's more," I continued. "He also sent us a news release about a lawsuit, a case eerily similar to what we would learn about Newberry. The suit was filed by the family of a vet who couldn't get his pain meds and killed himself in a VA parking lot in Georgia. According to Petroff, Newberry knew about this case. Ted then found out from one of Newberry's friends that he was injured while in the Navy and getting his meds was a constant problem for him, and he was in tremendous pain without them. A few days before the shooting, his coworker said that he was complaining about the VA.

"So, here's the thing: Now we are wondering if the

Newberry case is, in fact, 'not exactly as it appears,' to quote the lawyer. Yes, it's indisputable that he went to the Waterfront with an assault rifle and scared the shit out of a lot of people. But when you talk to his friends and people who knew him, they say he wasn't crazy, wasn't a white supremacist, wasn't radicalized. Mainly, he was a regular guy who was in a lot of pain."

"He owned a lot of weapons," Ted said, "but he also bought and sold guns, and mainly knives, at the local gun show—low-key and under the radar."

"Jacksonville cops confiscated a bunch of weapons from his apartment, but people who understand the gun business say that he really didn't have a lot of stuff," I explained. "You could probably find a gun safe within a mile of here, owned by a doctor or lawyer, with just as many guns in it. Basically, we learned that Newberry wasn't a terrorist."

I paused again. I couldn't tell what Rod was thinking, but I went with it anyway. "Okay, so let's roll with this idea that Newberry decided to go to the Waterfront to commit suicide by cop. He owned an assault rifle, collector or not. He took it to the Waterfront. He was wearing a motorcycle helmet. Trust me, it was a scary ensemble. He started waving the gun, stalking around, and then he fired a shot in the air, scattering everyone and causing more chaos. What if his plan was to get shot by a cop as a VA protest? He's wearing a Navy sweatshirt. He knows that other vets have committed suicide in VA hospital parking lots, but it's barely registered as a blip on the national radar. So, he went to the Waterfront on the busiest night of the year to make a statement."

"But then it doesn't go according to plan," Ted said, "because Walter Swanson takes him out, not a cop. All the attention goes from the would-be mass shooter to the armed bystander."

"And this is all fine by the VA," Olivia said, "because if word gets out that this is a suicide, then all hell is gonna break loose in Washington. The president is already pissed at the VA."

"Okay, I'm gonna stop you there," Rod interjected. "I get it. This is very dramatic, and I understand where you are going with this, but your comparison to the Zapruder film might be right on. 'Newberry on the grassy knoll.'" He made air quotes with his fingers, not a good sign, before continuing. "I'm not sure how much of this you can prove. And I don't see much of anything that we can put on the air. It's speculation on top of speculation. It might be true, but I need verified facts. Let's start with something fundamental to your story: How can we say with certainty that this guy was committing suicide?"

"I found out last night that the magazine was empty," I said.

"Wait, what?" he asked.

"When were you gonna tell us this?" Ted asked.

"Uh, yeah?" Olivia chimed in.

"I'm telling you now. He went to the Waterfront with one bullet," I affirmed.

"Get outta here," Rod said. "Who told you that?"

"Rebecca Dawes," I said before adding in a lighter tone, "on deep background. I think he brought the assault rifle for maximum effect, not maximum damage. You can't do a mass shooting with only one bullet."

"Damn. That's really interesting. But deep background, really, Pete?" Rod was clearly getting agitated.

"Yeah, I know we can't use it until we get more sources," I said.

"What about the lawyer? Can we get him on the air to say that Newberry was suicidal?" Rod asked.

"We haven't heard back from him since Tuesday," I said. "And he has never said that he was suicidal. He said he was 'troubled' and 'in pain,' but he pointed us to all these theories. He was dancing around attorney/client privilege."

"Okay, so you know I love to play the devil's advocate/dick editor role, right?" Rod said. It was rhetorical. We all know that every reporter who ever became an editor loved that role. "You have an interesting theory, a cagey lawyer, and a deep background-supporting fact. It's thin, Pete. You know that."

"I do," I said. "Part of the issue is that when this happened, the VA and the feds swooped in and delayed, and then slowed the information flow because, conveniently, thanks in part to yours truly, Walter Swanson became a cult hero. The narrative changed in their favor, and they want it to stay that way. The story works for them: Newberry is a gun nut, a crazy person, like every other mass shooter, and Swanson is the national folk hero. Works perfectly for the VA."

"What are you basing that on?" Rod said.

I had just said too much. Frank Martinez's steely gaze

flashed in my head.

"We haven't been able to get the VA to say anything, and Rebecca basically confirmed that they are slow-walking a lot of information," I said.

Maybe I'd just righted the ship.

"Okay, like I said, this is all very interesting, but here's what we need: the lawyer on the air confirming Newberry was suicidal and confirmation on the empty magazine. Once we have those two things, then we can go to the VA for comment. At that point, we will have the story, and we won't need them if they choose not to talk to us. Make sense?"

"Yes," I said.

"Why don't you see if you can get Dawes to go on the record?" Rod asked. "Can we get her to come over here to run through what you have so far? Maybe then we can get part of this story on the record."

For once, "Rod the Story Killer" had a good suggestion.

Chapter Seventeen

3 p.m., Thursday, WJAX

I CALLED EVAN for an update on the agreement with the Wheelers. He said he was going back and forth with them on the contracting entity as well as my new demands but thought we might get the deal done today. I told him to text me as soon as he had a document that I could review.

I called Rebecca. She picked up immediately.

"Hi, Peter—can I call you Peter?" she asked, still riding that line from last night. "What's going on?"

"I actually have some new information on Walter Swanson and Kyle Newberry that I found out today. I think Swanson may have known Newberry."

"Wait, what?" she said. "He told us he didn't know him."

"Then I think he lied to you. I have guys at the gun show who think they knew one another. He nearly admitted it to me yesterday, and this morning, I learned that Swanson was in Newberry's building on the morning of the shooting. Friday."

"He didn't say any of those things to us. Pete, I'm gonna need you to go over this with Detective Howard Steele, who's been running point for us on this."

"I'm happy to. Do you guys want to come to WJAX after work and we can run through it with the news team? Rod Kirby will fawn all over you and Detective Steele."

"We will be there," she said.

I had plenty of time to run a quick errand and stopped by Olivia's desk.

"Can I borrow a portable hard drive?" I asked.

"Yes, of course," she said. "But lose my pictures and you're a dead man."

"How much can it hold?"

"It's ten terabytes, so a lot. Why?"

"I'll be super careful, I promise."

She reached into her bag and pulled out a plastic-encased hard drive, not much bigger than a mobile phone. It was electric pink.

"If you need to download a lot of data, be sure to use the USB C port. Otherwise, it will take a hundred years to fill this thing up."

"Thanks, I appreciate it." I gingerly placed it in my briefcase and headed to the Kennesaw Bank building.

I WALKED INTO the building and flashed my press credential to the young guy at the security desk. I told him that I was with the local TV station and wanted to talk to the head of security about a story I was doing on cyberhacking.

I was greeted by another young guy who didn't look like a security guy at all. He was about five-foot-ten, wearing stylish glasses, jeans, Converse sneakers, and a polo-style shirt with the building's name and logo on it. He had brown hair down to his shoulders, a goatee, and a full sleeve of tattoos on his right arm.

He gave off an intimidating nerd vibe. But he was all smiles.

"How can I help you?" he asked.

"I'm looking for the person who oversees security for this building," I said.

"That's me." He extended his hand. "Gus Intriago...and you are?"

"I'm Pete Lemaster with WJAX. Is there somewhere we can talk?"

"How about my office?"

He led me through a labyrinth of steel doors and hallways, swiping his key card three times along the way until we were somewhere in the bowels of the forty-two-story tower. We sat in a small, windowless office with a stack of old personal computers and laptops piled in a corner. Gus had a triple-screen computer setup that either monitored everything in the building or was ready to launch an air strike. I noticed a photo of Gus and a pretty brunette in front of the famous Bull Gator statue at the University of Florida.

"I like that picture," I said and gave him a slight Gator chomp, like a secret handshake or a mobster's wink. "Did you go to the game?"

"Yeah, tough one. We are getting out-recruited, and until that gets turned around, there are going to be a lot of sad games here in Jacksonville for us," he said.

"That's spot-on. Kills me to agree with you, but the best plays don't consistently beat better talent." He nodded. I paused for a beat to see if he had a followup point about football. Most guys can go all day, myself included. But he looked at me with an expression that told me he was a busy guy.

"Listen, I'm interested in doing a story about cybersecurity for businesses here in Jacksonville at some point in the future, but I'm really here to talk about the shooting at the Waterfront. The shooter, Kyle Newberry, worked in this building."

"Yeah, the cops were here over the weekend. They searched his cubicle upstairs but didn't find anything."

"I'm not surprised. He didn't seem like the kind of guy who would have left much at his workplace. I'm actually more interested in the armed bystander who shot him, Walter Swanson. He was supposed to have been working here last Friday. Did you know that?"

"Oh yeah, I know Walter." He paused, clearly thinking for a moment. "Walter's a bit of a dick if I'm being honest."

"Oh, really?" Gus, my Gator compadre. I've hit the jackpot. "Did the cops ask about him?"

"No, I actually didn't talk to the cops. One of my guys let them in here on Sunday, and they never talked to me. But yeah, I have dealt with Walter a few times. He thinks he's hot snot. I agree that what he did was really brave and heroic, but you can be a hero and a pain in the ass, too, don't you think?"

"Well, I have met him, and I got the same impression."

"Yeah, he works for a big private security company, and he thinks he knows way more than I do. Honestly, I don't think he likes that I'm younger than he is and probably have a better job. I also don't give two craps about all his gun stuff. I work for a security company. I have a gun too. I just don't talk about it all the time. I go to the range a few times a year. I qualify for what I need to qualify for and hope that I will never have to fire the damn thing."

Me and Gus: Simpatico.

"Okay, here's the straight story. I have this theory that Swanson and Newberry knew each other, and I'm trying to see if they may have talked to each other on Friday when Swanson was here."

"You think they knew each other? That's pretty crazy."

"I'm thinking it's a bit thin myself."

"My fiancée has a true-crime podcast. She's been all over this thing. Wait till I tell her about this."

"Well, there's nothing to tell unless I can prove it. You have a bunch of video cameras in this building, right?"

"More than a hundred."

"Can I see the footage?"

"Well, even if I was allowed to share it with you, it would take hours to go through it all."

"Listen, I'm not going to put this on the air. I mainly want to see if they were ever together on Friday. If I want to put it on the air, I will go through all the official channels to get it." I paused for a second. "If you let me see the footage, I will go on your girlfriend's podcast and maybe even get a local cop to come with me. What do you say?"

"She would love that. You realize there are hours of footage from dozens of cameras, right?"

"I do. Can you download it to an external drive?"

"Do you have a huge external drive in your bag?"

"I do." I pulled out Olivia's bright pink hard drive and handed it to him. "My colleague says to use the C port or something like that."

"USB-C is one of the newer formats, yes. Theoretically, it can move data at ten gigs per second but not quite that fast in practical terms. But this is good."

"Great."

"So, give me a couple hours. I will need to get one of my guys to download the footage from the cloud and load it on the drive. Without any hiccups, it should be done by the end of the day." And then, it was his turn to pause. "And none of this goes public without approval of the building, and you do my girlfriend's podcast no matter what you find?"

"Yes." I shook his hand. "Thank you, Gus. And one more question." His eyebrows raised. "What do you drink?"

"Oh." He paused. "Scotch?"

"Excellent. See you in a couple hours."

As I headed back to the station, I realized I had a missed call from my mom, and I called her back.

"Did you speak with Denise?" she asked.

"Yeah, that ship has officially sailed."

"You okay?"

"I'm fine, Mom, I'm deep into the Waterfront shooting story right now, and it has gotten incredibly complicated. It's very murky and a little weird."

"Weird how?" she asked.

"Well, everything is happening so fast that I can't seem to get a handle on it. This story is spinning and spinning. I just need it to pause long enough so I can really understand what's happening. But I think I'm getting there."

"Take your time so you don't make any silly mistakes, Peter. You know, I could have sent some business deals to Denise if you had dated her long enough."

"Sorry that didn't work out for either of you," I said.

She laughed. "What's going on with Rebecca?"

I sighed. "That's a story in progress, and I also don't want to get into it. Goodbye, Mom." I hung up.

ON THE WAY back to WJAX, I stopped at my favorite liquor store and went straight to the counter because what I wanted was going to be behind it. I told the clerk to pull down a 750ml bottle of Johnnie Walker Blue, the best scotch that exists as far as I know.

I'm not a big scotch drinker, but Johnnie Walker is a can't-miss with my friends who do, and Blue is at the top of their lists. When something is aged with such care that it ends up costing $250 a bottle, it will taste incredible even if it's not your go-to drink. To me, an average scotch burns my throat a bit, has a kind of sour taste, and you're not supposed to mix it with anything except ice, maybe a splash of water, or more scotch. As a beer-drinking, rum-and-Diet Coke sort of guy, it's just not on my Christmas list.

I tapped my credit card at the checkout device and exited the store with a brown paper bag filled with liquid goodness.

I sat down at my desk and put the bag next to my computer screen.

"What's in the bag?" Ted asked.

"Insurance."

I GREETED BOTH Rebecca and Detective Howard Steele with a handshake as they entered our conference room. Olivia had her laptop at the ready to help me make my presentation and keep this little operation moving.

Rebecca was wearing her uniform with her hair in her now-familiar ponytail. Steele, a light-skinned Black detective in his mid-fifties, stood about five-foot-seven, and you could tell that he was in very good shape. He had a few wisps of gray in an otherwise enviable head of hair. He wore a charcoal-gray suit with a striped tie. He looked like a police detective straight out of a TV cop show.

Steele had an extremely friendly disposition. He gladly accepted our offer for coffee and then claimed to be an unabashed expert about all things coffee, donuts, barbecue, and soul food in Duval County. I chose not to ask him if he knew about Dixie Chicken—after all, we had work to do.

"I understand from Rebecca that you have found some new information about the shooting at the Waterfront," Steele said. "As I think she told you, we have had our own challenges with the feds on this one. A lot of folks at the national and state level offering their opinions. But I'm curious to hear what you've got."

"Well, I think the most important thing is to start with a phone call I received two days ago from an attorney in California named Barry Petroff," I said. "Olivia will put his website up on the screen. Petroff does all manner of injury cases, but he also specializes in cases dealing with veterans and the VA."

"Interesting," Steele said.

"There's a section on his website where he talks about veterans and suicide," I said as Olivia clicked on that page on the site. "And then he sent us a bunch of press clippings and some legal filings that basically say that veteran suicide has grown to epidemic proportions in America. And while that's interesting all by itself, a number of vets have actually committed suicide on the grounds of VA hospitals as a form of protest."

Steele's eyebrows raised, and he looked at Rebecca, who nodded.

"We reviewed a bunch of these articles and documents," I said. "And I will spare you all the details of the deep dive and say that the long and short of this is that veterans are more likely than regular citizens to commit suicide. And the VA knows this, but it is such a bureaucratic mess, these guys get frustrated and can't take it anymore. They have PTSD, other mental issues, pain issues, and they decide their only option is suicide. Petroff sent us a news release about a case he won a year or so ago regarding a young vet in Georgia who couldn't get his meds, and he was so distraught that he shot himself in the chest, sitting in his car in the parking lot of a VA hospital."

Ted chimed in, "The family won a million-dollar verdict against the company that was providing hospital phone operators. Get this: The family of this young man knew he was suicidal, and they called the hospital, but the operator didn't take action, and a few minutes later, the guy shot himself."

"That's awful," Rebecca said.

"Mm-hmm." Steele looked like he already knew some of this.

"So, what does that have to do with why we're here today?" I asked rhetorically. "Well, Kyle Newberry's situation turned out to be eerily similar to the Georgia case. He was injured while he was in the Navy; hurt his back really badly. He was honorably discharged. After he got out, he was constantly in pain, and he was regularly in dispute with the VA about his medications. We learned from his friends and coworkers at Southern Regal that Newberry had chronic back issues and was regularly in pain."

"One of my cop buddies has a back injury. So painful," Steele said.

"His closest friend from work said that the last time she saw him last Wednesday, he was complaining about the VA," I said.

"We interviewed a bunch of his friends and the people at Southern Regal," Steele interjected. "None of them talked about the VA. They were all shocked."

"Well, his closest friend was out of town until the other

day," Ted said. "So, she probably wasn't there when you did your interviews."

"Fair enough."

"So, here's what I think happened," I said. "I think Newberry had been dealing with incredible back pain for years, and he became fed up with the VA. The situation was impacting his ability to earn a living. It was impacting his ability to have relationships—a woman he dated said he couldn't go to the movies because he couldn't sit still for two hours. And it was impacting his quality of life. Nobody likes being in pain and having to be on meds."

Everyone except Rod seemed to be following right along, so I soldiered on. "I think he learned about the Georgia case and reached out to Petroff in California. They started to talk about legal options, but it was too little, too late. A couple months ago, he was assigned a new VA doctor who cut his medicine back, and he started regularly running out of pills. We learned from the Georgia case that the VA hospitals shut down at four p.m. on Fridays. If you don't get your prescription figured out by Friday afternoon, you probably have to wait until the next week to get your meds. In other words, you're screwed. I think Newberry was in pain, he was frustrated, and he was upset with the VA, and he decided to put his plan into place."

"What plan?" Steele asked.

"My theory?" I said. "Kyle Newberry decided to go to the Waterfront to commit suicide by cop. He put on a Navy sweatshirt, which would help to identify him as a veteran. He put on a motorcycle helmet to conceal his face and to look intimidating. He absolutely was, by the way. He might have also thought he would be less likely to be shot in the head if he was wearing the helmet. Maybe wanted to be able to have an open casket."

"What are you talking about?" Rod jumped in.

"We didn't share that with you, but the guy in Georgia and several others shot themselves in the chest.

Steele had a quizzical look on his face. Rod was simmering.

I kept at it. "Okay, so Newberry had an assault rifle because he wanted to be intimidating. I had a long conversation with some guys at the gun show, and they told me that he mainly sold knives from the booth he had there. But he did sell guns too. You guys confiscated his inventory."

Steele threw me a look.

"Sorry, that came out wrong," I said. "My theory is that the weapons taken from his apartment were not a personal arsenal. They were the guns and knives he was planning to sell at the gun show—his inventory."

No reaction from Steele.

"Here's another important part," I continued. "Newberry was not a white supremacist or a terrorist or some type of zealot. No one has found any crazed social-media rantings."

Rebecca chimed in, "He had no social media accounts to rant on."

"Right," I said. "No manifesto in his apartment either. You didn't find anything radical on his computer. He wasn't using his Xbox to talk to terrorists in the Middle East like in the Tom Clancy movie. He was troubled, for sure, and in pain, which is my theory and also that of his lawyer in California."

"All believable," Steele said.

"Okay, so Newberry goes to the Waterfront to scare people and provoke the cops into shooting him," I said. "What solidified it for me was learning fairly recently about his weapon and his ammo."

"The empty magazine." Steele looked at Rebecca and then back at me.

"We talked," she said.

"Here's the recap," I said. "Newberry goes to the Waterfront, looking scary and intimidating. He fires one shot in the air. Everyone scatters and drops. He figures the cops will close in. He will aim his empty gun at them, and then he will get shot dead. Then once the media find out the magazine was empty, all hell breaks loose, and the VA suicide story hits the front page. But there are a couple of problems."

"Walter Swanson," Steele said.

"Precisely," I said.

"And the VA," Rebecca added.

"As we have since learned, yes," I said. "Now, for us to take this story to air, we need more than speculation. We are working on getting the lawyer on the record to confirm that Newberry was suicidal, but we haven't heard from him in a few days. If we can get it on the record that Newberry's gun was empty, that he brought only one round, that would be a big help."

"Well, this is all very interesting, and I appreciate the work you've put in," Steele said. "Obviously, I can't confirm that he was suicidal like the lawyer can, but I can tell you that his magazine was empty. But you can only attribute it to a source at the JSO, not either of us personally."

"That story helps all of us," Rebecca said.

"The VA guys have been leaning on us for a week," Steele continued. "And I'm sick and tired of it. The amount of jurisdictional BS they have been spewing is making me crazy."

Rod chimed in, "That's great, Detective Steele. That's incredibly helpful and exactly what we need. I can't thank you enough for coming over today."

"But there's more," I said, interrupting Rod and taking this way further than anyone but me expected. He scowled at me, which made me briefly pause. But, nope. I was crossing the Rubicon. *Here goes.*

I said, "We have been working this suicide angle for a few days, and for a while, we thought it was thin. So, what's thinner than thin?"

"Too thin to share," Rod said. He had surpassed scowling and was now seething.

I kept at it.

"I think Swanson and Newberry may have known each other." I paused. "I told you that I spoke to some guys from the gun show. Well, my brother-in-law owns Patriot Guns on the north side of town."

"I know it," Steele said. "It's right next to Dixie Chicken."

I smiled and turned to Rebecca. "You didn't tell me he was a Renaissance man."

"I didn't tell you anything," she said. "What's Dixie Chicken?"

"Never mind," I said.

Note to self: Perfect second, or perhaps fifth, date.

"Okay, great chicken aside, I sat down with my friends at the gun show on Monday, and the word on Facebook is that Swanson used to attend the gun show too. And we know Newberry had a regular booth there. No one knows if they knew each other, but Swanson confirmed to me yesterday that he used to go to the gun show because it was a way to attract clients to his courses. So, it's possible that they could have met there.

"The other thing, and this is new to everyone here, is that when I showed Newberry's picture to the guy who runs the gun show, he recognized him but said he knew him as Chip."

Puzzled looks all around.

"Okay, so Chip is short for Charles. What does that have to do with anything?" Rod asked, surprisingly calm at that moment.

"So, I'm just crazy enough that when I finished my interview with Swanson yesterday, I turned off the camera and asked him if he ever met Chip at the gun show. And he said, without hesitation, 'I told the cops I never met the guy.'"

More stares and a look of consternation from Steele.

"He didn't flinch. He didn't say, 'Who's Chip?' Which is what I was expecting him to say."

"But you don't have that on camera?" Rod asked, clearly unhappy.

"The guy was not being helpful to me," I said. "He was just spewing sound bites at that point. I was trying to get him off-guard. And I think it worked."

"So, he may have lied," Steele said.

"Right," Rod said. "But we can't use that because we don't have it on camera." He was starting to get indignant.

"Yeah, but I can," Steele said.

I added, "I also interviewed his boss, who confirmed that Swanson was working in the Kennesaw Bank building on Friday. What do you make of that?" I directed the question to Steele.

"That's where Newberry worked, right?" he responded.

"Affirmative," I said, immediately regretting that I was getting too collegial.

Rod's glare intensified. "Swanson knowing Newberry is not a crime, by the way." Now he was just digging in for the sake of it.

"Lying about it to the police is," Rebecca said.

"And I would like to ask him if he knew he was in the same building with the shooter last Friday," Steele said. "This is definitely interesting, Pete. Rebecca said you were a pretty bright guy."

I could see the wheels in Steele's head spinning. Rebecca kept a solid, professional expression on her face. Ted and Olivia were smiling. Rod continued his slow burn.

"We talked to a lot of Newberry's friends, and plenty of them knew that he had these pain issues," I said. "I'm thinking that Swanson was a regular at the gun show and knew Newberry. But not only did he know him, he knew about his 'plan.' But we can't connect him because Newberry was a total throwback—no social-media accounts, didn't text, and even Olivia and her friends on the dark web found nothing but some speculation by the gun-show crowd."

"His phone records were completely clean," Steele said.

"And his phone records were clean," I repeated deferentially. "But somehow, Swanson knew this was going to happen. Maybe Newberry confided in him and Swanson took it from there. He got himself to the Waterfront, positioned himself outside, and waited."

I asked Olivia to put the video up again.

"Let's watch the video again," I said and began to narrate. "Newberry comes to the Waterfront with one bullet. He stalks around. He fires the shot in the air. Everyone hits the dirt. Then Swanson approaches. He's not super scared because he knows that the magazine is empty. The single shot was almost a signal to Swanson. Then Swanson takes him out. Bang, bang, bang."

Rod interjected, "It would be a lot better if he actually said he knew Newberry, like a declarative sentence. A thumbs-up or thumbs-down, maybe? We can't base a story on the fact that the guy didn't question you when you brought up a name he may have never heard before."

"That's another way of looking at it, yes," I said. Rebecca was watching me closely, sympathetically, right along with Ted and Olivia.

"Beyond thin, like microscopically thin," Rod said.

"Now, you do have something else interesting here that has to do with the third person in this case, Stephanie

Singleton," Steele asked. "If Swanson knew Newberry was coming to the Waterfront with an assault rifle, he had an obligation to tell the police. And if he knew it and decided to take the law into his own hands, then the death of Stephanie Singleton might be manslaughter."

I gave a slight smile.

"We can't arrest him yet," Steele said. "But we can talk to him again and ask some pointed questions at the sheriff's office. I think he definitely lied to us, and we should talk to the girlfriend again too." Then, looking at, Rebecca, he added, "I bet she knows more than she's saying."

"Well, you'll have more luck with her," I said. "She flew back from New York already. I have a feeling they had a fight."

"That could be good for us," Rebecca said.

"What about Swanson?" Steele asked.

"He's in New York until Monday," I said. "At least that's what he told me."

"Well, the sheriff isn't going to fly us up to New York on a private jet, so we will have to wait," Steele joked.

"News travels, I see." I laughed.

Rod scowled.

"When are you going to run this?" Rebecca asked me.

"Well, I withheld half of this from my boss, so I'm not sure when we're going to air or what we can air or even if he's gonna let me keep my job," I said with a half-smile at Rod.

"It looks to me like you have some information worth checking out," Steele said. "But you need to sort out the rest of this with Mr. Kirby. In the meantime, like I said, the JSO can confirm that Newberry's magazine was empty."

Ted and Olivia chose to walk Steele and Rebecca out, leaving me alone in the conference room with Rod.

As the door shut, Rod's face turned a bright red. If it was a color in the crayon box, it would be called "rage."

"I don't know which is making me more angry right now," Rod said. "The fact that you withheld all of this information from me or that I was stupid enough to hire a guy who would fucking run down these imaginary roads and then have the fucking balls to bring in the police and unload a whole mess of theories without any evidence the cops can use, much less anything that we can put on our air."

"Rod," I said, "I'm sorry if I caught you off-guard."

"Off-guard?" He turned an ever deeper shade of red. "Pete, this is way beyond off-guard. This is more like insubordination. More like undermining my whole news operation. We are supposed to be playing together here, and you are bombing three-pointers from half-court with no one under the basket. It makes no sense."

"I'm sorry, Rod. This story has become intensely personal to me."

"Well, not anymore. You're off of it."

"What do you mean?"

"I mean you are no longer working on the shooting story. While you were smugly playing Agatha Christie or Encyclopedia Brown or whatever the fuck that was, I was assigning you to cover the turtles tonight."

"No, no, no. Rod, I need to finish this story."

"Pete, you are in no position to make demands with me. You did some great work here. Your footage from last Friday is already legendary. But this wild-ass, rabbit fuck hole you have gone down is not gonna happen. You are out of your depth, Lemaster."

He stared at the ceiling and then at the computer monitor, which still showed an image of Newberry holding his assault rifle. He took a breath. "Get me a good story on the turtles tonight, and maybe, just maybe, I will let you follow through on this suicide angle."

"Okay," I said, completely and utterly defeated.

"Yeah, exactly, Pete. Go find Bobby. He drew the other short straw on the turtles. Maybe this will help you remember who signs your paychecks."

Chapter Eighteen

7 p.m., Thursday, WJAX

ROD'S PLAN TO run me ragged as punishment was working to perfection. Shortly after our meeting, I hauled butt over to the Kennesaw Bank tower and traded the bottle of Johnnie Walker, which Gus Intriago did not seem to fully appreciate, for Olivia's now fully-loaded hard drive. I also reaffirmed that I would indeed be a guest on his fiancée's podcast but to just give me a week or so. Apparently, she recorded it from a heavily blanketed, makeshift studio in their shared Bay Meadows townhouse.

Gus also told me we could crack open the "bourbon" I had just given him when I did the taping. I bit my lip and began to question my motivation—and even the meaning of life. But he was a nice guy who did me a favor, so his alcohol ignorance could slide. No good deed went unpunished as I tried to erase from my thoughts the possibility that this guy might make some kind of ridiculous cocktail with the Johnnie Blue. Alas.

Unfortunately, I wasn't able to do anything with the hard drive because I had to immediately go meet Bobby to cover the turtles.

On its face, turtle nesting season in Florida is a heart-warming tale. For thousands of years, if not longer, mama sea turtles of several different species have been crawling up onto coastal Florida beaches and laying their eggs in the soft sand. Two months later, if all goes according to plan, cute little baby turtles come rushing out en masse and make a sprint for the water. Without question, it's a lovely "circle of life" kinda story. But it also has a hard edge as environmental groups blame overdevelopment and pollution for destroying turtle habitats. Crowded beaches scare off turtle moms, and city lights confuse the babies, who sometimes crawl toward the lights, streets, and people, mistaking them for the moonlit ocean.

Local environmentalists are incredibly diligent when it comes to efforts to preserve the existing turtle population, and they're aided by Florida Fish and Wildlife, probably one of the most underfunded and understaffed agencies in the state.

We arrived at one of the few remaining pristine sections of beach in North Jacksonville, which might coincidentally be the site of the future condo I'd been dreaming about. The last thing the environmentalists wanted was another gleaming residential tower, with its accompanying ten-story shadow covering the turtle nesting areas, not to mention hundreds of pairs of sunburned feet slogging through the dunes.

As journalism assignments go, this one is quite the crap shoot. Over the past few months, the turtles have come ashore and laid their eggs, so the turtle enthusiasts have tracked the activity. The turtle folks "think" they know when the babies will pop up through the sand, but they are never quite sure. So, getting assigned to cover this story might mean that you stay up all night and then get nothing to put on the news. If you were filming a nature documentary, you would spend a couple of weeks waiting out the turtle babies, but we don't have that luxury. In my case, Rod felt like he had something of an obligation to the turtle crowd, and he believed that when done correctly, the story could get a ton of clicks. As a bonus, he could punish me at the same time.

Either way, I didn't get any sleep.

As we were setting up our gear near the beach, my phone rang. Rebecca.

"Hey, how's it going," I asked as waves crashed not far behind me.

"I'm doing well, just got home. Are you at the beach?"

"Yeah, I'm covering the turtle hatchlings if you can believe that. What's going on? Anything new on the case?"

"We've made some progress, but I just called to see how you're doing. Rod was getting a little hot at the end there."

"Well, it's ten o'clock at night and I'm on the beach looking for baby turtles when I should be investigating the biggest story to hit Jacksonville in years. So, I guess I'm doing kinda lousy right now."

"He took you off the shooting story?"

"For now, but yes. He's pissed at me for not clearing everything with him and following my nose a little too closely, I guess."

"Wow, that stinks. I have to say, watching you explain what you guys have learned was," she paused, "impressive.

You seem really invested in this story."

"You have no idea," I said, realizing that I had just opened the door and wanted her to come through.

"What do you mean?"

"Um, yesterday you told me a specific one thing, about the magazine, remember?"

"Yeah."

"Well, I kind of have my own one thing I haven't shared with anyone else."

There was a noticeable pause. "Pete, you're making me a little nervous here."

"I'm sorry." I paused this time. "That's not my intention, but here it is." I took a deep breath and just told her. "My father was in the Army. He took his own life when I was a kid."

She gasped. "Oh my god, I'm so sorry, Peter. That's awful."

"Um, yeah, it really is." I took another breath. "I'm sorry if that was just super heavy, but it has been dragging on me."

"That's okay… Well, it's good if it makes you feel better talking about it," she said. "We learn a lot about different types of trauma in law enforcement. Everyone handles it differently. If you want to talk about it, I'm happy to listen."

"I appreciate that," I said. "Not sure why I just shared that when I should be focusing on turtles."

She laughed. "Well, it's good if you can keep perspective, I guess." Another pause. "That's a lot to process, but I'm glad you shared it with me. Does Rod know?"

"Shit no. Who knows how he might react? Honestly,

you're the only person in Duval County who knows."

"Ah, so that's a really good one thing too," she said. I could sense her smile.

"I guess so," I said, feeling more relaxed than I had in days.

My phone pinged—a text from Bobby.

"Hey, I gotta go," I said. "Bobby just texted me. He's combing the beach right now, and I'm thinking it's even money that we see even a single turtle. He will probably have one of his eruptions later tonight, which are very entertaining."

"Okay, Pete. Go cover the important turtle story," she laughed. "Oh, and I had fun last night. Let's do it again."

"We will," I said. "Have a good night." We hung up.

Slowly advancing, like the turtles, with Ms. Dawes.

Bobby and I interviewed several nice folks who were on turtle watch, and we covered all the known issues and warnings. Residents near the beach should turn off their lights so the babies trudge to the ocean and not a condo or the surf shop/pizza joint across the street from the beach. No greater tragedy than baby turtles crushed by cars or beach cruiser bikes. Beachgoers needed to be aware of the marked nesting sites and make sure not to disturb the nests, the turtle moms, or the babies—it carries a fine of up to $5,000 and up to five years in jail.

And then be sure to come out in force to prevent future development, they will say, even though most of the do-gooders own condos down the street. They already own their piece of paradise and figure that others shouldn't have theirs if it puts turtles at risk. I have covered many Not In My Backyard—NIMBY—groups since I started in TV journalism. I always find it interesting because I'm sure there were prior generations of NIMBYs too.

As feared, I stayed up all night and listened to Bobby swear for nine hours because we saw not a single baby turtle emerge. Bobby would likely be stuck going out there again the following night.

I got home as the sun was creeping up and then slept for a few hours before groggily getting ready for work. The one bright side of leaving the apartment at midmorning was that there was little chance of running into Denise.

Evan had sent me the contract from the Wheelers. They agreed to all of my new demands. Interesting. They might be stringing me along by agreeing to let me string them along. I also might be losing my mind because I'm really tired.

They were to wire $75,000 upon execution of the agreement, which was nullified in five days if the money didn't arrive or if I chose to back out.

I called Evan to congratulate him on getting everything I wanted and to confirm that he was ready for me to pull the trigger. He said it was "go time" and to let him know once I signed it. I closed my laptop. Not yet.

I arrived at the station, still dragging ass, and sat down across from Ted, who immediately started to mock me.

"You look like a shell of your old self," he said. "Like you have been shellacked."

"Did you stay up all night dreaming of that line?" I asked. "If so, a waste of good sleep, which I didn't get.

What's the latest?"

"Barry Petroff got mugged a couple days ago," Ted said. "I just got a text from him."

"Get outta town! What happened?" I had a sinking feeling. *Is this Frank Martinez's doing?*

"I don't know very much. I got a text that he was mugged and in the hospital until yesterday. No idea who did it. He's in pretty bad shape—a few broken ribs and a fractured arm. I tried to call him but no answer."

"No idea who did it?" I asked. "Santa Barbara's not well-known for street crime, is it?" I knew the answer. "Damn. So, any chance of getting him on the air anytime soon is shot to hell. Man, this story has suddenly become a slog, and I'm not even supposed to be working on it. What about the girlfriend?"

"You said she was in town, right?" Ted asked.

"Yes," I said. "See if you can track her down."

I wandered into the breakroom. This story was on life support. I'd reached too far and got smacked down. There was nothing solid I could put on the air, and it was all just as Rod said—rumor and innuendo. I hated when that guy was right more than I hated being wrong.

I opened the top of the coffeemaker and dropped in a capsule. Was there an "extra strong" button?

As I waited for the coffee to brew in the empty breakroom, I realized how much tension I was feeling in my neck and shoulders. The easy choice was to take the money, assuming the Wheelers were good for their word, and just let the story go. It was in dire straits anyway, and Rod had me on a short leash. All I had was speculation and my gut, though I knew I was right. And I also hate bullies.

I opened my email on my phone and electronically signed the Wheeler contract and then texted Evan that it was done. He immediately responded with a thumbs-up emoji and a beer mug emoji. "Cheers," I guess?

My coffee was still in the coffeemaker, steam rising.

I can't let this story die while I'm covering more fluff.

I abandoned the coffee cup, walked outside to my car, and called Kamari Small at the governor's office.

Buckle up, Kamari. Today, you will raise your boss's national profile after all, courtesy of your friends in Jacksonville.

Chapter Nineteen

11 a.m., Friday, WJAX

I WANDERED INTO Rod's office and was greeted with a big smile.

"Did you see any turtle babies?" he asked. "My wife loves the turtle babies, and her college roommate runs the rescue foundation."

"Not a single one," I said. "With all due respect to your wife, her roommate, and all the people who patrol the beach all night, I think their science is super suspect. Each year, we go out there, and either their timing is way off or global warming is messing with the turtles or something. I just taped a story about sea turtles without any damned turtles in it."

"Think of it as part of your community service," he said.

I got the joke but chose not to acknowledge it. I said nothing and let the silence fill his office.

"Okay," he said finally. "I'm giving you and Bobby a little treat to go along with your all-nighter. Putting you on the pageant story." He handed me a piece of paper.

Again, I knew exactly what was going on.

"I'm on it, boss," I said. *Eye on the prize, Lemaster.*

"Smile, Pete," he said. "Pretty girls at the Marriott. Perfect for my two favorite bachelors. And remember, keep it light—it's mainly a scholarship pageant since they dropped the bikinis. Have a little fun and then get back here."

A few minutes later, I was zooming down the expressway headed for the Marriott resort in Ponte Vedra, the site of this year's Miss Northeast Florida and the Beaches pageant. Bobby was stoked. Me, not so much. Normally, this is my bread and butter: a fun little story showcasing overachieving pretty girls who, for some reason, were still participating in a so-called beauty pageant. But today, there's real news to report, and I was stuck working on a story with the goal of generating web traffic. Rod is focused on clicks, and pretty girls still get clicks. *Alas.*

Putting objectification to the side for a moment, I was happy for Bobby. The overnight turtle assignment sucked for him, too, so he would get to have some fun talking to the girls. He's funny and charming when he wants to be, and he soaked up the girls who preened for his camera.

After speaking to the organizer of the pageant, a fairly young guy who inherited the event from his parents, I learned a little bit about the economics of a beauty—ahem—scholarship pageant. Apparently, the money is in the broadcast rights, and streaming video might be the death knell of the pageant industry—not the issue of whether we should be grading girls on how they look in cocktail dresses. He pledged to keep doing the pageant as long as girls signed up and as long as he could continue making money from it.

I interviewed a few contestants along with some pageant parents. The common theme was girls likening pageants to a hobby like dance or a sport like cheerleading, and they also saw it as a way to get scholarship money for college. The parents saw it as a way for their girls to learn life lessons, make some friends, and actually have to speak with judges and communicate one-on-one versus talking and texting on their phones. They also seemed to universally lament the impending end to pageants as girls can get more fame and fortune from being an Instagram or TikTok influencer than the pageant could ever provide.

I sensed that the real story here might be the changing-of-the-guard aspect of this tale. Posting on social media might be a much shorter pathway to the fame once afforded by the pageant circuit, but I knew that I wasn't getting out of Rod's doghouse by going philosophical on a story he wanted purely for views.

Bobby and I ended up with a nice little story package highlighting the seemingly noble goals of scholarship pageants while showing off plenty of bright, smiling young women who were ready for a weekend of friendly competition. Just what Rod ordered.

On the way back, I called Evan. The Wheelers had countersigned the contract, which was good news, but he hadn't yet received the money. I asked him to call me as soon as the funds arrived.

Back at the station, I sat down across from Ted, who matter-of-factly announced that Hailey Marsh wanted to speak with me.

"She returned my call and said that she was available tomorrow to be on camera and talk about what has happened since the shooting," he said. "She's back in town, and Swanson is still in New York, but it sounds like things have gotten weird with them."

"So, tomorrow what time?" I asked.

"Do I look like your hot secretary? I will have her text you directly, Mr. Lemaster."

I wasn't planning on working the next day, but if I wasn't on the clock, I didn't have to justify my time to Rod. Maybe, just maybe, I'd learn something from her that we could use to bring the story back to life.

A moment later, as I was collecting my thoughts, the monitors in the room were all tuned to the governor's mansion in Tallahassee, awaiting Governor Jim McManus.

That was quick.

He stepped to a lectern, flanked by the Stars and Stripes and the State of Florida flag, and began:

"Good afternoon. It's been an interesting week here in Tallahassee, as we have all been dealing with issues regarding the aftermath of a shooting at the Waterfront. I know that many of us had thought that this incident was over and that we had put it behind us. But today, my office has uncovered a startling and disturbing development in the shooting case. As most of you know, I'm a Navy veteran, and I was a proud member of the Navy's Judge Advocate General's Corps, known as the JAG Corps. And I'm proud to say that my dress uniform still fits."

What is it with military guys and their old uniforms?

McManus continued: "I was stunned to hear the information that my office uncovered. The gentleman who went to the Waterfront last Saturday, Kyle Charles Newberry, was a Navy veteran who served with distinction until he was injured in an on-base car accident. After leaving the Navy, he came to Jacksonville, and he dealt with, as far as we have learned, unrelenting pain due to his accident. But sadly, he also had ongoing issues with the U.S. Department of Veterans Affairs regarding his care.

"On a regular basis, he was denied pain medications, and the VA messed up its diagnosis and even violated his rights as a veteran. While none of this justifies any actions that Mr. Newberry took last week, we have learned that his intention was not to perform a mass shooting at the Waterfront but, in fact, he was trying to send a message, a message to the Veterans Administration and ultimately a message to Frank Martinez, the Secretary of the VA.

"Mr. Newberry wanted the world to know that the VA was not doing a good job taking care of our nation's veterans.

"How do we know this? Why are we discussing it today? Because my office has just learned that while Mr. Newberry went to the Waterfront with an assault rifle, he also went with only one bullet. Mr. Newberry went to the Waterfront to commit suicide—and send a message about the abysmal care many veterans receive.

"Now, I don't agree with what Mr. Newberry did. There are better ways to communicate your problems than waving an assault rifle around during a crowded event. But we have learned that the VA was fully aware of Mr. Newberry's struggles and almost immediately began to cover up the agency's culpability. The VA allowed the false narrative that Mr. Newberry was acting as a domestic terrorist to be propagated by the media. They deceived me and other public officials. They deceived the American people. All because the tragic situation and now tragic death of Mr. Newberry, while still a crime, is also an absolutely horrible indictment of how veterans are treated in America.

"I have already reached out to the President, asking him to convene a full and thorough investigation of the VA and Secretary Martinez. This coverup is unconscionable.

"Most of us did not know how significant the issue of suicide is among veterans. In fact, vets are one-and-a-half times more likely than average citizens to commit suicide, and many have chosen to commit suicide in highly visible ways as a form of protest. As I said, it's a tragic situation, made all the more abhorrent by the actions of the VA to cover up Mr. Newberry's true intentions.

"While I can't do anything more nationally than ask the President to make a full investigation of the VA and Secretary Martinez, in Florida, we are going to take action.

"I have set up a special task force, website, and 800 number that will enable the State of Florida to offer immediate counseling and assistance to any veterans who are in need of services or who need assistance getting their rightful benefits, treatments, and medications from the VA.

"If you have been honorably discharged from the United States military, be it the Army, the Navy, the Air Force, or the Marines, and you don't feel like you are getting advocacy from Secretary Martinez and his department, then you can call us in Florida. We promise to help you."

I was pretty sure Rod Kirby left his office screaming my name, but I couldn't confirm it because I had already left the building.

Chapter Twenty

7 p.m., Friday, Pete's Apartment

I IGNORED MY phone and drove toward home in a deep funk. It wouldn't take a well-trained investigative journalist to figure out who leaked information to the governor. I may have just lost my job and torpedoed my career.

Inside my apartment, I thankfully found a beer and cracked it open before turning on my laptop and plugging in the pink hard drive. There were dozens of folders and hundreds of files in a larger folder labeled "Kennesaw building." Yikes. No idea where to start.

I called Gus Intriago, who thankfully answered at the fairly late hour.

He explained that each folder was a different camera, and each file was a different period of time for the specific camera.

"Any idea how I might slay this dragon?" I asked.

He laughed. "I did think about it a little. You should look at the main common areas and the elevators. I would say try to see if you can catch them entering the main lobby. Unless you take the stairs, everyone entering or exiting the building goes through the lobby. And check the elevators.

That footage might be better because usually the cameras are closer and in better focus."

"Ah, okay, that's good advice," I said. "Just so I'm clear, each folder is a camera and then the files in the folders are timestamped video files?"

"Yes," he confirmed. "The cameras stop recording if there's no movement, so you won't have to stare at hours of nothing on some of them. If I had more time, I could have had the files better organized, but you wanted them right away—which was yesterday."

"Yeah, yeah, I know," I said. "I thought I would have some help with this, but the past two days have been a blur. Anyway, thank you, Gus. And I'm all in on doing the podcast. Just give me a few days. Have a good weekend." We hung up. I turned off my phone.

I started clicking on files. Another puzzle. I opened up several files and tried to figure out what I was looking at.

Parking structure? That wouldn't help me.

Outside a bathroom on one floor? Seemed invasive.

What looked like the catacombs where Gus worked? I didn't think either guy would be there.

Still, after a few minutes of head-scratching, I was able to find three cameras in the main lobby plus the four main elevator cameras. I then had dozens of files to review instead of hundreds. Gus had given me good advice.

First, I watched the main lobby. The video started at midnight last Friday and had little activity until about 4:30 a.m. when some new security guards came to work. Things started to cook around seven a.m. and built at a steady pace throughout the morning hours on the timestamps. But I did not see anyone who looked like Newberry or Swanson.

One key nugget emerged. Many of the Southern Regal employees appeared to wear royal blue shirts. So, I could rule out women and anyone not wearing royal blue, which seemed to speed things up.

After watching for several hours, I started to get tired and felt like this was a fool's errand. I had watched the equivalent of eight hours of footage of people going in and out of the lobby, and nobody looked like Newberry or Swanson.

I switched to the first elevator and watched people going in and out. Up and down. Thankfully, lots of women and guys in gray suits work at the bank. Plenty of delivery drivers too. I could rule all of them out.

By about midnight, I was wiped. Operating on about four hours of sleep from the turtle trek, I decided to call it a night. Should have drafted a bunch of interns to do this. *Alas.*

I FELL ASLEEP quickly but then woke up a few times in the middle of the night. By five a.m., I was staring at the ceiling. Wired and rested enough, I got up and made coffee.

I went back to the laptop and started on the second elevator. More people. Bursts of activity first thing in the morning, around lunchtime, again at about four p.m. for coffee breaks, and then a healthy bustle between five and six p.m. But no sign of Newberry or Swanson.

THE BYSTANDER

At about seven a.m., before tackling elevator three, I wandered to my refrigerator and pulled out a frozen croissant that might have been purchased by my apartment's prior tenant. If I was gonna be unemployed, I might as well start eating bread again. I threw the croissant in my toaster oven, and with some butter, it wasn't too bad. Yes, it would have been greatly improved with some jam or marmalade or whatever, but my bachelor pad completely lacked any sugary, preserved fruit products.

I decided to turn on my phone and face the reckoning.

I'd missed calls from Ted and Rod, naturally, plus a text from Rebecca asking me to call. I couldn't bring myself to call her. My head was just too scrambled.

Ted had unrelentingly texted me about five times, the most unnerving being: "If I have to, I will even come over during the football game."

My phone pinged, and it was a text from Hailey Marsh: "Are you available at 11 today? 457 Tanglewood Court in Yulee."

I had almost forgotten about her. I replied that I would see her then.

I had enough time to review more footage, take a shower, and still have a few minutes to collect my thoughts for the interview. Should I even interview her? I wasn't even supposed to be on the story. But Rod couldn't really get mad at me for meeting her on my own time, right? If I was even still employed…

My only hope was that she could provide some clarity and maybe even help me bring this story in for a landing. I was sure she must have heard about the governor, but who knew what she would make of that.

Okay, back to the laptop: Third time lucky, as the British say?

More elevator monotony and then, breakthrough. The timestamp of the footage from the third elevator read 8:48 a.m. as Kyle Charles Newberry entered. Royal blue shirt. Khakis. A camera captured his face. *Gotcha.*

Dang, in eight hours, he'll be dead.

Newberry exited, presumably on his floor, with no sign of Swanson. I was excited, adrenalized for the first time in days. Newberry was in the building, which we knew, but now I had eyes on him.

I kept watching. Still monotonous, but at least it felt like I had hope.

I dug deep into my pantry, looking for something else to eat. A mini box of cereal—some kind of bran flakes. Yuck. What I would do for some chocolate-covered sugar bombs to go with my bizarre adult equivalent to Saturday morning cartoons.

And then I saw him. At the 12:43 timestamp, Swanson entered the elevator, wearing the blue baseball cap I would never forget. He turned toward the camera. Definitely him. Wow.

A moment later, on the camera that I was calling the third elevator, in walked Newberry. They stood shoulder to shoulder. Looked like they were talking. No physical contact. Definitely talking. And then they exited.

I wrote the timestamp information on my pad and noted

the name of the file.

I had them in the elevator and leaving together, but was there more?

After a few miscues, I found the lobby camera that had a view of the elevator bank. I wrote down the name of the file and then opened it. Sure as shit, at the 12:44 timestamp, Newberry and Swanson exited the elevator and stopped to talk to each other in the lobby.

They moved toward a corner, fortunately still in view but a bit farther away. They were very close to one another, well within the realm of personal space. I had no way of knowing what they were saying, but you don't get that close to a person you don't know.

I could use a lip reader or one of those British royal family body language experts.

Looked like things were wrapping up and then, oh my god, they bumped fists.

Chapter Twenty-One

11 a.m., Saturday, Yulee, Fla.

I TOOK A shower and headed to Yulee with my one-man-band equipment.

An old Florida town that is evolving into a Jacksonville bedroom community, Yulee is best known for being on the way to Amelia Island and Fernandina Beach. It's a nice enough little suburb about thirty minutes north of downtown, and one of its main benefits is that it is still outside the sprawl of Greater Jacksonville.

Hailey's house was a typical Florida ranch-style home, painted a pale yellow and likely built in the 1960s or '70s. It looked to be about three bedrooms but was sitting on a big lot, probably an acre, in an area that most city dwellers would call the middle of nowhere. I would say remote, for sure.

She lived on a quiet street with a mix of homes with well-manicured lawns along with places that didn't look like they'd been touched in years. Bass boats and RVs that hadn't seen action in quite a while were plainly visible in the neighbors' yards, but I also saw several kids playing outside and parents doing yard work. Soon to be typical suburbia, I guess.

When I knocked on the door, I still wasn't sure if I was going to put Hailey on camera, but I also wondered if she might have gotten made up for the interview. Nothing worse than telling a lady who spent time and energy at the salon that she won't be on television.

Not to worry, though, because I instead found myself, forgive the cliché, staring down the barrel of a gun, in the hands of one Walter Swanson.

"I guess I don't have the wrong house," I said.

"No, you sure don't," he said as he waved me into the home. He directed me to a wooden chair in what looked like a living room. The sun sifted in through faux wooden blinds on large bay windows.

He took my phone and turned it off.

The home was tidy but a bit lived in. It was decorated in early-2000s farmhouse style. Lots of wooden furniture, a sunken living room, and a large open kitchen with a big dining table and about a half-dozen chairs. And lots of cows. Cow kitchen towels, coffee mugs, coasters, trivets, you name it. And a whole farm scene of saucers and plates on a sideboard. Your grandma would love it, though she'd first want to dust it.

"Why are you aiming a gun at me?" I asked.

"Because you fucked up my life," he said.

"I fucked up your life? Okay. Walter, you are clearly upset, and I don't want to make this worse, but please put the gun down. I'm sure we can work this out. When we were at the Waterfront, I just did my job. I'm sorry if that messed up your life. Please put the gun away."

"It's not that, you fucking idiot. You're not doing the deal with the Wheelers, and you're asking all these questions about Chip Newberry."

My eyebrows must have lifted or something, because he gave me a silly grin.

"Yeah, I fucking knew Chip Newberry."

I knew it. Calm down, Peter. Gun, remember.

"I met Chip at the gun show," he continued. "He didn't sell anything that I liked or needed. Had a shitload of cool knives though. He was a good guy. We talked a few times at the shows. And then one day, we decide to go grab a coffee at the convention center's shithole cafeteria. He tells me about all of his issues with the VA and how tons of vets have committed suicide but the government isn't doing shit about it."

Oh my god, he's monologuing, like the villain in *The Incredibles*. Life imitates art.

Dude, gun, remember?

"He tells me that he's in the same boat as all these other vets," Swanson said. "If he doesn't get his meds, it's basically unbearable pain. And then he says to me not to be surprised if one day you hear that 'I went out in a blaze of glory.' I told him that it was crazy and that it couldn't possibly be that bad, but then he told me about his idea to fake an active shooter incident and get killed by the cops. *That* would get attention. And on Friday, he did it. I just happened to be there."

"You knew he had only one bullet?" I asked.

"Yeah, that was my idea," he said proudly.

Uh-oh, this guy's sick.

"I told him that one shot would scare everybody," he continued. "And then he said it would shock and surprise everyone that the cops shot a guy with an empty gun."

"But you shot him instead, Walter."

"Yeah, and..." He paused with a sly grin.

"And what?"

"I told him I would back him up and take out some cops," he said.

"What? You were gonna back him up? You want to be a cop killer? What the fuck?"

"No, fuck no. But that way I knew his plan and made sure he didn't wimp out."

He didn't just know him. He set him up.

Homicidal double cross.

"You knew all along that you were gonna take him out?"

"Yeah, I did," he said. "And I'm the hero."

I didn't know what to say.

He noticed the pause and said, "He was gonna die anyway."

He's a psychopath. I got that part wrong. I'm so fucked.

"Okay," I said, trying to compose myself. "Okay, okay, I see how this happened, but this is not the way to solve this." I paused again. *Think, Peter.* "How does hurting me help you?"

"I will feel a lot better when I punch you in the fucking face."

"Okay, I guess I get that, but you don't need a gun to punch me in the fucking face, right?"

"Yeah, but you're a pain in the ass, you know. Everything was fucking perfect. Everything was fucking great until you showed up in New York and started asking questions. And then you backed out of the documentary deal, and the Wheelers are now fucking me."

"Whoa, whoa, whoa. I haven't backed out of anything, dude. That documentary is supposed to make me a lot of money. I signed the contract."

"Bullshit. Don't lie to me."

"I'm not lying to you. What did they say? What did they tell you?"

"Yesterday in New York, I'm sitting with the Wheelers, and all of a sudden, they get a phone call. And they look pissed, and they're basically saying you're not going to play ball."

"Walter, I signed the agreement yesterday. I can show you on my phone."

"Bullshit. And you're not gonna trick me into letting you turn that thing on."

I sighed.

"They then said the documentary was off," he went on, clearly getting more agitated. "You fucked up the whole deal, and they start asking me all kinds of questions about Stephanie Singleton because now they think I'm gonna get fucking sued. The family and that preacher freaked them out, and then the governor gets on TV, and that was the last straw."

Martinez pulled the plug after the governor's press conference. I was never getting any money. *It's all academic from*

THE BYSTANDER

here, except I have to figure out how to not die.

"So, one day, I'm running for fucking Congress and making all this money off my courses, getting ready to be a fucking TV star," Swanson said. "And then the next day, I'm SOL."

Shit outta luck.

"You didn't make any money?" I asked.

"Oh no, I made money. I made money, but those motherfucking Wheeler brothers took most of it. They took 40 percent of my fucking GoFundMe money. You want to know why? Because they set up the fucking GoFundMe page before they even knew me."

"Those fuckers know how to make money," I said. *Maybe I can make them a common enemy, but Swanson is ranting like crazy.*

"The GoFundMe page raised something like one hundred grand, right? Those assholes took fifteen thousand of it for their costs for working with me. Investing in the courses, my airfare, my hotel stay, the theater tickets, everything. They took it right off the top. Then they took 40 percent of what was left, leaving me with about fifty grand. But then they withheld another 20 percent for the government because they wanted to be sure I paid my taxes. Do you believe that shit? So, I ended up with a little over forty thousand dollars of one hundred thousand that was raised—for me!"

"Dude, that sucks," I said.

Keep him talking—at least that's what they say on the cop shows.

"They're worried about me paying taxes," he said. "So I'm sitting in that fucking conference room, fuming at these assholes, and I just said, 'That's it. I'm done. I'm out. Write me a fucking check.' Then I said, better yet, forty thousand in cash, and I will go on my merry way."

"What did they say?"

"They had already wired the money into my account. It was take it or leave it. Motherfuckers. I said goodbye to those assholes, got the fuck out of there, and came down here to see Hailey."

"Where is Hailey, by the way?" I asked, realizing that I wasn't the only one who had to deal with this lunatic today. "Is she okay?"

"I get down here, and who do I find she is getting ready to meet? My fucking sworn enemy, Pete Lemaster from WJAX."

"Walter, is Hailey okay?"

"She's fine. I gave her a handful of hundreds and sent her to the fucking spa. She'll be there all goddamn day."

Whew.

"Walter, I don't want to upset you, but I signed the deal with the Wheelers. They promised me a bunch of money, too, and I haven't seen any of it. Please put the gun down."

"You can calm the fuck down, Pete. Can I call you Pete?" His voice was dripping with sarcasm.

"Walter, you can call me whatever you like. Just let me go. You can break my phone into a thousand pieces and send me on my way. Dude, I'll leave my car. I'll walk out the door, and you will never see or hear from me again. Believe me, this whole situation has not been a bed of fucking roses for me either. Let's just agree to, like, part ways."

"I really don't give two shits what you think. I didn't come down here to fuck with you. It's just a nice convenience that you are here, and I know where you are, so you can't fuck this up for me any worse. I'm gonna leave you here. Take my money and go to Costa Rica. Fuck you. Fuck the Wheelers. Fuck everybody. I'm out of here, and you're never gonna see me again."

I withheld any thoughts I had about the fact that he was probably gonna get charged with manslaughter at least and there was absolutely an extradition treaty with Costa Rica. So, he'd completely misled himself on that part of the plan.

Keep it to yourself, Peter.

"You can just let me go now," I said. "I don't want to cause you any more trouble."

He then reached over the counter and pulled out a handful of industrial-sized zip ties.

"Are you seriously going to fucking tie me to a chair like we're in a cheap thriller novel?" I asked.

"No, you're gonna tie yourself."

"You are fucking kidding me, man. Walter, let me go. I know the cops. I'll tell them what happened. You tried to do the right thing, but it got outta control and then you got fucked over by the Wheelers."

Total lie—he planned the whole thing, and he was going to prison.

"Nope, too late for that shit. Start with your legs."

He threw me a zip tie, which I caught, like an idiot.

"Okay." I leaned down and wrapped the tie around my leg and the chair.

Can't fucking believe this.

He tossed me another one, which I bobbled and dropped.

"No fucking around, Lemaster," he yelled.

As I reached down to grab the second tie, wondering how I was gonna get out this mess, I heard a crash, and then *boom!*

Chapter Twenty-Two

11:30 a.m., Saturday, Yulee, Fla.

THE IMPACT KNOCKED me to the floor. My head throbbed and my ears were ringing. I couldn't see.

My head felt like vegetable soup. My ears were still ringing, and now my eyes stung.

What the fuck just happened?

I curled into a ball. Fetal position. My hands over my ringing ears.

What happened?

It was one of the loudest noises I'd ever heard—way louder than my first concert, the Foo Fighters.

I heard another loud noise and then footsteps. I pulled my legs and arms in closer. A tighter ball. Heavy steps went past me, and then a hand rested on my shoulder.

One guy in tactical gear was looking at me and talking, but I could only hear the ringing. He looked at me right in the face and mouthed what could have been "are you okay?" and then did a thumbs-up or thumbs-down gesture.

I gave him a weak thumbs-up. I could hear a little bit better. Lots of voices now.

"Can you stand?" the cop asked. Or at least that's what I thought the cop said.

"I don't know," I sputtered. "My head is spinning."

"That was the stun grenade. We have Swanson in custody. Can you stand?"

"Sitting is pretty good right now."

"We want to get you out of here, away from the tear gas and into the fresh air."

"Okay," I said as he and another officer lifted me to my wobbly feet.

The second officer produced an automatic pocketknife, and a blade shot out of the side of it, which he used to cut the zip tie still holding my ankle to the now toppled chair.

They got me to my feet and basically dragged me outside. The moment the fresh air hit my lungs, I immediately felt better, and then I collapsed on Hailey Marsh's lawn. A SWAT team member wiped my eyes with a wet towel and offered me a bottle of water.

I slowly started to process what had happened, and then I noticed a dozen police cars parked in disarray around the property. Walter Swanson was getting similar treatment a few yards away from me, except he was in handcuffs.

An EMT approached me and said, "Everything will be okay."

"I can sort of hear," I said, probably very loudly.

A moment later, I felt the hand of Detective Howard Steele on my shoulder.

"Sorry about the flash-bang," he said, "but we had to get you out of there. Are you okay?"

"He knew Newberry," I said.

"What?"

"Swanson told me that he knew Newberry from the gun shows. He knew Newberry was going to the Waterfront. He knew all about the suicide plan. He murdered him."

"He told you that?" he said, handing me another bottle of water for my eyes.

"He did. With a gun in my face and right before the asshole tied me up."

"Dang. Criminals never cease to amaze me. Okay, Pete, let's get you checked out by the EMTs, and then we can go down to the station and take down all the info. We learned a lot about Swanson in the past two days, but he clearly told you more. I told Rebecca you were okay. She was worried about you."

"Thank you," I said as I took a deep breath and wobbled again as I got to my feet. I saw Ted and Bobby standing in the distance with a camera pointed at the chaos. I strained to see if any other media outlets were around. Nope.

I will never get tired of an exclusive even if I almost die getting it.

TED AND I entered a meeting room at the sheriff's office, and Detective Steele, Rebecca, and Olivia were milling around the conference table, waiting for us. A police transcriptionist and a videographer were set up to document my statement. Ted had told me Olivia wanted in on this meeting and wouldn't be denied. She gave me a big hug, asking if I was alright. Rebecca approached me and put her hand on my arm. A hug would have been inappropriate, but her gentle squeeze lingered long enough for me to notice but not draw attention from the others. She reached up as if she was going to touch my face but then brushed some dirt from my sleeve before pulling back slightly.

There's something going on here.

"How are you feeling?" she asked with a concerned look I hadn't seen from her before.

"I think I have had my share of loud noises for a while. My ears are still ringing a bit," I said.

"Too much trauma for one week, that's for sure." Her eyes never left me.

Definitely something.

"Aside from your ears, everything else…physically, I mean?" she asked.

"Pushing through everything else as best I can," I said, with a quick eyebrow raise and a forced grin.

She nodded sympathetically, holding her gaze.

Amid all this insanity today, at least this part feels good.

"My eyes still kinda sting though," I said, trying not to stare at her.

"You will be okay in a few minutes, Pete," Steele interrupted. "It only hurts until it stops."

"Well, I guess I must be in alright shape if you're joking with me," I said, still feeling dazed and trying to piece everything together. I turned to the group and asked, "What happened?"

"Since we met on Thursday, we've been tracking Swanson," Steele said. "We wanted to question him, but we didn't

THE BYSTANDER

have enough evidence to pick him up and certainly not enough to go and arrest him in New York. We figured that sooner or later, he'd come back to Jacksonville. His girlfriend was already back, so we decided to wait."

"I guess it didn't take too long," I said. "Wait, what about Hailey? Did you find Hailey?"

"We found her at the spa. Took her out mid-massage. We don't think she knew about any of it, or at least she's not acting like she knew," Steele said.

"Okay, sorry for interrupting," I said.

"That's understandable," Rebecca said. "In the meantime, we tried to reach Barry Petroff in California, and we stepped it up after we learned that he was mugged. He finally called me back last night, or actually early this morning, around one a.m. I talked with him for about twenty minutes. He didn't divulge anything specific about Newberry, but he gave us enough to solidify the suicide-by-cop theory. He said he'd been continually harassed by the Veterans Administration. Nothing illegal, but the VA has been pushing back on him for years. And it's only gotten worse lately."

"So he, sort of, confirmed part of the theory?" I asked.

"Yes, that's one way of saying it," Rebecca said. "I guess it was implied that he believes Newberry went to the Waterfront as a type of VA protest, but Petroff never said that specifically. That's about as much as I could get, because he was super wary of his attorney-client privilege even though Newberry is dead. He also said that he wanted to talk to you guys, and he reminded me that he called you first, Pete. When he was assaulted outside his office, as you might imagine, something like that can change your perspective."

"We were then at least feeling like we were on more solid ground about the suicide theory," Steele said. "I also talked to Mr. Aronberg from the gun show."

"You're checking my facts," I said.

"*Our* facts," Olivia said. Ted chuckled.

"Yeah, we had to, Pete. We can't arrest a guy based on one observation from another person even though it might turn out to be right. As you might imagine, Mr. Aronberg, like a lot of people, was more forthcoming when talking to the police than he was with you, who he called the 'fake news media.' But he likes you, by the way."

"I bought him lunch," I said. "Usually helps."

"Well, Mr. Aronberg said with conviction that he had seen Newberry and Swanson together. He couldn't remember when and didn't know what they were talking about or anything specific. But, to us, it was looking more and more like they knew each other."

"He was more evasive with me," I said. "Trying to keep the identities of his vendors private. Seems like part of the gun culture."

"Well, that admission gave us more reason to bring Swanson back in," Steele continued. "He lied to us."

"I have more on that," I said. "I mean, aside from what he said to me an hour ago." I handed Olivia her pink hard drive and my notebook with the file names and timestamps. In short order, she opened the first file and played the elevator video stamped at 12:43. We gathered around her laptop as she hit play.

"On the left is Newberry, on the right is Swanson," I said. "Last Friday at the Kennesaw Bank building."

"I'll be damned," Steele said.

"You dumpster-diving junkyard dog," Olivia said.

"How'd you get it?" Ted asked.

"Charm." I smiled. "Bribery and charm, but mostly charm. I promised that I wouldn't put it on the air without permission."

"Is there more?" Rebecca asked.

"Go to the next one, Liv," I said. She cued it up and hit play.

"They depart the elevator here in a moment," I said. "And they chat for a second. They look like they know each other to me. You guys agree?"

"Smoking gun," Ted said.

"Wait for it," I said.

They bumped fists on the video.

"Wow," Steele said.

Rebecca was looking at me with a piercing, incredible gaze that went right through me.

"The legend continues," Ted said. "You are gonna be intolerable."

"Hard work, play 'em one game at a time," I joked in Ted's direction. He punched me in the arm. Kinda hard, actually.

"Okay," Steele said. "Further proof that they knew each other. This is really valuable for us, Pete. Thank you. Okay, so as I was saying, we've been tracking Swanson since our meeting the other day. As best we can figure out, everything started to unravel yesterday. He got into an altercation with the Wheelers."

"He told me that they pulled the plug on the documentary and took most of the money from his GoFundMe page," I said.

"I'm not sure about the money, but I guess that's not a surprise." Steele sighed. "Did he tell you that he punched Stephen Wheeler?"

"Wow. No. He left that part out," I said.

"Again, not a big shocker," Steele said. "Stephen told the NYPD that he and his brother met with Swanson after watching the governor's press conference. They said the financial backers were getting nervous about the allegations against Swanson regarding Stephanie Singleton and the blowback on the VA. Jason also said there was a dispute about money but that they had just wired a substantial sum to Swanson that morning."

"Swanson lost it then," Rebecca added. "Jason said the project was just going to be temporarily paused, but Swanson got angrier and angrier, and then he clocked Stephen and took off. The Wheelers said they were shocked and scared, so they had their private security team lock down their offices."

"Of course they did. They probably have their own militia," Ted joked.

"A couple hours later, they finally called the police and filed charges against Swanson," Rebecca said. "But by then, he could have been anywhere."

"That made us nervous," Steele said.

"A highway camera caught Swanson's rental car near

THE BYSTANDER

Brunswick, Georgia, a few hours ago," Rebecca said. "We think he flew to Charlotte and then rented the car. He traveled all night."

"We were coming to pick him up when you ambled in," Steele said.

"Holy crap, I'm so sorry," I said. "What a nightmare."

"We got the bad guy," Rebecca said. "That's what matters. And that you are safe." She gave me another electric smile.

OUTSIDE THE JSO offices, Rebecca's team had scheduled a press conference to discuss the raid and subsequent arrest of Swanson. Olivia joined Bobby and Jill Thompson among the cluttered mass of reporters. Ted and I stood in the wings as I had no interest in getting caught up in the press pool. I knew we had more on this story than any other station could even imagine and wanted to keep it that way.

Rebecca quickly offered the details on the raid, announcing that they had tracked Swanson to Yulee after they learned of the assault in New York. When it became apparent that a visitor to the home was in danger, they sent in SWAT.

Most of the questions involved clarification of what happened during the raid and what was next for Swanson.

Angie Irwin piped in, "How come we weren't notified about the raid?"

"We are not in the business of inviting media to our covert ops, sorry," Rebecca said.

"Then why was WJAX there?" Angie asked.

"I can't stop one of your competitors from doing their job, Angie."

A clearly miffed Angie then asked, "Can you confirm that Pete Lemaster from WJAX was in the house with Swanson?"

"At this time, we are not releasing any information on that," Rebecca said. "We are processing Mr. Swanson and holding him for an assault warrant out of New York."

As soon as I heard my name, I tapped Ted and then went back into the police station, figuring that the vestibule would provide a bit of a sanctuary from Angie.

My phone rang. My mom.

"Hey, Mom," I said.

"I just heard what happened. Are you okay?" she asked.

"I'm fine," I said. "The ringing in my ears is going away. The EMTs say it will be gone by tomorrow. Kind of like after a rock concert."

"Why didn't you tell me about the VA and the governor, Peter?"

"I didn't want to stress you out. I have to deal with some of these things on my own."

"Have you talked to a counselor?" she asked. "You know these things have the potential to cause"—she paused and I heard a deep breath—"these things can cause long-term problems."

"I know, Mom. I actually talked to the cops about it, and they have a counseling program for victims, and I'm gonna have a short conversation in a few minutes with them.

Apparently, I can talk to them whenever I want to after that."

"I'm coming to Jacksonville tomorrow," she said.

"You don't have to do that, Mom."

"I already booked the flight. It arrives around eleven a.m. Can you pick me up at the airport"?

"Of course I can."

"You understand that I'm worried about you, Peter."

"I do," I said.

"Okay, I will see you tomorrow then. Maybe I can take you and Rebecca to dinner tomorrow night?"

"Not a chance." I groaned. "Thank you for the call, but I'm hanging up now. Bye, Mom."

Back in the conference room, I answered a few more questions from Detective Steele, who told me that I would likely have to testify against Swanson. I told him it wouldn't be a problem. He thanked me for all the work I had done and again apologized for the stun grenade.

"Pretty sure you saved my life, detective," I said. "You shouldn't apologize. I'm thankful you were there."

Rebecca came into the room with a look of relief on her face.

"That was a tough one," she said, looking directly at Steele and then giving me a quick glance. "It's harder when you know the people involved in it." He nodded.

Rebecca exhaled and then looked at me, Steele, and Ted and said, "Okay, boys, my assistant is going to finalize this and deal with any other followups. The Gators kick off in a few minutes, and I hate missing kickoff. Will you guys join me at the Mustache, or do I have to watch the game alone?"

My Gators were playing Ted's Mississippi State Bulldogs.

"I'm in, absolutely," I said. "Wouldn't dream of leaving you to watch alone. That would be quite rude."

"Are you sure you want Pete there?" Ted asked.

I shot him a look of complete consternation. *What the hell, Ted?*

"He yells at the TV during Gator games," Ted said. "It's pretty obnoxious."

"That's okay," Rebecca said. "So do I."

Chapter Twenty-Three

One Week Later, Northern Duval County, Fla.

IN THE SHADOW of an Elvis, we waited. Customers and staffers hustled out takeout orders, carefully packed in large brown paper bags, and the line outside started to grow. We had arrived just ahead of the lunch rush.

On crunchy, brownish leatherette seats in a tight, ancient booth, I sat across from Rebecca. The sweet tea in front of her somewhat aligned with my Diet Coke on the chipped and stained tabletop as the unmistakable aroma of hot, frying oil permeated the restaurant. Could be vegetable oil. Could be lard. Could be some form of addictive narcotic. But I wouldn't dare ask.

Her anticipation was building, and I assured her that it would be well worth the drive and the wait.

I'd built this place up pretty good. Hopefully, not too much.

It was the first time we had seen each other since the day of the flash-bang raid, as I had taken to calling it, though we had spoken and texted regularly.

"Will you tell me about your dad?" she asked. I think she had been waiting for the right moment, and this was it.

"Uh, yes. But gosh, where to start?" I said.

"Wherever you want," she suggested.

"Okay. Well, the first military campaign I ever learned about was Operation Desert Storm, which began in 1990 after Iraq invaded Kuwait. I studied it in great detail as a teenager. The United States and our allies dropped nearly ninety tons of bombs over a six-week period, and the air bombardment was so successful that the ground campaign that followed was over in one hundred hours. The United States lost 212 men and seven women in what we now call the first Gulf War. Given the number of missions flown, ground gained, soldiers deployed, and bombs dropped, it was remarkable that more lives weren't lost."

"It was a big win," she said.

"Yes," I said, "but then there's the PTSD."

She listened intently as I continued.

"About fifteen percent of soldiers who go to war experience some form of post-traumatic stress. The numbers have been consistent since these things were first tracked following the Vietnam War. Before that, they called it shell shock. No matter what you call it, sadly, it's become part of the military equation. But the good news is that it can be treated and doesn't have to be debilitating, even though it sometimes is."

I paused and took a deep breath. "My father, Army Sergeant Major Stephen Lemaster, was one of thousands of Americans who fought heroically in the first Gulf War. According to my mother, he came home physically uninjured. She was relieved, joyous. But he had emotional wounds that never healed."

Rebecca was an incredible listener, absorbing everything.

I was completely smitten—no big surprise.

"I have recollections of him that are bolstered by video clips and photographs," I continued. "But mainly, it's too painful. Honestly, I almost never talk about it."

"It's okay," she said.

"It's odd not knowing much about a person so significant in your life. The emotions are complicated."

"I can only imagine," she paused, still gazing into my eyes. "Please keep going if you want."

"As a kid, I couldn't understand why it happened, and I really still don't, even though as an adult I have a better grasp on how challenging the pressures of life can be. And after everything that's happened in the past two weeks, I now have a profound understanding of the overall impact of trauma." I took a deep breath. "But if I had to give one reason why my father did what he did, I guess I would have to say PTSD. To me, it's the only thing that makes sense of something...so senseless."

"I'm so sorry, Pete. And your poor mother."

"My mother? Deep down, it had a huge impact, but she rarely shows it. She taught us to keep a stiff upper lip, work hard, lean on her and the family when necessary, and never be afraid to talk about things that were bothering us. She believes you should face all of your challenges head-on, whether they are physical, mental, or emotional."

"That's good advice," Rebecca said.

"Looking back, it's hard to argue with her philosophy. She's turned her lemons into the equivalent of a lemonade conglomerate. She's been incredibly successful, and I do my best to generally follow her guidance, though we frequently disagree on the specifics."

"So you've told me." She laughed.

Out of the corner of my eye, I saw our waitress approaching.

"Here we go," I said.

She placed two steaming plates in front of us, and as I unfurled my paper napkin to release my plasticware, I could see the glistening, golden brown skin that is the hallmark, the centerpiece, and the culmination of the best meal one will ever have in Jacksonville. And it's all nestled between generous helpings of perfectly seasoned collard greens and the creamiest mac and cheese.

Rebecca picked up a drumstick and took a discerning bite. I stared, waiting for the verdict. She smiled, and her brown eyes gleamed in yet another way that I had never seen before.

Yes, on our second date, I took Rebecca to Dixie Chicken.

Epilogue

THE AFTERMATH OF the arrest of Walter Swanson came swiftly.

He faced legal charges for manslaughter, conspiracy, reckless endangerment, lying to law enforcement, and assault (of a political hack). A felony manslaughter conviction would mean that he can no longer own or possess a firearm, but Craig and Lenny pointed out that in Florida, he could still own a gun classified as an antique.

The family of Stephanie Singleton filed lawsuits against Swanson and the developers of the Waterfront. The family's lawyers said that Swanson was responsible for the wrongful death of Singleton, and because he committed a criminal act, he was afforded no protections by the Good Samaritan law. They believed they had a negligent security case against the Waterfront, saying that the retail center didn't take reasonable precautions to safeguard its customers and guests. It would likely be years before either case reaches any type of resolution.

Frank Martinez resigned as Secretary of the VA. During a media availability, the president claimed to have barely known him but promised an inquiry into not only the disturbing level of veteran suicides but also mismanagement, budget overruns, and the use of government resources for personal gain by Martinez. Despite an impending indictment, Martinez received a lucrative consulting contract to go back to work with WestStrike.

Barry Petroff's mugging remained unsolved. He added some security cameras around his home and office, and when I spoke to him shortly after the news broke about Frank Martinez, he said he believed his safety was no longer in jeopardy. He's still recovering from bumps and bruises, but nothing that couldn't be cured by some beach time with his wife and dogs.

Martinez's fall played perfectly into the hands of Florida Governor Jim McManus. He was now the clear national frontrunner to succeed the president and had seized on veterans' issues as key planks in his platform. Kamari Small never called to thank me.

On the Monday following the arrest, Bo Rodgers went on a twenty-minute rant on his podcast about the perils of vigilante justice and how Walter Swanson may have set the pro-Second Amendment movement back decades.

Over at CNN and MSNBC, commentators attacked the president for his lack of attention to veterans' issues, condemned acts of vigilantism, and asked Congress to ban assault rifles and close the gun show loophole.

Switching to FAN News, Skip Kennedy chose to run an hour-long special about an Idaho school district that required daily nondenominational prayers and reintroduced corporal punishment. To date, the network never again mentioned Walter Swanson.

THE BYSTANDER

The Wheeler brothers *were not* being investigated for misappropriating Swanson's GoFundMe money.

While I was being held at gunpoint, Bobby and Ted filmed the entire thing, which included the flash-bang explosion, my teary, wobbly extraction, and Swanson's arrest. The footage drove another huge click-storm to the station's website. The attitude of Rod Kirby, who was still miffed at me, was greatly softened by the money that came in as a result. Later—like three weeks later—he told me he appreciated my newsgathering instincts.

A few days after the flash-bang raid, I again appeared on *The Morning Show*. Cathy Merrick said I "fucking killed it," and was recommending me as a future guest contributor. My mom was ecstatic.

The station's marketing team asked each of us to tape a personal postmortem they could use for a daytime Emmy application. That first part was easy for me.

The U.S. Veterans Administration spends billions of dollars each year treating psychological issues related to PTSD and other traumas impacting the armed forces, usually with noticeable success. The agency is keenly aware of the issue of veteran suicide and continually works to improve its offerings for veterans who need assistance.

I guess what I'm trying to say is that Kyle Newberry didn't have to die. Help was nearby for him, but he didn't know it. Yes, the VA system is sometimes a disorganized morass, but the agency has been managing these types of issues for decades. Had he been more vocal, told more people, and leaned on his friends and loved ones, then most certainly there would have been a different and better outcome.

And Kyle Newberry certainly didn't have to die at the hands of Walter Swanson. A call to a suicide hotline or a conversation with the police or any number of actions could have made Swanson an actual hero. He could have saved the life of a troubled yet eminently savable man. Let that sink in. When he could have been a bona fide hero, he chose to be a manufactured one. Instead of being a friend, or even just a compassionate person to Newberry, Swanson was an opportunist, a liar, a piece of human garbage—and a murderer.

I don't know what final justice will look like for Swanson, but I will do everything I can to make sure he faces it. I will share every bit of evidence that we found. I will be deposed. I will testify. Whatever it takes.

And I will soldier on.

The End

Acknowledgments

Writing and publishing a debut novel was one of the most challenging things I have ever done, and it would have been impossible without the support of many during the three-year journey from first draft to publication. From page one, my beautiful wife Pamela believed in it, saying *The Bystander* was the best thing I had ever written. Publishing veteran and early editor Robert Astle offered a deft guiding hand as I honed the manuscript. The BPA First Novel Award judges put vital wind in my sails when they longlisted it. My kids, Emma and Jack, didn't hate it, which is saying something. And my friends and early readers, Karen Janson, Lisa Shaheen, and Richard Candia, offered thoughtful critiques and, more importantly, unrelenting encouragement. Too many friends and family members to name also deserve my thanks.

I will be forever grateful to Julie Sturgeon, executive editor of Tule Mystery, for plucking my manuscript from the slush pile and sending me the greatest email ever—seriously, I should frame it. The entire Tule Publishing community has been incredibly supportive.

And to my readers, thank you and enjoy—and feel free to drop a loving review!

Finally, for aspiring authors out there, the publishing journey can be an intimidating and even soul-crushing slog, so I would suggest leaning on these words appropriated from legendary college basketball coach Jim Valvano: "Don't give up. Don't ever give up."

About the Author

John David is a long-time public relations and crisis communications consultant, author of a non-fiction business book, and a corporate ghostwriter. His debut novel, The Bystander (The Lemaster Files Book 1), was longlisted for the BPA First Novel Award. When not working or writing, he enjoys fishing, talking about politics, and following the Florida Gators. He and his beautiful wife Pamela live in Pinecrest, Florida.

Thank you for reading

The Bystander

If you enjoyed this book, you can find more from all our great authors at TulePublishing.com, or from your favorite online retailer.

Made in the USA
Las Vegas, NV
26 August 2025